LIKE FALLING STARS

Roselin Books
California
www.roselinbooks.com

This is a work of fiction. Names, characters, places, and incidents are a product of the author's imagination. Any resemblance to actual persons — living or dead — or to businesses, companies, events, institutions, or locales is completely coincidental. The author claims no responsibility for readers whom explore mysterious forests and make gifts of bread to strangers.

The characters of Cecil and Tanya are adapted from characters belonging to R. Hamlin. The character of Oberon is adapted from a character belonging to S. Buckhalter. All are used with permission.

Editing and book formatting provided by Elana A. Mugdan
www.allentria.com

Like Falling Stars / Avalon Roselin – 2nd ed.
ISBN-13: 979-8-9869284-0-1

Content warnings for this book include:

Amnesia, Anxiety, Bullying; Brief Disturbing Content;
Mentions of Animal Death and Suicide

Visit www.roselinbooks.com for more information.

TABLE OF CONTENTS

"ONE OF THE ELEMENTS I LOVE ABOUT FAERYTALES IS THE FOREST. EVERY TIME A CHARACTER GOES INTO A FOREST, THEIR LIFE IS GOING TO CHANGE FOREVER."

LISA STOCK

*For everyone who ever searched for home,
and found it in the company of a friend.*

*With special thanks to M. Boucher, T. Pilgrim,
C. Conway, F. Fleecy, K. B. Cook, A. Dockery,
J. Hinderman, and T. Roget for their support.*

1

THE EQUINOX FESTIVAL

ONCE UPON A TIME, Prince Nicolas Rasmussen made the biggest mistake of his life.

The sun had set on summer, and the evening that followed was clear and crisp. A soft breeze wound through the ancient treetops and down the thick trunks, carrying with it a chill that would usher autumn into the world. For now, the few leaves that departed from their branches to dance with the wind were still green, but soon they would be transformed into bright, fiery hues.

That night, the usually calm forest was filled with light and laughter as faeries gathered to honor the changing of seasons. Throughout the woods, the faeries that bloomed flowers in the spring, brought the light and warmth of summer, and froze the air in winter came together to help the autumn fae celebrate the arrival of their season. Some lived in the forest year-round, while others had come from the farthest reaches of the Northern Realm to take part in the festivities.

As per tradition, the Ruler of Autumn and Regional Prince of the Autumnal Floral Fae, Julius Erlich, hosted

the grandest of these parties. And he had been sure, under no subtle direction from the Eldest of their realm, to invite *all* of the important faeries of the Northern Realm.

Including—begrudgingly—the Regional Prince of the Frost Fae, Nicolas.

A muddle of high, cheerful voices assailed Nicolas's ears. The garish orange candle light that emanated from the strung-up pumpkin lanterns made him narrow his eyes beyond his usual glower. The pumpkins, squashes, and stalks of barley and rye used to honor the autumn season for centuries had been thrown together haphazardly with the crude decorations of the modern era: orange and black streamers and tacky stuffed crows. Nicolas would have ignored the streamers if not for the fact that they kept brushing against his head and mussing up his hair. He kept it in a ponytail, and every tug at the top strands meant his band had to be readjusted. Fixing it was nothing short of an awkward movement in a crowd.

Smiles and laughter surrounded Nicolas. He could find no reason for the other faeries' mirth and merriment. Did they see how uncomfortable he was? Had he done something to make them laugh at him?

Nicolas felt his mouth begin to tug into a frown. He covered it with the back of his hand, pretending to wipe away a stray crumb, despite not having touched a single morsel since arriving at the party. The food smelled too overwhelmingly of pumpkin and allspice, and hard candies in garishly bright wrapping were scattered across the banquet tables.

Nicolas wouldn't go near the crowd if he could help

it. He instead kept to the outer rim of the party, which was easy enough given that they were celebrating outside. All manner of creatures were able to come and go as they pleased, and while it was an ingenious way for Julius to prevent dirt and stray leaf bits from being tracked through his home, it did entail far more exposure to said refuse than Nicolas liked.

He glanced up at the trees. Still green. He could not excuse himself yet. He had to wait at least until the leaves began to change color so as not to be perceived as rude. Julius had, apparently, gone *out of his way* to make sure Nicolas felt *welcome* because they *wouldn't want a repeat of two decades ago, now would they?*

As if it had taken Nicolas more than a wingbeat to recognize the chiding tone of Drew Wright in the invitation, using his place as the Eldest Ruler of the Northern Realm to try to make everyone get along. If only Nicolas were a few centuries older and could claim that title for himself, he would focus on work rather than forced camaraderie. And yet, for all his talk of teamwork and the bonds of their ranks, Drew had never acknowledged that *Julius* was the one who had spilled the punch and therefore caused the 'incident' two decades prior. Nicolas had not, and would not, set aside his pride for the convenience of those who wronged him.

What was taking so long? The sun had set some time ago, and the changeover from autumn to winter never took place longer than an hour after sunset. The party had gone on for nearly two now, and all signs indicated it was still summer.

He scanned the throng of dancing, laughing, singing faeries for the Ruler of Autumn, but saw no sign of the younger Prince. He did not recognize a single one of the guests, nor should he. They were mostly floral fae that frittered their time away growing flowers and making garlands with them, or littering the ground with dead leaves. A few light fae moved among them, equally as unknown and annoying to him, little more than over-grown fireflies. The frost fae in attendance were all too low-ranking to ever have spoken to him directly.

At the very least, the Autumnal Equinox meant it would soon be time for Nicolas's season. He envisioned the forest covered in snow, everything a pristine, spar-kling white, just the way it ought to be. He saw him-self ruling over an eternal winter, bringing forth a new masterpiece of snow banks and frost-covered trees each and every morning. In his mind, everyone loved it, and loved him for it. There was no frostbite, no huddling by fireplaces, no staying inside to wait out the snow and wish for hot summer days and balmy nights. Everyone would see his world and never want to leave.

The intrusive sound of laughter jolted him from his reveries. This time it was coming from just behind him, and he found that he did recognize the darkly tanned faerie responsible for the distraction. He barely had time to hide his frown.

Jack Barnaby had been appointed as the Ruler of Summer and Regional Prince of the Light Fae in the Northern Realm sometime in the last few decades. Nicolas could not recall how many years ago exactly, but he could recall being made to pause his own off-sea-son preparations in order to attend the new Prince's cor-onation — an irritatingly sunny event to say the least.

'Irritatingly sunny' was a perfect way to describe

Jack Barnaby, all the way from his yellow and orange wings to his sandaled feet.

"Jack," Nicolas said flatly.

"I was wondering how long it would take you to realize I was standing there," Jack chuckled.

Nicolas forced his mouth to remain in a flat line. Showing his aggravation would be akin to admitting defeat.

"I did not think to look for you," Nicolas answered, a sharp edge creeping into his carefully curated mono-tone. "Do you have some business with me?"

"Business?" Jack's wings fluttered, radiating flecks of light. "Do the Rulers of Summer and Winter usually have business with each other here?"

Nicolas bit back the urge to sneer when he answered, "No, they do not."

The blaring glow in Jack's wings faded a bit at his icy words. That gave Nicolas the slightest amount of pleasure, though the idiot kept right on smiling at him. Nicolas could not tell if being obnoxiously cheerful was common to all light fae, or if it was a trait unique to Jack.

"Maybe we could change that," Jack offered. "I already finished the whole transfer-of-season blessing thing with Julius, so I'm free for the rest of the party." He pointed out the golden leaf that floated over a cornucopia on a pedestal behind the central banquet table. In spring, the leaf shone pale green to represent new growth; in summer, it darkened to vibrant emerald to represent the vitality of life; in autumn, its golden hue symbolized the abundant harvest of autumn.

Nicolas glanced at the trees again. Nature's leaves were still green. If Julius had already received Jack's ritual blessing and the ceremonial leaf had turned gold, then why had the seasons not changed over yet?

Upon closer inspection, Nicolas found the reason. The gilded edges of the leaf reflected the flickering candlelight, but the center was still a verdant green.

"What do you say?" Jack pressed. "Want to dance, or grab some food, or do something other than standing off to the side looking intimidating and broody?"

"I need to speak with Julius," Nicolas said tersely.

He strode away from Jack to look for the Autumn Ruler more thoroughly, just barely catching Jack mumble, "Oh, okay, see you later then?"

Nicolas struggled to maneuver through the near solid mass of revelers. Most of them moved out of the way, though some obstinately remained where they were, brushing against him as he passed. He scarcely noticed the hindrance, too intent on finding Julius. It should not be so difficult to find a party's host, but Julius was a small creature and easy to lose in a crowd.

Poor, pathetic Julius, born only half Nicolas's size and ill-fitted for his oversized wings.

Nicolas's concentration broke when someone grabbed his hand.

"Hey, there! Want to dance?"

He jerked his hand back without looking at the speaker and kept going, but now he could hear bits and pieces of the conversations around him.

"Is that him?"

"He looks different from what I expected."

"Isn't it odd for a frost faerie to have gold in his wings?"

"He's so *tall* in person!"

Nicolas forced himself not to react. If he responded to them, if he even gave any indication that he'd heard what they'd said, they would all know that they had gotten to him. He gritted his teeth and kept moving, lowering his gaze to seek the smallest, most infuriating floral faerie in attendance.

He finally spotted Julius standing at the food table, ladling soup into a hollowed-out gourd and chatting with a few others—probably lower-ranking faeries by the look of their unadorned clothes. His entourage melded into the crowd when Nicolas approached.

Julius's smile dropped and he curled in on himself when he saw Nicolas, folding his drab orange and brown wings in tightly. "What do you want?" he asked, pretending to be uninterested and spooning soup into his mouth.

"Why have you not changed the season yet?" Nicolas asked.

Julius shrugged. "I don't feel like it yet. Why should I change the season right this second? Summer won't come again for almost a year, everyone's having fun, and all the vernal and light fae want to enjoy the party as much as the rest of us before the autumn season weakens their magic. A little more summer won't hurt anyone."

"You are intentionally delaying autumn?"

"I would hardly consider a day to be a serious delay," Julius quipped. A conniving smile grew across his face. "I might not even consider a *week* to be a serious delay. Who knows?"

Loathsome brat! Nicolas thought. "I see. Well, then, I should think you would not consider it any problem if

I start winter early this year. A day or a week is not too significant a head start, is it? Perhaps a month would be more appropriate." He extended a hand toward the gilded leaf. The cornucopia beneath it gained a layer of white frost, and the edges of the leaf itself became a bit paler.

"I didn't say you could do that!" Julius protested, his wings flaring out.

"I hardly need *your* permission," Nicolas said. "The ritual blessing is only a show of goodwill. I can start winter any time I wish. *I* am the most powerful faerie in the Northern Realm, and if you will not perform your duties as you are meant to, then I see no reason to hold myself back. You are already giving up part of your season for summer. Why should I not expect you to do the same for winter?"

Julius's face twisted into a frown of indignation and then defeat. As silence settled between them, Nicolas noticed that the rest of the party had also grown still. All the gathered faeries watched the two of them, their faces full of an emotion Nicolas saw only too often: fear.

One moved forward with determined steps. Nicolas immediately recognized Drew, the Prince of the Floral Fae, Ruler of Spring, and Eldest Prince in the Northern Realm. That did not mean he was more powerful than Nicolas, only older. He held more authority in title, but soon he would experience the yearly weakening that all vernal floral fae experienced through autumn. He would be hardly more powerful than any one of his underlings.

Drew was known for his charming smile—his charming everything, really—but if Nicolas had ever

13

seen it, he did not recall. The only interactions he had with Drew typically involved the older Prince knitting his brows in frustration and disappointment, as he was doing now.

"Are we having a problem?" Drew asked, setting his glass of rose wine on the table next to the punch bowl. Nicolas wanted to roll his eyes at the simpering tone. Drew always said 'we' whenever the slightest conflict reared its head. It was meant to stress the importance of togetherness, or some similar sentimental nonsense, but it only ever made Nicolas want to call him a coward.

Before either of them could answer, Drew stepped protectively in front of Julius and placed his hands on his hips in an attempt to look commanding. Even with his mottled pink wings spread to their fullest, Nicolas towered over Drew to the point where his stance was almost laughable.

"Are we having a problem?" Drew repeated.

"None that I am aware of," Nicolas responded. "I am simply reminding young Prince Julius that if he is not going to carry out his duties *properly*—"

"It is not up to you to decide whether he is carrying out his duties *properly*," Drew said. "And if he were not, it would not be up to you to decide his punishment, nor would you be justified in carrying out *your* duties improperly." Drew lowered his wings so he could look at Julius, then back at Nicolas. "Are we clear?"

The whispers began. Nicolas spared a glance at the watching crowd. He caught the slightest hint of laughter.

"Crystal clear." Nicolas forced the words through gritted teeth. Julius nodded and returned to the crowd, joining Jack as the Summer Ruler tried to lighten the tense mood that had consumed the party.

Drew sighed, lowering his voice so only Nicolas could hear. "What are we going to do if this keeps up, Nicolas? You cannot continue to threaten Julius like this just because he's smaller and less powerful than you. Do you realize that this is the twelfth time in the past two decades that you have tried to bully him into starting winter early? And publicly this time."

"Was my public humiliation not enough retribution?" Nicolas snapped.

"I don't know," Drew said, shaking his head. "Is it enough, Nicolas? Are you done with this grudge yet? Or do we have to bring this to the attention of the King and Queen?"

Nicolas's wings flared despite himself. "Is that a threat?"

"Don't be ridiculous!" Drew answered.

"I am not the one being ridiculous. I am not the one extending summer as a petty, childish slight against my superior."

"But you are accusing me of making a threat, when the only one who has done any threatening is *you*," Drew said. He placed a hand on Nicolas's shoulder. "I wish it weren't necessary, and I don't want to see any-thing bad happen to you, but…I'm sorry. If you carry on this way, we'll have to do something about it."

Nicolas shrugged off the other Prince's hand. "So it is a threat."

Drew frowned and shook his head again. "If that is what you *want* to believe. And it does seem like you want to believe it." He looked up and made eye con-tact with Nicolas briefly before the frost faerie looked away. "When did you start seeing us all as your ene-mies, Nicolas? I thought having Julius invite you to the Autumnal Equinox would help you get over this petty feud. Perhaps I was foolish to hope for that much." Drew again tried to look him in the eye, but Nicolas hastily turned his face the other way. He hated forced eye contact. "I pity you, Nicolas."

"Pity me?" Nicolas's wings shimmered and the temperature began to drop.

Drew stood his ground. "Yes, Nicolas, I *pity* you. When I look at you, I see a brilliant, handsome, talented young faerie who could be spending time with friends while enjoying the celebration of another autumn's arrival, but has instead chosen to wallow in bitterness and misery and let himself believe that everyone in the world is out to get him. I feel pity for that faerie, and the faerie he *could* be."

Nicolas was too stunned to respond. Drew sighed and walked away, calming the nervous floral fae he passed and trying to encourage the crowd to resume dancing. A few of them cast lingering, pitying glances at Nicolas, then turned their backs to him.

Everyone turned their backs on him.

The temperature continued to drop. Drew could say what he liked about trying to be friends, but Nicolas knew the real reason Julius had agreed to invite him. He had done this deliberately, he had provoked this response from Nicolas by not changing the seasons on time, and he had known that Drew would be there to embarrass Nicolas with another dose of self-righteous scolding.

A frown formed before Nicolas could stop it. The temperature plummeted.

"So, you pity me, do you?"

The drinks and soups froze solid. Frost formed on the tablecloth and ground, spreading out from Nicolas.

"Save your pity for yourselves."

Nicolas spread his wings to their full span. Ice spiraled through the small clearing, coating everything around him with a thin, white glaze. Even the pumpkin lanterns froze over, their merry glows extinguished. Heavy gray clouds obscured the light of the moon. He would not make it snow just yet; the vanishing moonlight was message enough.

"Enjoy your autumn while you can, for it shall be short this year. Winter will begin on the day of *my* choosing with a blizzard the likes of which none of you have seen before. We shall see who is deserving of pity then."

He flapped his wings and was gone in a rush of

17

glacial wind, leaving a party full of frightened faeries behind. All of them looked to Drew, who fluttered his own wings and rose, hovering high enough that the whole crowd could see him.

"There is no reason for alarm," he said. "Nicolas has made these kinds of threats before, and they are always dealt with swiftly and fairly. No harm will come to any of you, we can all be sure of that."

He drifted back to the earth, where Julius and Jack were waiting for him. The other guests moved away, allowing the Princes room to discuss the matter. Most left the party altogether to tend to their respective plants in the wake of the sudden chill, shooting dirty looks at the frost fae. Those poor souls were torn between their desire to help remove the frost, and the loyalty their Prince demanded of them.

"You are going to do something this time, I hope?" Julius asked. "I'm tired of him getting away with nothing more than a slap on the wrist. I don't care if his threats are empty, they're still threats."

Drew nodded, the reassuring smile disappearing from his face. "I had so hoped things would go well tonight. However, I don't think he's left us any other option at this point. It's time the King and Queen were involved. Jack, what do you think?"

"Me?" A few sparks of light flickered off of his wings in surprise. "I haven't been here all that long, and I don't know the whole situation. If this is normal behavior for him, then I guess it's the only thing to do." Jack's tone did not match the certainty of his words. "What will the King and Queen do to him?"

"We can't know for certain," Drew admitted. "It

could be a minor punishment, or they might…remove him. He hasn't broken any major law yet, so they wouldn't execute him."

However, as Drew looked at the now starless sky, he wondered if perhaps this fit of rage did count as breaking a major law. Faeries had few rules, but those were treated with the utmost reverence: obey the King and Queen, maintain the balance of nature, show hospitality when recognized, and avoid keeping humans beyond the scope of hospitality. Nicolas had attempted to change the ceremonial leaf to its winter white, even if only a little, even if only to prove a point. Something like that could easily be seen as a declaration of defiance to the balance of nature.

"I suppose I had better go speak to them now. The celebrations will have the King and Queen in high spirits, and they may be inclined to show mercy," Drew said.

"Or they might be upset that their festivities were interrupted with bad news, and decide to have Nicolas executed," Julius pointed out. There was no eagerness or hostility in his voice, but the indifference was almost as bad.

Drew winced. How had things come to this? "We'll just have to chance it. This needs to be dealt with as soon as possible, for time's sake if nothing else. I don't want to watch the Northern Realm be made into a desolate, frozen wasteland while I'm too weak to defend it."

"We won't let that happen!" Jack said. "I'll keep an eye on Nicolas until the King and Queen are able to do something. That way Julius can manage autumn in peace, and you can conserve your strength for next spring."

"Thank you, Jack." Drew gave each of them a short hug. "Don't let him intimidate you. There is nothing he can do that we cannot."

"Except make blizzards that can destroy the whole forest, or freeze us from the inside out, or…" Julius quieted when Drew gave him a warning look.

"Let me rephrase. Nicolas has amazing powers, but so do the rest of us. Don't let him make you believe otherwise," Drew said. Then he hopped twice, letting his wings unfurl and lift him skywards on the second jump. He maneuvered past the branches until he was above the treeline. Once he had risen high enough, he summoned a warm spring breeze to dispel the dark gray clouds. Then he shifted the direction of the wind and rode the gust toward the palace of King Oberon and Queen Titania.

He had been there only a few times to witness the funerals of different Princes and Princesses in the Northern Realm, and to take part in Nicolas's and his own coronations centuries ago. He couldn't help but think back to Nicolas's coronation as he flew.

In those days, Drew had not yet been the Eldest Ruler in the realm, and he had seen himself and Nicolas more or less as equals. He wondered if Nicolas had already resented the fact that someday Drew would hold more authority than him. That crowning ceremony had been Drew's formal introduction to Nicolas, and what he remembered most was the frost faerie's eyes, less for their lovely ice-blue color and more for their loneliness.

Nicolas had always been withdrawn and a little

odd. His predecessor, Princess Bethilde, had spoken of him little, though her few mentions of him had been full of praise. The impression she had given was that Nicolas was quiet and shy, nothing like the tall, broad-shouldered, intimidating faerie Drew had come to know. When questioned about why he was so rarely seen, Princess Bethilde had only said that he had a hard time socializing and was happier by himself. It made Drew wonder if Nicolas had ever been close to anyone but her — if even that — and how he must have felt when she passed on. Upon her death, Nicolas had taken her place as Winter Ruler and Drew had assumed her role as the Northern Realm's Eldest Ruler.

Nicolas had always been *different*, it seemed, but his tremendous power had made him the perfect candidate for the Ruler of Winter almost from birth. King Oberon and Queen Titania had made sure that someday he would take that role, just as they did for all the Princes and Princesses of their Court — it was an appointed position of authority and responsibility, bearing no blood connection to the royal family themselves.

And yet Drew wondered if Nicolas saw it that way. Maybe he believed that, as a Regional Prince, he ought to have a special connection to the faerie King and Queen that would allow him to get away with misbehavior.

Perhaps it was Drew's own fault for not nipping it in the bud when he'd had the chance a century ago, when this feud between Nicolas and Julius had begun for…some reason. If either of them had ever told him what it was about, he had long forgotten.

Apparently Nicolas had not, no matter how much anyone wished he would.

It was nearly dawn the next day when the waters of the crystal lake appeared beneath Drew, and the knowledge that he was nearly there gave him the strength to keep flapping  his wings. The golden spires of the King and Queen's castle rose in the distance. The beauty of the palace still left him breathless.

If only he were there to celebrate once more. Now the high, diamond towers felt unapproachable and ominous, filling him with dread. He could only hope the King and Queen were in a good mood, or not there at all, and that he would not soon return to this magnificent and fearsome place for the coronation of a new Ruler of Winter while Nicolas's funeral roses were being cleared away.

He stood in front of the palace doors for a moment, ruminating. He could still turn away and try to resolve the issue privately. He could give Nicolas one more chance to prove that he could be reasonable and accept the company of the other faeries. Drew couldn't forget those lonely eyes, and couldn't help but wonder if things might have been different had he done something, *anything,* sooner.

Drew took a deep breath and rapped the door knocker firmly against its frame. He had promised Julius he would consult King Oberon and Queen Titania if the threats continued, and he had done all he could to assure Nicolas that they meant him no harm. It was out of his hands now.

His wings folded and he dropped his head as he heard echoing footsteps on the other side of the doors. His woven flower crown slipped to the side.

He had no way of knowing what would happen as a result of his or Nicolas's actions. He did not know what the King and Queen would decide to do once the news reached them. All he could do was hope that everything would turn out for the best.

2

THE WOMAN IN THE WOODS

ONCE UPON A TIME, in a land far, far away, there was a forest as old as time itself.

The trees of this ancient wood were nearly tall enough to pierce the clouds, and their roots stretched deep enough to tangle with the heart of the world. There were no marked paths through the trees, only faint trails made by animals so wild that most had never seen a human before.

Humans rarely strayed into this isolated part of the world. A small settlement sat at the edge of the wood, but few people stayed there longer than it took to pass through. As such, no one could remember the town's official name. It was known only for its vicinity to the forest, and was so called "the town next to the woods." It had been a grander mark of human civilization once, as evidenced by the dilapidated houses and a well that had been retaken by the forest, in days far beyond any living memory.

A heavy iron gate ringed the town's current limits. No one living there had been in the area long enough to remember *when* exactly the gate had been built, but everyone knew why it was there.

Faeries were not always kind, to trespassers or each other.

If the thickness of the growth wasn't enough to keep curious humans out, the many signs posted around the trees' perimeter reading "Danger: Faerie Land" and "Faeries: Enter at Own Risk" usually finished the job. Anyone brave or foolish enough to venture into the woods was never seen or heard from again. Whether that was the work of the fair folk, or whether foolish explorers just got lost and were eaten by wild animals, was up for debate; in either case, the woods presented clear danger.

However, the forest still charmed those few who had made it their permanent backyard. The plant life was varied and beautiful, especially as autumn was just beginning. The air was not yet cold enough to drive people inside, but it made their cups of morning coffee or tea that much more enjoyable. The leaves on the trees had transformed from green to an array of orange, yellow, red, and brown almost overnight, interspersed with touches of dark pine needles. It was enough to make travelers linger a day or two more.

Within this forest, there was a secluded cottage built into the side of a hill. It was small and dark, but not confining; in fact, the woman who lived there thought the aroma of the earth and the plants that lined the dirt shelves made the place cozy. A fire crackled in the hearth at the center of the single room, and its fragrant smoke was drawn out through the chimney. The cottage couldn't fit much more than the chimney, the jars of aromatic leaves, and a tiny cot.

The woman closed her eyes and let her head drop

onto her cot. All was well and peaceful right where she was. She didn't feel like getting up, though she knew her legs would soon grow restless for the open road. Then she would pack up her things and set out to find a new place to build a new little cottage, and she would be just as content there until it was time to move again. It wasn't in her nature to stay still for long, no matter how much she might come to like a place. Though she did enjoy the woods, and the town next to them—she'd even let herself get caught up in superstitions of fair folk in the forest—she knew she could not stay forever. Eventually rumors would spread, and the people of the town would come to view her with suspicion. It was best to leave before that started.

Perhaps one day she would come back for a visit. For now, she was beginning to feel that she'd overstayed her welcome. She'd spent a few months here, far longer than she had ever spent anywhere else, due to a pressing need in town for her services. With those services now rendered complete, she was determined to leave after the party tomorrow night.

She wasn't sure why she had even agreed to go. She was not the type to attend such events, and since the festivities were taking place in the evening, she would have to delay her departure by a full day. Still, she hadn't been able to turn down the invitation, offered in earnest by the host as thanks for her work.

One party—one day—couldn't make that much of a difference.

Her satisfaction faltered and anxiety seized her heart. She *couldn't* go! She had never been to a party in her life, much less been a guest of honor, and she knew

26

she was going to make a fool of herself.

The once domestic flames grew and consumed the room. Smoke filled her vision and her nostrils; the fresh air became ash in her mouth. Her body burned with pain, so overtaken with searing agony that she wasn't sure where her limbs or torso or head were anymore, only that they hurt.

Heat boiled her blood and blistered her skin. The fire had overtaken all of her senses. She struggled to find a way out of the flames, only to discover that her hands and feet were bound and her back was straight against a wooden pole. She fought harder, struggled more, and though she went nowhere, she was sure that she felt something shift and give way to her clawing hands.

Ann awoke from the nightmare with a start, disturbing the cool grass beneath her and sending a small moth flittering into the light breeze.

She sat up to look around, examining her body first. The dark vision had not fully faded, and she was worried that she might find herself covered in burns. There were none. All she found was a pair of pants, a light shirt, a beat-up satchel, bare feet, and hands so caked with dirt she could hardly see her fingernails. Her fingers had gouged little furrows into the ground; the sensation of digging must have brought her out of her dream. Raising her hands to clean her nails, she noticed that the dirt caught beneath them was nearly the same color as her hair.

She was sitting on top of a low hill. Trees of every sort surrounded her, and between them grew clumps of fern and tall grass. Leaves in vibrant shades of red and orange littered the forest floor. From the way the sun was shining through the branches overhead, she guessed it was midmorning. There was a slight chill in the air that made her rub her arms.

It was a calming scene after such a horrific nightmare, and Ann decided to take her time cleaning the dirt out from under her nails to enjoy it. She listened intently to the bird calls in the branches above, and tried to find each serenading songbird. She managed to spot a bright blue jay, but the rest were too well concealed among the leaves.

She opened the satchel and rummaged through it. Inside were some spare clothes, a few tools for personal hygiene, and a coin purse full of gold. She reached in as far as she could, all the way up to her shoulder, but there wasn't anything else in the bag. It certainly was deep for such a small thing. Odd, but she shrugged it off.

Ann stood, dusted off her pants, and slung the strap of the satchel over her shoulder. She had seen all there was to see from where she was sitting, and there must be more to see beyond the small clearing. She chose a direction at random and started walking, the fern fronds brushing against her hands as she passed through them.

While she walked, she couldn't stop staring up at the canopy above her. She was mesmerized by the bright sunlight that occasionally broke through interwoven branches, each tree displaying its own unique coloring. When she did finally look away from the treetops after tripping over a few rocks, she discovered that the ground was far more than simple dirt. It was a patchwork of brown earth and green moss, littered with patches of light, clusters of leaves, and half-buried pebbles.

Ann licked her lips and headed downhill. Her nightmare had left her mouth and throat uncomfortably dry, and a drink of cool water would be welcome. She came across a stream soon enough, and sank to her knees in the soft mud while she cupped her hands to drink.

Once she had swallowed a few handfuls of water, she noticed a pair of boots sitting by the river. They were travel-worn and beaten up, like her satchel. Maybe she had been here before!

Ann fished a pair of socks out of her bag and donned both them and the boots. She set off again, walking along the stream. She couldn't feel the mud squelching between her toes anymore, which was a shame, but the boots looked nice and protected her feet from rocks, so she decided it was better to wear them.

She came across a fallen tree that was nearly as tall as she was and long enough to span the stream. She dug her nails into the soft, rotting bark and hauled herself onto the top of the great log. Mushrooms sprouted on and around the trunk, and from her new perch, Ann spotted clusters of yarrow and rue flowers growing on the other side of the stream. She traipsed across the tree with a little bounce in her step and made her way through the white and yellow flowers, pausing for a moment to enjoy the sweet smell.

The farther Ann went, the more she noticed the abundance of flowers on the forest floor. The yarrow, heather, and rue were not unexpected, and she was pleased to find raspberries on a bush that she passed, even if they were a little sour when she sampled them. However, some of the flowers were out of place. Gladiolas were autumn flowers, but Ann felt a distinct sense of strangeness when she came across a clearing of wildly different gladiolas all growing together. The pinks, yellows, purples, whites, and hybrids were all beautiful, but there was no chance of such a garden occurring naturally. With only a mild chill in the air, Ann thought it was too early in autumn for them to all be in full bloom.

She pushed the thought to the back of her mind, excusing it as the work of an overly enthusiastic gardener, but she couldn't ignore the blooming dog roses that she passed. It was too late in the year for them to be flowering, even with a gardener's best efforts. Besides, the forest didn't seem like a place where someone would plant a garden.

Her suspicions were soon confirmed when she came across a squirrel that didn't run away from her until she was close enough to touch its fuzzy tail. She had no doubt that the squirrel had never seen a human in its life. However, the lovely-yet-strange flowers were immediately forgotten as she jumped at the squirrel. It raced up a tree before she could catch it, sending down a few leaves as it chattered in irritation.

She chased it anyway, climbing as far as she could until she lost sight of the squirrel. Figuring she might as well keep going, she then kept climbing until she lost sight of the ground.

One she reached the canopy, she found there wasn't as much of a view as she had thought there might be. Still, she was pleased enough to see how high she had managed to climb.

Getting down took a little longer, and Ann had to stop her exploration to clean her nails once again. At least the slivers of bark under them helped remove the last bits of mud. Once they were clean, it was time to walk again, her path marked by the clumps of vibrant blossoms.

She walked for far longer than she thought she would. The shadows of the trees grew darker and denser, and the once pleasant breeze started to nip at her exposed arms. She put on a sweater that she found in the bag, and kept going.

Twilight cast a red glare over the sky. The pine trees were hardly affected, but the deciduous leaves, once bright and warm, now looked like the glowing embers of a fire. They reminded Ann of her nightmare. The wind had grown more furious, and even with her sweater, she had to keep her arms clutched close to her chest for warmth. She tried to keep her back straight as she walked, but couldn't stop herself from hunching her shoulders inward.

The sun set quickly, or perhaps she lost track of the time again. Soon it was completely dark, save for the fireflies hovering around her. She could hear animals much larger than squirrels moving through the thick underbrush, marked by the occasional snapping of a twig or frightened shrieks of smaller creatures.

A flash of red caught her eye, darker and shapelier than the leaves. In the near distance Ann glimpsed a figure in a scarlet cloak, though it was obscured by the tree trunks between them. The figure's back was to her, and they had their hood drawn up; Ann could have crept by, and was considering doing just that, until the figure turned and revealed the profile of a sturdy woman with a stern expression. A basket hung from the crook of her arm.

Ann watched the woman, captivated, and the woman saw her.

Their gazes locked. Ann knew that if she was going to run, she had only a few brief seconds to make up her mind and do it, but she stayed put. There was something in the woman's eyes that kept her still. They were deep, and somehow older than the rest of her. Her age was difficult to discern, especially in the dark; she had a round, dignified face framed by light blonde hair. She could have been anywhere from twenty years old to forty. Ann had no doubt that her plump frame was reinforced with muscle.

Her pale blue eyes appraised Ann, and in that moment, Ann wanted this woman's approval more desperately than she could explain.

"Excuse me," the mysterious woman called, "what are you doing so far in the forest, alone?"

Ann opened her mouth. It took a moment to muster her voice, and she realized that she hadn't spoken a single word since she had woken up. "I didn't know that I was alone."

"You surely are not now," the woman said as she approached. "But that only answers one part of my question. What are you doing in the forest?"

"I was following the flowers," Ann answered. "And after that I was chasing a squirrel. Then I followed the flowers again, and now I'm talking to you."

The woman examined her, then leaned in for a closer look. Ann froze, worried that if she made a wrong move, she might displease or offend the woman in some way.

"You smell of earth," the woman said, pulling twigs out of Ann's hair with gentle care. "Have you been in the forest all day?"

Ann nodded. "Yes."

"How very odd. Now that it is dark, you must be on your way back to where you came from. The forest is not safe at night. Which way is your home?"

Ann thought for a long moment. She thought about what color the walls of her room might be painted, how far it could be from the kitchen, and the face of the person she must have said goodbye to when she'd left for a walk in the woods. Her memory showed her nothing. She felt like she ought to know all those things, but couldn't recall any of them.

When she didn't answer, the woman asked, "Are you lost?"

"I think so," Ann responded. "Could you point me in the right direction? I must live in a town nearby. I got carried away exploring and lost track of where I am, that's all."

The woman gave her a small smile and patted her head, this time removing a leaf from her hair. Ann felt her face heat up and she realized how messy she was, covered in dirt and bark and leaves. Her hair was nothing but tangles.

"There is a town to the west of here," the woman explained. "It is small, but there are a few permanent residents. Unfortunately the gates close at dusk, so you will have to wait until morning. You should be able to reach it tomorrow, if you set out when the sun is high. That still leaves the matter of where you will stay tonight. Ordinarily, I would offer my home, however…" She smiled. "I think I know just where you should go."

"You do?"

The woman gave a curt nod. "Before you go, I must prepare you. There are things you should know, and things to be done."

The woman set her basket down and adjusted the cross-stitched cloth that covered the items inside. The light from the rising moon glinted on a sharpened blade beneath. Though the woman took care to move the ax out of the basket and into the folds of her skirt, Ann noticed it, and she gave the woman a curious look.

"Wolves," the woman offered by way of explanation. "In fact, that is the first thing you must know. This forest is a wonder to behold by day, but at night all manner of dangerous animals and dark creatures emerge. This makes it unsafe for the unarmed, such as yourself." She retrieved a comb from the basket. "Hold still, now. You need to be at least somewhat presentable."

Ann stood as still as she possibly could, but to no avail as the combing tugged her whole body this way and that. The comb was barely able to make any real change to her tangles, though it did get a few locks a little straighter. After quite some time of pulling and fighting with the mess of waves, the woman gave up with a sigh. "That will have to do."

"Where am I going?" Ann asked, rubbing her sore scalp.

"The home of a faerie," the woman said.

"A *faerie*?" Ann gasped. She did know about faeries, or at least she had an idea of what they were like: tiny people with butterfly wings. How would she ever fit into one of their homes?

"And now for the rest of what you must know," the woman went on. "Faeries are capricious by nature, but even they have rules that they must follow." She placed the comb back into the basket and retrieved a loaf of bread. "For example, if you greet a faerie by offering a gift and call him what he is, then he will be obligated to treat you with hospitality for one week. This should be far more than you need, if you live in the town next to the woods. So long as you pay your host the proper respects and have good manners, he should not be inclined to play tricks on you."

Ann accepted the loaf of bread, holding it carefully. "Thank you."

"You are welcome, my dear. Unfortunately, I cannot make the journey with you. I am sorry to leave you to walk the distance alone. Keep going north, into the pine forest, until you can see the mountains over the treetops. You'll be close then, and you will be able to climb a tree and see the towers of his castle."

"What sort of faerie is he?" Ann asked.

"You need not worry about that," the woman said. "Remember, he is bound by law to show you hospitality once you offer the bread and reveal that you know what he is."

That was not the most inspiring answer, but it was the one that Ann was given, and she accepted it. She held the bread loaf closer. "Thank you again, ma'am."

The woman frowned briefly at that, and Ann thought that she must be on the younger side of her possible age scale. "Forgive my manners. You may call me Tanya."

"Tanya. That's a beautiful name," Ann replied. "Mine is Ann."

"Thank you. Yours is a good name, as well. Quite fitting." Tanya tried once more to smooth Ann's hair into place. Then she readjusted her cloak, picked up her basket and her axe, and said, "You really should get going. Remember, north until you see the mountains, then look for the castle towers."

Ann nodded. "I've got it, and I won't forget!"

"Farewell for now, my dear."

Ann started walking toward the northern end of the woods, turning to wave over her shoulder at Tanya as she went. The red-cloaked woman waved back cordially, and soon Ann's stride took them out of sight of each other.

Though the hoots and howls should have worried her, Ann found herself much more at ease. Perhaps that had something to do with the flares of a red cloak that she caught in the corner of her eye as she walked, or the warm smell of the bread loaf in her hands that reminded her of a cozy hearth, her nightmare forgotten for now.

Before long, the leaves at her feet gave way to dark green needles, and soon she was walking through nothing but pine trees. The forest was sparser here, and in no time at all she was able to peer between the tall, angular treetops to see moonlight reflecting on the distant, snow-capped mountains. She took a moment to look for a tree with low, sturdy branches. She found a suitable one, tucked the bread loaf into her satchel, made a running start, and clawed her way up its trunk.

It took a moment for Ann to find anything resembling a castle tower, but she did spot them. They were pure white, and blended in with the wintry forest and mountains, but they were definitely towers. And the castle wasn't too far!

She carefully descended the trunk until she was close enough to the ground to let go and land on her feet.

The knowledge that the castle was so close gave Ann fresh vigor. She practically skipped toward the glassy towers she had seen.

By the time she reached the castle's gated courtyard, the moon was high in the sky. At first she wondered how she would scale the locked gate and clear the sharp spires at the top, especially since the gate appeared to be made of ice. Then she realized that she was small enough to slip between the bars. Easing through them, she entered the courtyard beyond.

A cobblestone path led from the tall gate through mounds of snow, circling a fountain where other paths branched out to western and eastern entrances. The fountain wasn't running; instead, the water droplets had been frozen in midair, creating an elegant ice sculpture. Other ice sculptures were arranged around the fountain—images of praying angels, prancing foxes, and stags with elaborate horns, all so meticulously crafted and detailed that at first Ann thought they were real.

She resisted the temptation to bound through the snow and admire the statues. She needed to deliver the bread and gain the faerie's hospitality. She doubted he would welcome her to stay in his home, even for a single night, if he caught her trespassing.

As incredible as the courtyard was, the castle itself was on an entirely different level. It rose from the northern end of the garden like a mountain. The architecture was deceptively simple—tall and square, with a few beveled towers. However, when looking a little closer, Ann saw intricate designs of individual snowflakes etched into the walls and stairs, all of which were made out of ice and glass. The whole place shimmered and sparkled as if it was a massive diamond.

Intrigued and excited about what sort of faerie must live in such a wondrous place, Ann removed the bread from her bag and knocked on the front doors.

Nicolas had nearly fallen asleep in his study when there was a knock on his door. He rose to answer it, back popping as he straightened his posture and stalked down the staircase to the entrance hall. Drew must have come to give him a private scolding in regards to his actions at the Autumnal Equinox festival, and another ludicrous speech about pity or scorn.

If Drew thought he could threaten Nicolas here, where he was most powerful, then the Eldest faerie was sorely mistaken. However, Nicolas would give him a chance to say what he wanted before sending him away.

He took a seat on his throne so he could glower impressively at the doors. With a wave of his hand, they opened. "Intrude."

The small figure at the door was not Drew. In fact, it was no one Nicolas had ever seen before: a woman, small and plain, her pale skin smudged with dirt that matched her earthy brown hair. He could not tell her eye color, but he could not imagine that it was at all significant.

Her only significant feature was that she did not have wings.

Nicolas waved his hand again to close the doors and keep her out, but she was already inside, so they closed and kept her in, instead. She glanced at the doors as they slammed, taking a few more cautious steps inside. She paused there to take in the sight of the entrance, at which Nicolas felt the tiniest spark of pride. He had been meticulous in the details of the castle's construction. The ice, opaque from the outside, acted as a window from within. The mountains, courtyard, and forest were in full, clear view at all times of day. Beyond the front door was a grand hallway that branched out into a vast ballroom. An impressive crystal chandelier hung from the center of its vaulted ceiling, catching every bit of light from the outside and scattering it across the room to illuminate the frozen décor. A banquet table stood off to the opposite side of the hall, but there were no places set, despite the ornate tablecloth that rested over it. At the end of the hall, displayed on a pedestal and directly between the ballroom and dining room, sat a high-backed throne from which Nicolas could oversee all. A staircase on either side of his throne led up to the second floor's many rooms.

The human lifted her chin in defiance, though she looked at him directly for only a moment. "Greetings, Faerie!" she called.

"Do not come any closer," Nicolas commanded. Thankfully she stopped, having covered almost half of the distance between his throne and the door. "Identify yourself."

She appeared to be baffled by the command. Then, with a little shake of her head, she said, "Oh, right! My name is Ann." She held up a loaf of bread. "And I've got this for you. It's rye, I think. So, uh…if it's not too much to ask, may I spend the night here?"

Nicolas gripped the arms of his throne. This had to be the most foolish human he had ever come across. True, he did not see them often, but usually when he was recognized by a human they cowered in fear and awe of him. This one—Ann, a simple name for a simple creature—was not only completely unafraid, but asking *favors* of him!

If the law were not protecting her, he would have thrown her out and cursed her with a nasty case of frostbite, but he forced his hands to remain on the throne.

Then again, perhaps she wasn't human at all. He could sense magical energy around her. Weak, but there. And she had found him so easily, perhaps by tracing his own magic. It might do more harm than good to reject her. Wanderers were supposed to be good luck, after all.

"You may stay, as the law demands," he answered finally, each word like losing a tooth.

She smiled, but there was no cunning in her round eyes to show that she enjoyed his suffering. If Nicolas had to guess, she was simply oblivious. "Thank you! I'll be gone in the morning, so you won't have to worry about me much. What should I do with the bread?"

"Take it to the kitchen." Obviously.

"Oh." She looked around, lifting herself up onto her toes as if that would provide a better view. She was still for a moment before adding, "I don't know where that is," at the exact moment that her stomach loudly growled.

Nicolas covered his mouth with his hand so she couldn't see him frown. He supposed he would have to feed her, too. Letting her starve certainly wouldn't be hospitable, and he didn't want her to think he didn't have food to spare. He checked his pocket watch. The human was already being a pain, but it was nearly time for his evening tea.

"Would you care for tea?" he asked.

"Yes!" Ann said, patting her stomach. "I don't think I've ever had tea, but I'm willing to give it a try. What does it taste like?"

The frost faerie rose from his throne and walked past the banquet table without answering. She followed him, her feet occasionally sliding on the ice floor. Thankfully she didn't fall; he didn't want the bread to be smashed. She managed to match him stride for stride as he passed through the hidden passage at the corner of the dining room that led to the kitchen. He probably should have remembered that it wasn't visible to most people—which was, of course, the point; he hated to have an obvious hall disturb the symmetry of the layout—but he so seldom had guests, it had slipped his mind.

Now that they were closer, and standing on even ground, Nicolas was surprised by how tiny the human was. Despite appearing to be fully grown, she only just passed his waist in height. He was certain he could pick her up with one hand if he so desired. The loaf that had at first seemed disproportionately large was, in actuality, normal-sized. It would be just enough to last the week.

Entering the kitchen lifted Nicolas's spirits, if only just off the floor where he'd left them. The kitchen was perhaps his most prized creation. He had fitted it with all manner of enchantments and spells so he could enjoy warm tea and confections without causing the castle to melt around him. Many of the walls were constructed from glass instead of ice, but the transition between the kitchen and the rest of the palace was so seamless that no one had yet guessed his secret.

He gestured to the small table placed near the oven. Normally it was used to place baking racks and cookie trays, but it would serve as a tea table for the time being. "Tea will be ready shortly."

Instead of walking, Ann slid across the floor and grabbed the edge of the table to stop herself, standing with her hands folded neatly on top of it. She smiled, full of pride. Nicolas made no comment.

Nicolas set the kettle on the stove and retrieved two bags of rose tea, placing them in teacups. The cup didn't match. He'd never felt the need to buy his teacups in sets, as he never had company. Now the mix-matched cups bothered him a little.

"Are you royalty?" Ann asked.

He looked over his shoulder at her. "Of a sort."

"What sort? And you haven't told me your name yet."

Nicolas took a deep breath. Oberon grant him the patience to deal with this pest! "I am Nicolas Rasmussen, Regional Prince of the Frost Fae, Ruler of the Season of Winter and *Second-Eldest Ruler* of the Northern Realm. You may address me as any one of my titles." Never mind that Second-Eldest Ruler was not a proper title.

"Your…titles? Not your name?"

"Of course not, unless you have a title of your own," Nicolas said. He looked over her again. Was that *mud* on her pants? "Which I highly doubt."

Still, he couldn't ignore the fact that a seemingly ordinary human woman had traces of magic around her, and recognized him as a faerie immediately. As far as he had heard, human adults were not supposed to be able to see the fair folk; only a select few could do that once they left childhood.

"Are you a witch?" he inquired. He tried to keep his nose out of it, but he had heard rumors from some of the more active frost fae under his command that witches had been spotted in the area.

"Nope, I'm not a witch. I'm just Ann!" she chirped.

"As I thought." The magic must be coming from an enchanted trinket — the purse, maybe. The crystals that studded the flap were indicative of that. She most likely did not have any actual powers, like most humans. But

43

the law was the law, and there was no going back on it now.

"But I suppose, in that case," she went on, "I'll call you 'Your Majesty!'"

"'Your Highness,'" he corrected her, though he couldn't expect a human with no grand position to remember the subtle nuances in addressing nobility.

"You don't have to call me 'Your Highness.' Just 'Ann' is fine!" she laughed back.

Nicolas shook his head and focused on the kettle, which would take some time to whistle. An ordinary human peasant had found and gained access to his home. He would have to find a way to make sure that this did not happen again. How had she managed to pass through the gate?

"Where should I sleep?" she asked. It was as if she could not withstand two full minutes of silence without opening her mouth.

"Any of the unlocked rooms," he answered.

"*Any* of them? But the castle is huge!"

"Then it will not be difficult for you to stay out of my way."

"But how am I going to know which doors are unlocked?" Ann asked, looking at him expectantly.

"They will not be locked," Nicolas answered. For some reason, this caused her to break into a wide smile. Had he said something amusing? He had not meant to, and he was not sure how to feel about her smiling like that. It didn't *seem* derogatory, but one could never be too sure.

The kettle finally whistled. Nicolas poured the boiling water into the cups, letting it steep for a few minutes before serving the tea and a thick slice of bread to Ann. In the few brief moments it took for him to walk from the stove to the table, the tea was already cool enough to drink safely. Not even the gloves he wore could prevent Nicolas's naturally cold aura from chilling the liquid, but that suited him just fine.

Nicolas intended to take his tea in the study, rather than remain in the woman's company for another moment, but she continued to speak—and only a rude host would leave the room while the guest was talking to him.

"Are you alone here?" Ann asked.

"I enjoy solitude," Nicolas responded, taking measured sips of tea. "Besides which, there is nothing wrong with being alone. What of you? Were you not alone?"

"I have been alone," Ann answered. She took a few sips after he did. "And being alone wasn't bad at all, but I'm much happier here with you than I was out there alone."

"You are happy here?"

"Yes. Why wouldn't I be? This castle is incredible, there's snow outside to play in, and I'm having tea with a real, actual faerie prince! How could anyone find a way to be unhappy here?"

"How, indeed. I do not understand it, either, and yet it is true." Ice began to accumulate on Nicolas's teacup. The tea within froze when he thought of the Equinox festival. He and his season were unwanted by both faeries and humans. "If they only saw things the way *I* do."

He cut himself off there. He was getting too emotional. He hid his face behind the teacup for another sip, only for the frozen solid tea to clack against his teeth.

"Can I see it?" Ann asked.

Her request caught Nicolas off guard. He was silent for a moment before coolly responding, "See what?"

"What you see."

"I doubt it." What hope did a mere human have of understanding him? Then again, every faerie he had ever tried to explain himself to had also misunderstood. She would be gone in the morning, so he had nothing to lose in trying again. "Once you finish your bread, I will try to show you what I mean."

Ann attacked the bread slice, shoving it into her mouth and tearing off half of it in one bite, which she chewed only a few times before swallowing. The other half was gone just as quickly, washed down with the remaining tea. Nicolas would have to remember not to allow his hand to stray near her mouth while she was eating.

"...If you will accompany me back to the throne room..."

Ann jumped up from her seat and slid toward the kitchen's entrance, back down the hallway and to the throne room. The fact that she had mastered moving around on the icy floor so soon was commendable, but Nicolas never did anything at anyone's pace but his own. He calmly walked to the throne room, taking his time.

He couldn't tell if Ann was shaking from the cold or excitement, and he inwardly scoffed at the fact that she was wearing only a sweater to protect herself from the frigid temperature. He did not relish the idea of removing her frozen corpse from the castle grounds, but offering her a proper coat would be beyond the requirements of hospitality. A gift like that would mean welcoming her to stay indefinitely.

Nicolas fluttered his wings, and the air around them chilled. He concentrated on making a small cloud, just big enough to hover over his hands. Ann stared with wide eyes as the cloud formed and crystalline flakes of snow fell from it into his waiting palms. Within a few minutes the cloud dispersed, and Nicolas let the collected flakes fall toward the floor. Ann reached out and caught them in her hands.

"It's cold!" she gasped.

"Of course. What else did you expect?"

The snowflakes melted slowly in Ann's hands, before dripping onto the floor and freezing again.

"That was fun! I don't see how anyone could get tired of that," Ann said.

"But you did not see it," he said. "Snowflakes are more than *fun*."

Ann shuffled her feet in response to the glare Nicolas gave her. Had she done or said something to offend him? She had thought that her enjoyment of the snow would put him in a better mood, but every indicator told her that he was even more frustrated now.

"I've never seen snow fall before. I thought it was wonderful," Ann offered.

"That is not the point." Why didn't she understand? Why didn't *anyone* understand? Then again, it wasn't as if he'd believed she would. "It melted too quickly for you to see it correctly. Your hands were too warm." That had to be the problem. Everyone else was too warm to truly appreciate the cold as anything but a fleeting novelty.

Ann frowned at his sudden defensiveness. "It was still amazing to me," she said. "If it's possible, could we tour the castle? I'd like to see more of it. Maybe then I'll understand."

"It is not possible," Nicolas responded curtly. "The castle is far too large, and I feel the beginnings of a headache. If you must be escorted, then I will show you to the empty rooms you may sleep in, but no further."

"That's fine," Ann said. "I'm feeling pretty tired. I wouldn't mind going to bed."

Nicolas stifled a sigh of relief and led her up the stairs behind the throne, to the western corridor. Solid slabs of ice stretched between arched frames along the walls. However, Ann could see that there were rooms beyond them. "How—"

"Hush." Nicolas tapped the center of one of the ice slabs. It split in a neat line down the middle to form a pair of double doors that opened with ease. The room beyond contained just a few wooden furnishings: a bed, a wardrobe, and a nightstand, all carved with images of the woods and snowflakes. The room itself was large, and had its own adjoining bathroom.

Ann pressed her hand on the mattress to test it. Thankfully, it wasn't made of ice. Instead it was soft, warm, and covered with goose down pillows and thick fur blankets. She smiled. "Thank you. I'll find a way to make this up to you."

"You need not bother. I trust you can find your way back to the kitchen for breakfast—no, make it the parlor, down the hall. That is a more proper room for mealtimes. Be there shortly after dawn, do not be late, and do not break anything. If you need me, I will be in my study in the east wing."

He left the room, closing the door behind him. Ann removed her boots and bag, then changed into one of the long wool nightgowns that hung in the wardrobe. She crawled into bed, tired from the day's journey. Resting her legs felt wonderful. She nearly sank into the mattress, and would have been content to do just that, allowing herself to be buried beneath the warm embrace of the furs.

Sleep was slow to come, and as Ann lay awake in the bed and stared at the ceiling, she became keenly aware of how high it was. Looking around, she realized that everything was far away, and the almost empty room filled her with loneliness.

She slipped out of the bed and walked into the hallway to get away from the bareness of her chamber. It was only a guest bedroom, and judging from Nicolas's comments about solitude, he didn't have much of a need to fill it.

However, she found more of the same in the hallway. When she thought about it, the throne room felt the same way. Despite the immaculate detail of the décor and furniture in every room, there was no life in any of it. If she and Nicolas left the castle, there would be no evidence that anyone had ever lived there. The whole palace was empty.

Ann began to understand Nicolas's surprise at the idea that anyone could be happy there.

She returned to her room, curled up under the blankets, and closed her eyes tightly while thinking of the forest, the flowers, and the sun that she dearly missed.

3

THE NAMELESS TOWN

ANN AWOKE AT WHAT SHE THOUGHT was a bright and early time the next morning, having not slept well the night before due to nightmarish visions of fire and wide, empty spaces. However, by the time she found her way to the parlor, Nicolas was already setting the table for breakfast. He spared her a glance before returning his attention to perfectly plating the coffee cake.

"Sorry, were you waiting long?" she asked as she took her seat.

"Four minutes. Did you sleep well?"

Ann shook her head and took a sip from the teacup at her place setting in an attempt to warm up. It was certainly hotter than the air, but too chilled to have much of an effect. Still, she liked the flavor, and kept drinking. Realizing that Nicolas expected her to respond verbally when he cleared his throat, she said, "Not really."

"Was the room not to your liking?" Nicolas asked more insistently than she'd expected.

"Oh, no, the room was fine! The bed was comfortable, and I liked snuggling into the blankets." Ann gave him a reassuring smile. That much was true, and she felt no need to bring up the haunting loneliness of the

cavernous castle. It was his, after all. He must like it that way. "Just…nightmares."

The parlor didn't feel quite as hollow, probably due to its smaller size. The two of them sat at a little table near a bay window overlooking the courtyard. The presence of a window offered a strange comfort, though the walls themselves offered almost the same view. A chaise lounge and a low bookcase completed the parlor, which was less a full room and more of a rest stop in the east hallway.

Nicolas did not smile or nod back to her. "I am relieved that you found your room enjoyable. I have never known any but frost fae to be comfortable here."

"What other kinds of fae are there?" Ann asked, perking up. She ought to have assumed that there were others. They couldn't *all* live in ice castles and control frost and snow.

"All sorts, some benign, some destructive. Most are small and tend to be reclusive. Our kind do not mix particularly well with humans, or even other fantastic beings, so we prefer not to be seen. I am sure you could find plenty of floral fae doing something silly, like painting leaves, if you looked hard enough. I, of course, am a frost faerie. I am responsible for snow, hail, and so on. You should know that already from yesterday."

Ann smiled wide in excitement. "There are more of you around?"

"There is only one of me."

"I meant—"

"I know what you meant. The other frost fae do not come here often. As Regional Prince, I am more than powerful enough to take care of this area myself.

I prefer to issue my orders by messenger, rather than have underlings swarming in and out at all hours of the day and night for their assignments."

"Solitude?" Ann offered.

"Complete solitude," Nicolas said. "I despise interlopers."

She fell quiet, her gaze downcast. "Have you *always* been alone?" she asked, her voice soft.

"No," Nicolas said. He sipped his tea, pausing to consider his answer before he gave it. Perhaps if he spoke more, she would stop looking so grim. "Almost, but not quite. Before me, Princess Bethilde held my title and made her castle here. She raised me on these grounds and taught me everything she knew. When she passed on, I inherited her position and made my palace here as well. That was nearly two centuries ago. I have established myself quite nicely, I think."

"What about other faeries?"

"They never got along with me," Nicolas answered shortly. "That was always how things were. Princess Bethilde brought me to the more remote reaches of the forest because of it. I have never felt any reason to leave. I am content here, and the castle is exactly how I like it."

Nicolas was surprised at how easily he could speak his mentor's name. Perhaps enough time had finally passed. He had always known he was being trained to replace her and that she would eventually fade away. That morbid knowledge had loomed over his entire apprenticeship. Despite that, he had a few treasured memories from his tutelage under her wings, and hated to think of her funeral. That may have been the last time he had spoken of her.

And yet, this strange human woman easily drew the name out from him. Perhaps his earlier assumption that she was a witch had been right, or maybe she was some other magical creature. He looked her over again, searching for the usual tells: pointed ears, pointed teeth, or mismatched eye colors. Nothing marked her as anything other than an ordinary, if semi-wild, human.

Ann looked as if she wanted to say more, but she returned to her cake, finishing it in two bites. Her questions confounded Nicolas, but he had to admit that he found them the slightest bit touching. Humans and their sentimental ways. She must be missing the company of other humans after her night in the woods, and would likely not bother him again once she found her way back to her own kind.

"I suppose I'll be off, then," she said, once the teapot was emptied and the coffee cake had been reduced to crumbs. "Thank you for your hospitality."

"You are welcome. I wish you good fortune."

Nicolas rose and saw her to the door. He watched her hop through the snow on her way out, slipping easily between the bars of the gate.

That had not been the worst ordeal of his life, but he was glad it was over, and he returned to the silence inside the castle. He would have to clean the room where she'd slept. That would throw off his schedule a bit, but it was necessary and he had best get to it.

The town was smaller than Ann had expected, not that she'd expected much. It consisted of little more than a library, a church, a hotel, a few boutiques and restaurants, an automotive repair shop that seemed out of place in a town with no paved roads, and a few dozen houses, not counting the living quarters attached to the shops. It was surrounded by a tall iron gate topped with sharp points. Signs posted in various places read, 'Practicers of magics not welcome here.'

Despite the gorgeous sunshine and weather, the town still managed to be gloomy. It filled Ann with a deep sense of dread, and she nearly changed her mind about passing through the entrance.

Ann inspected the houses first. None of their old wood planks and shabby roofs brought her any comfort or sense of familiarity. It was hard to say who would actually want to live in such houses, and Ann was certain that she didn't.

Only a few people answered their doors when she knocked, and they turned her away with scorn. One old woman even struck her with a broom and yelled at her to go back where she came from, as if that wasn't what Ann was trying to do!

Most of the other houses sported large locks, but her bag held no key, so they couldn't be hers. A few others were uninhabited, their insides bare of furniture, food, and any other signs that anyone had lived there in weeks. She got the feeling that these houses were for travelers looking to stay a week or two, not permanent residences.

She supposed she could move into one of the empty houses while she searched for her own, but that eerie feeling grew each time she entered one. And the incident with the broom wasn't endearing her to her potential neighbors.

Ann hoped she didn't live in this town. It didn't feel like home at all. Perhaps that was why she'd gone into the woods. If that were the case, she would have to roam farther to find a place to call her own.

And she'd have to do it all wearing the same pants and sweater. She didn't love that idea.

On that note, she decided a quick stop at the clothing boutique was in order.

The shop owner regarded her coolly from the moment she came in, and she shrank under the woman's frigid stare. Did she intimidate her customers into buying her merchandise? Ann couldn't imagine a smile on her face.

Instead of perusing the aisles, Ann swiped a pair of gloves from the front rack and brought them up to the counter.

"Thirty dollars," the saleswoman snipped.

Ann opened her bag and pulled out her wallet. Were there dollars in there? Were there *thirty* of them?

She reached into the wallet and pulled out a handful of what she thought must be money, dropping six gold coins onto the counter. Judging from the woman's shocked and unamused expression, Ann felt safe making the guess that those wouldn't do.

The woman picked one up and bit it between her teeth, then gave Ann a bewildered look. The gold looked real, ever so slightly dented by the woman's bite.

"Is this some kind of joke?" she barked. "What are you playing at?"

"I'm sorry!" Ann said quickly, ducking out of the store with the gloves. The amount of gold she'd left on the counter should more than cover the cost of them.

She heard the woman yelling at her from the door and hurried away from the shop, barreling down the main road to the biggest building in the city. It was a whole two stories tall, and the outside looked well-maintained. Ann met with the musty smell of old books as soon as she opened the door. A desk sat to the right of the doorway, bearing a stack of books waiting to be reshelved, and a small brass bell.

Ann rang the bell and, delighted by the sound, continued to do so until the librarian appeared. She knew he was the librarian because it was written on his nametag. That was also how she knew his name was Cecil. The gap between his two front teeth told her that he had a goofy smile, and she liked it.

"Someone's enthusiastic," he said with a laugh.

"Actually, my name is Ann."

He snorted, and Ann knew without a shred of doubt that they would be friends. He was the only person in the town that didn't make her want to run back into the woods as fast as she could.

"I haven't heard that name before. Are you new in town?" he asked.

"You mean I don't live here?"

"It wouldn't be unusual if you didn't. I've met plenty of travelers who are just passing through. Aren't you one of them?" Cecil asked.

"I...don't know."

"Oh, my. That is unfortunate." His tone was light, but Ann could see concern growing in his eyes. She could see the same look on her own face, reflected in his thick glasses.

"My family must be somewhere nearby," Ann said. "Are there any new families in town?"

Cecil opened a thick leather-bound tome that sat on the desk. Its pages were yellow and brittle with age. He flipped to the back and scanned all the signatures and dates near the end of the book. "No new visitors since last month, and it looks like those two left about a week ago. They were an elderly couple, and I don't think they had any of their children with them."

"That just can't be right. Are there reports for missing persons?"

"Missing persons, yes. *Reports* for missing persons? No."

Silence descended on the library. Ann stared hard at the book, willing it to reveal something about her missing family. Cecil gave her a brief look of open concern, then closed the ledger, smiled reassuringly, and patted her head. "Cheer up, there, Ann. It's not so bad. You're in a library!"

"What's so great about that?"

"I'm going to pretend you didn't say that." Cecil reached under the desk and removed a small paper card and pen from a cubby hole. "Here, write your name on this."

Ann took the pen and scrawled all three letters of her name across the line on the back of the card, stretching them out so they took up the whole space. She didn't think to ask, "What's this?" until she was already done signing her name.

"A library card. With this, you can check out as many books as you want, as long as you return them in two weeks."

Ann examined the card, not quite sure why he had given her one. How would this help her find her way home?

Before she could ask he stepped around the desk and took her hand. "Come with me."

Ann followed Cecil faithfully through row upon twisted row of bookshelves. At the center of the maze stood a table, though it hardly looked like one with the half dozen blankets that were draped over it. A lamp and some encyclopedias had been placed on top to keep the blankets from sliding off. Cecil pulled one of the blankets aside and disappeared under it, finally releasing her hand. Ann dipped down to follow him without hesitation.

Underneath the table were more blankets, pillows with floral prints, flashlights, stuffed dragons and unicorns, and rows upon rows of books that filled the space between the table legs.

"This is one of many book forts I have set up

around the library," Cecil said with a proud grin. "I figured this one would be the best to start you with. Now, let's see…" He drew his finger along the spines of the books, quietly murmuring their titles as he passed them. "*Alice in Wonderland, Tales from Moominvalley…* Ah! *Classic Fairytales.* Perfect." He flicked on a flashlight and removed his glasses, which hung by a chain around his neck. The book's spine crackled from age when he opened it, and handed it to her so she could follow along. "Now you just get comfortable. *Once upon a time…*"

Ann wasn't sure whether it was the soft blankets and pillows, the smell of the old books, or Cecil's melodious voice rising and falling with the introduction of each new character, but she found herself drifting away into a world of beautiful princesses, magic spells, evil step-mothers, and clever animals. She was equally enchanted and horrified; in one instant she was happy that Snow White had been awoken by true love's kiss, and in the next she was pitying the evil queen who was forced to dance in red-hot shoes until she died (which was a little too close to being burned alive for her liking). The step-sisters in *Cinderella* cutting off parts of their feet and having their eyes pecked by birds was hard to sit through, and she found herself clutching the little dragon plush closer even as Cinderella was getting her happily ever after. And she had expected someone to save Red Riding Hood and her grandmother—perhaps someone like the woman she had met in the woods, who also wore a red hooded cape and carried an ax—but the wolf ate them up, and that was the end!

She didn't know what to feel about *The Little*

Mermaid, but she found it hard not to shed a tear.

And these were meant to be stories for *children*?

By far, the tale that captivated her most was *The Snow Queen*. No one was horribly maimed, there were talking animals, and the power of true love conquered all without really hurting anyone in the process. A happy ending to a beautiful love story.

Ann would be lying if she tried to convince herself that she wasn't thinking of Nicolas as she listened. She found herself wondering what his and her roles would be if they were the ones in the story.

"That's enough for now," Cecil said finally, putting his glasses back on. He glanced at the watch on his wrist. "Goodness, it's been hours! I'm terribly sorry, Ann, but I have to get ready for a lunch date." He pulled a few books out of the piles and led Ann back to the front desk, scribbling their titles and the date into the ledger. "I think these books would be good for you to read on your own. Remember, they'll be due back in two weeks. Even though I just read it, I included *The Snow Queen*, since you looked like you enjoyed it so much. And this one." He pulled a book from one of the nearby shelves of non-fiction. "Read them over and we'll discuss them when you make the return!"

"I, ah...okay, then!" Ann replied as Cecil thrust the books into her arms.

"I'm really sorry, but my boyfriend will kill me if I'm late again. Last time I got too caught up in *Don Quixote* and almost missed our lunch entirely." He said all this while pulling a mirror out from under the desk, smoothing his hair just for his bangs to fall back where they'd been, and straightening his tie. "How do I look?"

"Handsome, and thank you for the books. Good luck with your date."

"You're more than welcome. I look forward to your next visit—feel free to stop by anytime. You don't have to wait the full two weeks, just so you know. And Ann..." He chose his next words carefully: "I hope you're leaving in a better mood than you arrived in. I'm sorry I can't help you more in terms of your family, but try not to let it get to you. Keep your chin up, and you'll find them."

Instead of walking out of the library, as Ann would have assumed was the direction of the date, Cecil instead dove back into the maze of shelves. She could only guess at where he was going, and she showed herself out.

The street was just as empty that afternoon as it had been that morning, and Ann was certain now from the record in the library that this was not where she lived. That fact brought her more relief than anguish. Cecil was nice enough, and she did enjoy the library, but the thought of *living* in this town was far too dreary. She much preferred to be a visitor.

Still, that raised the ever-present question of *where* exactly she'd come from. There were no roads in the forest to lead her elsewhere, and she had the suspicion that there were no other towns within walking distance. She had to live somewhere close by, but *where*?

Missing persons, but no reports, she recalled. Gazing out into the thick woods, she could all too easily imagine hapless victims braving a hike only to get lost in the forest after dark and left to the mercy of whatever lived there. Their families would never think to file a report in a small, nameless town, if they had families at all.

Even more worrisome was the fact that she couldn't remember what she'd been doing in the woods in the first place. It was easy enough to assume that she had fancied a walk through the beautiful early autumn trees and had decided to take a nap, but she was only *assuming*, and that frightened her.

She looked down at the books Cecil had given her. They included the book of fairy tales he'd read from, the individual copy of *The Snow Queen*, *Treasure Island*, and one that was unlike the rest. One that didn't have colorful illustrations on the cover.

Coping with Amnesia.

Nicolas was surprised when he heard a knock at the door and found that Ann had returned. The sun had begun to set, and though she had arrived before nightfall, she wouldn't be able to make it back to town now without risking her life against night hunters and the more treacherous fair folk.

She had probably come to give him the good news that she had found her home. She wouldn't have wanted him to worry about her getting lost or attacked. It was only a cheerful, air-headed courtesy, and he would extend an invitation to her for another night's stay in the castle due to her mistake in judgment.

One more night. Then she would be gone. He could stomach that.

Why she had come carrying books, of all things, was

a mystery he decided not to question. Humans were a strange and altogether frivolous species; that was explanation enough.

Besides, he hadn't even asked, and she was already telling him everything about her day.

"…And then he showed me this *incredible* book fort and told me some stories for a few hours, and it didn't seem like that much time had passed, but he was going to be late for a date so he gave me some books to read and sent me on my way. A good day, all in all. I learned where I'm *not* from, which is more than I knew before. And now I'm back. What have you been doing?"

"Nothing out of the ordinary." With his season yet to come, and the vast majority of his subjects still recovering their magic in the far north, there was not much to do around the ice palace besides bake, drink tea, and read from his own personal library. Ordinarily he would paint, too, but lately he could not think of anything that stirred his brush hand.

Not that he was complaining—far from it. He enjoyed the serenity of being alone with his thoughts, without talkative faeries or humans pestering him.

"What do you mean by 'you are back'?" There was a finality to her statement that struck him as out of place. She had met another human, after all. Hadn't that been the purpose of her going to town in the first place? Whether she lived there or not was beside the point.

Ann shuffled her feet against the ice. "I didn't find my home, so I came back. I hope that's alright."

Nicolas gritted his teeth, but kept his voice even. "And you came here instead of staying in town, where there are other humans who could look after you?"

"I did a little reading on my way," Ann said, flipping open the book at the top of the stack with one hand. "And it says here that I should stay close to people, places, or objects that make me comfortable, to minimize stress."

"And what book is that?" Nicolas turned the cover over and saw the title. His frustrations were almost instantly abated. "Oh. I see."

"I'm sorry. I know you don't want me here. I promise I'll try my hardest to get my memories back and find out who I am and where my family is! But until then, may I stay here?"

Her eyes were wide and pleading, and now Nicolas could see that they were dark blue, like shadows falling over fresh snow. They held an honest look, and her plea was sincere. He could not turn her away.

"I suppose that you may, so long as it is purely temporary," he sighed. How long would it take her to remember where she lived? A few days? A week? If it were any more than that, he would have no choice but to put her out, lest Oberon and Titania discover her presence. For a faerie of his station to break the law, the punishment would be nothing short of execution.

She bowed. "Thank you, Your Royal Majesty, Ruler of Snowflakes—"

"That will suffice," he said, raising a hand to cut her off. An official-sounding salutation like that from her was nothing short of ridiculous. Perhaps he should have let her use his name, after all. "Evening tea will be held in an hour in the parlor. Do not be late."

THE WANDERER IN THE CASTLE

BEFORE HE REALIZED HOW FAST the time was passing, it had been a full week since Nicolas had taken Ann into his home. Come midnight, he'd have to make the decision as to whether she would stay or go.

The dreary weather made the choice no easier. Every time he imagined himself telling her firmly (but not unkindly) to leave the palace, he saw her walking out into the dark, damp forest, alone and unprotected from the unruly faeries of the Unseelie Court.

His uncertainty concerned him. It should not be so difficult; the week of hospitality had passed, the last slice of rye bread was soon to be eaten, and she had to make her own way in the world. He was under no further obligation to house her, and had more than enough reason to shoo her off to town and tell her to find someone else to watch over her. Surely the librarian she'd mentioned could help find her a place to live.

Still, this cheerful creature had wormed her way into his routine. She was there every morning for breakfast, if a few minutes late, and they would share their plans for the day or opinions on books they were reading. He had to assure her more than once that fairytales were only stories, even amongst the fair folk, and there was a stark difference between 'fairies' and 'faeries'.

After breakfast, Ann spent most of her days searching for clues to her identity, and returned in the late afternoon to have tea and talk again about the discoveries she made in the woods. There were no leads about her past yet, but she did delight in regaling to Nicolas the stories of how she found a family of squirrels or narrowly escaped a swarm of bees after knocking over their hive. If nothing interesting had happened during her wanderings, Nicolas would answer her questions.

The number of Ann's questions never failed to stun Nicolas. Where he had once passed his afternoons in silence and solitude, Ann filled his time with an endless symphony of *how* and *why* and *what about*. Almost in spite of himself, Nicolas told her more about Princess Bethilde and how long she had reigned as the Eldest Ruler due to her old age, which was almost a given since frost fae lived longer than floral fae, and light fae rarely stayed in the Northern Realm for long. Once Nicolas told Ann all that, he had to explain that the Eldest Ruler was the leader of the Regional Princes and Princesses, a title Nicolas would one day claim for himself after he inevitably outlived Drew. He avoided talking about the other Regional Princes currently ruling at any length, keeping them to mere mentions in his descriptions of faerie society and the role they played in managing the seasons throughout the world.

Between the two of them, they would speak until the sun began to set. Then they would eat a slice of the bread for dinner, say good night, and part for the evening.

It would be more accommodating for her to stay than for him to readjust his life *again* around her absence, but the law was the law. Oberon had forbidden faeries from keeping humans in their homes any longer than they were required to by the Law of Hospitality. Ann had spent her week in the castle, and now it was over. He risked execution if she was not gone by midnight.

Nicolas had considered making something for Ann as a token of the end of her stay, but no inspiration came to him—at least, no inspiration for anything practical. He'd considered sewing her a beautiful dress fit for one of her fairytale princesses, or painting a landscape of the castle courtyard so she would not forget the view, but every time he found himself idly sketching concepts he remembered that she had no idea where she lived and these extravagant gifts would only slow her down.

On this day, Ann had broken her usual routine and decided not to leave the castle. Perhaps she knew what he was going to tell her by the day's end.

Nicolas had known that it wouldn't be too long before the human came to pester him. It was the first time that she had spent a full day in the castle, and from the moment he'd seen heavy gray clouds in the sky, he'd known she wouldn't be able to make it to lunch without growing restless. He had been relaxing in his private study, as always, distracting himself with a book of coat patterns and so deep in thought that at first he didn't notice her enter. She had become so accustomed to moving around on the ice that it was as if she had been doing it her whole life, and she rarely made noise when she walked.

"What are you doing?" she asked.

He set his book down, not feeling any need to mark the page—none of the patterns appealed to him that day, either. "Nothing in particular, though I would not advise that you make a habit of barging into my study."

"Sorry. I was just wondering if you would come outside with me today."

"Why? I can see the outside just fine from here."

"That's hardly the same thing," Ann countered, folding her arms. "There's snow on the ground in the courtyard."

"There is always snow in the courtyard," Nicolas pointed out.

"So let's go enjoy it!" Ann said. "Please?"

Nicolas sighed and stood up, grabbing a tailcoat that was displayed on a nearby mannequin. He did not need it, but on the off chance that someone were to happen by, he did not want to go outside half-dressed. Of course, most faeries didn't wear as many clothes as he did, since slipping wings through the narrow slits in the back could be a hassle. Nicolas found it fairly easy with practice, and he liked his suits. "Alright."

"Great!" Ann cheered. "Race you there!"

She darted out of the room, slid down the staircase banister, and sailed along the frozen floor toward the door. With a bit of effort she managed to wedge the heavy slab of ice open and squeeze herself out into the courtyard. Nicolas did not care for races. He followed at a more dignified pace, giving the door a small push to open and close it.

Ann was already frolicking in the snow. He watched

her with amusement and bewilderment as she dove into snow banks and rolled through the soft powder. She tossed snow into the air and leapt after it, a huge smile plastered on her face.

As he watched, he felt the creep of embarrassment. Didn't she know she was making a fool of herself?

Nicolas turned to go back inside when a snowball burst against his shoulder.

He stopped.

He heard muffled footsteps retreating through the snow. When he returned his attention to the courtyard, he caught a glimpse of Ann's leg disappearing behind one of the statue pedestals. He waited for a moment before stalking toward the statue, readying his magic. She was right to hide. He would bury her in snow and leave her to dig herself out for that insulting display.

A giggle sounded behind the statue. Nicolas paused again.

She wasn't cowering in fear or trying to run away. She was enjoying this.

Nonetheless, Nicolas had built up a snowball roughly half her size and he meant to use it. He maneuvered around the statue.

"You made a grave error."

"So did you," Ann said. She lobbed a snowball in an arc over his head. It struck the snow-laden tree branch above him and powder poured down in a great lump, showering his shoulders and head. He dropped his snowball and heard a squeak of alarm as Ann was covered, too.

Nicolas shook himself off, fluttering his wings a few times to clear the ice crystals from them. He knelt and brushed some of the snow off of Ann. She was still grinning.

"Caught you in my trap," she said proudly.

"I think it backfired on you considerably."

"But it still worked, more or less." Ann fluffed up her sweater to shake the rest of the snow off before it could soak into the fibers and freeze them stiff.

Nicolas wondered why she wasn't succumbing to the cold. Eventually all humans took shelter from the snow and ice, but she seemed almost as at ease in the frigid temperature as any frost faerie. Once more he examined her for signs that she might be a magical creature. Before he could say another word, she was back on her feet and staring into the trees.

He followed her gaze, but saw nothing.

She crept forward.

"What are you doing?" he asked.

"There's a bird in that tree. I'm going to catch it."

Nicolas sniffed. "You cannot be serious."

Ann continued forward as if she hadn't heard him. When she was halfway to the tree, she broke into a sprint. She was fast and sure-footed, but not as fast or sure-winged as the cardinal. The bird took to the sky, circled them once, and flew away over the courtyard gate.

Ann stopped at the base of the tree. "Shoot!"

"What were you trying to do?" Nicolas asked, half to himself. "What would you have done with the bird if you had caught it?"

"I would have let it go, probably." Ann shrugged. "I wanted to see it closer, that's all. It was so *red*. Maybe the second reddest thing I've ever seen."

"And you thought you could grab it from the tree?" The idea almost made him laugh, but he quelled that urge. Stoic, unfeeling, cold—those were the traits that defined a frost faerie of his standing.

"Why not?" Ann said. "I think people have caught birds before. And you must have caught wild animals, too. Just look at these statues." She pointed to a sculpture of a swan. "Like this one! The detail on the feathers makes it almost look real."

"I did not catch the swan, I merely watched it from the shore and sketched it," Nicolas explained.

"And the deer? The fox?"

"Observation. You might do well to spend a little more time watching from a distance, and a little less time chasing after everything. Someday you might chase something that chases back."

She merely smiled in response and strolled through the yard to examine the statues. When she was done, she returned to his side with her chin lifted proudly. "There, I spent time watching. Now you need to spend time chasing after something."

Nicolas frowned. "And what, if I were to entertain this foolishness, would I chase?"

"Anything!" Ann said. "How about it? We could go for a little run through the woods and follow whatever we come across. I do it all the time. It'll be fun!"

Gray clouds still loomed overhead. It would rain soon. However, this game would get her away from the castle, and once she was away, he could inform her that she was not to return. She knew the woods well, and would have plenty of time to reach the town. It was a perfect plan.

"Very well. But do not expect me to strain myself." He was not going to debase himself by getting dirty and sweaty in order to keep up with a human. He gave her a moment's head start, then began walking.

Ann bounded along the path ahead, looking back at him whenever she grew concerned that he wasn't following. A few times she tried to break away from the even, clear ground to pursue a squirrel or a bird, but she stopped when she realized that Nicolas refused to go crashing through underbrush and dirty his slacks for the sake of trailing vermin.

Eventually she slowed her pace to walk beside him.

"You don't go outside much, do you?" she asked.

"I have no need to mingle with the faeries that reside in these woods," Nicolas answered. Faeries that would gladly do horrible things to Ann before they killed her, if they even gave her the dignity of death. Nicolas was glad to have been born of nature and granted a place in Oberon and Titania's Court, rather than being born a cruel trickster or mindless, bloodthirsty beast.

"Not even for the snow?"

"I can observe the winter well enough from the castle." Nicolas stopped. "Why do you ask these things?"

Ann kept walking. "Because I want to understand you. I want to see what you see—and I want *you* to see what *I* see. For instance…"

She pointed at a large oak growing farther down the path. The leaves were mostly orange, appropriate for early October, but Nicolas noticed stubborn tinges of dark green remained among the leaves, and the branches weren't nearly as sparse as they ought to be. The leaves that had fallen crunched gratingly under Nicolas's shoes when he humored Ann and followed her to the trunk.

"This isn't *just* a tree. This is an adventure!" Ann wove her way up the branches, climbing with more grace than Nicolas thought a human could possess. Once she was a few branches up, she called down to him, "Come up! You can fly, can't you?"

Nicolas stared up at her from his place on the ground. She had barely given any thought to scaling the tree, or going into the woods, even when humans had every reason to fear them. She charged blindly ahead into everything, and somehow left him trailing in her wake despite the potential dangers she faced.

What do you see from up there? he wondered.

Nicolas scoured the area for hiding pixies or brownies before giving in to a moment of foolishness. It had been a long time since he had flown for the simple enjoyment of it. He spread his wings and gave them a few test beats, then rose to join her.

Once Ann saw that he was coming along, she scampered higher up the tree and found a branch near the top where she could sit. The branches were too thin to hold Nicolas's weight, so with a shimmer of faerie dust, he transformed himself into a light blue hummingbird. He had to take a moment to right himself in the air; it had been *decades* since he'd transformed, and it was far from his favorite trick.

Ann was both startled and amazed. She held out a finger, allowing him to perch on it. "Sometimes I forget that you're magical in more ways than one," she breathed. "Can you still talk like that?"

"I can," he said, his voice much quieter. "Most faeries prefer to become butterflies or moths because their wings are similar to ours, but I have never been too fond of insects. Ordinarily I would take the form of a swan, but that form would not be advantageous in this location, either."

He didn't mention that taking on the form of a feathered creature was a tad presumptuous, as it was common for the royal family to transform into birds. Oberon specifically was known to favor the swan.

Ann smiled and rotated her wrist so they were no longer facing each other. Now he could see the view of the forest and beyond, as she did. From the treetop, they could look upon the glistening towers of the castle and the mountains in the distance. They had ventured farther than Ann had perhaps meant to, but not too far.

She kept her free hand on the trunk of the tree, letting her legs sway in the wind. For a moment, Nicolas allowed himself to enjoy the scenery. Varying shades of silver and white mingled to create a marbled sky, cut occasionally with striking blue. A few light rays peeked through in these places, and when the wind moved the clouds, the golden glow shifted over their tree, creating a halo around Ann. She closed her eyes, enjoying the slight warmth, and Nicolas took note of her illuminated flyaway hairs.

Just once, he wished she'd let him brush that tangled brown mess. Whenever he offered to do so, she only laughed and said that she liked her 'tangled mess' the way it was.

The light drifted away again, and Nicolas would have frowned if he'd had a mouth at the moment—less so because this was not as ideal a time to tell her about the time limit as he'd thought, and more because he didn't usually think over how he said things this much. A Prince did not mince words or worry over hurt feelings. Yet he worried anyway. Here, perched on her finger, small and protected, he wondered how she might feel around him. He had no idea what she thought of him. He knew from her behavior that she most likely didn't fear him, but what she *did* feel for him and what she did *not* were two entirely different things.

She spoke before he could even try to gather himself. "The view from here is amazing, isn't it?"

"Yes, it is. And even this is nothing compared to how it will look after the blizzards," Nicolas said, imagining the snowy landscapes he used to fly over every winter. He had stopped some time ago, though he couldn't remember how far back, preferring to conjure from his castle and allow the frost fae in his service to handle storms farther afield. "I shall craft the most magnificent winter this year."

Ann looked down at the earth and imagined all the colors erased and replaced with white and shades of blue. "Blizzards... I think I must have witnessed a blizzard at least once in my life, but I can't remember it now. In the stories I've read, humans are always together with their loved ones by a fireplace when blizzards happen."

Nicolas looked away. Huddling inside instead of enjoying a perfectly good blizzard, of course. Ann might be tolerable, as far as humans went, but Nicolas would not forget humanity's disdain for his beautiful creations.

"I suppose you have the power to bring people together," Ann went on with a smile.

"Is that how you see it?" he asked.

"Don't you?"

Nicolas thought back. He and Princess Bethilde had never sat by a fireplace together during a storm. They had no need of the warmth, and were more than likely the ones conjuring the snowstorm in the first place. He could so clearly recall her lessons.

"No. I suppose not."

"I wish I could remember being warm like that," she said, and with that, fell silent.

Nicolas expected that she was in quiet contemplation of pleasant things, pondering over the words of her storybooks. She was such a strangely happy creature, perhaps too simple in mind to comprehend loneliness or sorrow. He might even go so far as to liken her to a light faerie, always full of optimism and giving no more thought to anything than she did when she recklessly raced out into the woods.

She stayed quiet too long. He saw another bird in the distance, and he expected her to comment on it, but she did not. Her face was tight, her lower lip pursed beneath the upper.

"You are quiet," Nicolas stated after a moment. Had she guessed what he was going to tell her next? "Have I said something to upset you?"

"No, you haven't."

"Then why are you so quiet?" Usually she was only silent while he spoke, and when he was not speaking, he could barely get her to stop.

"Just thinking."

"About what?"

Ann took a deep breath. "I've been studying maps at the town library and yours, from as far back as I can. There is another town that's a little ways off, but its name doesn't sound familiar at all, and why would I have walked for over two days just to nap in the woods, by myself? It doesn't make sense. I *have* to come from the town at the edge of the woods, but Cecil says there's been no new people and no missing person reports."

Nicolas felt a twinge of guilt. She truly had nowhere else to go. Was she going to plead with him to let her stay?

"Then I got to thinking, maybe I don't have a family. There are lots of characters in stories who are orphans, and maybe I am one, and that's why I can't remember my parents. But aside from that…someone must have noticed I'm missing, even if I lived alone, right?"

Her voice began to crack as she continued. "I wish I could remember who I am and why I'm here, but at the same time I'm glad that I don't, because I don't think there's anyone who cares that I'm gone! How awful must I have been, to not have a single friend that would care enough to go looking for me? Did anyone even notice? Were they happy when I disappeared? And maybe…maybe I don't have any memories of being with my loved ones because I don't *have* any loved ones."

Nicolas watched her, taken aback by her words. In that brief moment, a feeling seized him, the same feeling he experienced when he used ice magic or painted or indulged in any of his other hobbies. The world aligned and made sense. He *understood*.

We are more alike than we are different, he thought, and was amazed by it. He had not felt such a connection to another living being for so long, not since Princess Bethilde's death, and his kinship to her had been expected. He had been brought into the world to take her place and rule over winter in her stead. Ann had been nothing to him.

She was far from 'nothing,' now.

"You will cease talking about yourself this way at once," Nicolas stated firmly. "It will begin raining again soon, and you do not have a proper coat. Come. We will return to the castle."

Ann climbed down from the tree carefully, her former dauntless attitude faded. Nicolas guided her down, hovering near each foothold to make sure she didn't slip and fall. He abandoned his hummingbird form at the ground and they walked back to the palace. Once they were indoors, Nicolas headed straight for his private library without another word.

Rather than follow, Ann went to her room. She rummaged through her bag again to search for any deeply sentimental items, anything to jog her memory, but it was empty aside from clothes and a coin purse, neither of which she remembered packing.

She bit her lip to keep it from trembling, curled up under the thick blankets, and opened *Coping with Amnesia*. Her eyes skimmed the pages, one turn after another. No matter how many times she perused this book, she never felt any better, but what else could she do?

One passage she had been fixating on came up again: "*Some people afflicted with amnesia never recover their memories.*"

Ann ran a finger over the letters as if she could coax more information from them. When would she know if she was going to get her memory back or not? And there was no book on the planet that could tell her if she'd be happier once she did.

Ann set the amnesia book aside and looked over the collection of fairy tales and myths. The old, cracked leather spine of *The Snow Queen* stood out to her. She'd read it dozens of times already, more than all the others, but she felt better the moment she opened it and the smell of old pages reached her nose.

She immersed herself in Gerda's journey for a while, still unsure if she was meant to be in the shoes of the heroine or the captive, until she drifted off to sleep.

It was the same dream again. It was always the same dream. The stake, the fire, the crowd cheering for her death and the deep ache in her chest from their betrayal. She wanted to say something, but she didn't know what, and the dry air sucked the breath out of her every time.

This time when she searched the crowd, she saw Nicolas's face. His expression was as apathetic as ever, but his eyes burned with scorn. He was a Prince, and she was just a common human girl. What was she to him but a nuisance?

Maybe the crowd was right to cheer. Maybe she was a horrible person.

She tried to search her memories for a reason why this was happening, squeezing her eyes tight, though she could still clearly see the crowd and the growing fire.

"Witch!" she heard them shouting. "Witch! Witch!"

Nicolas's voice joined the crowd, standing out from theirs, "Identify yourself."

"Witch! Witch!"

"Identify yourself!"

The fire swallowed her, so hot that somehow her shoulder felt cold.

She woke to Nicolas gently shaking her arm.

"Your Majesty?" she gasped.

"You did not respond when I knocked," he explained. "You were whimpering in your sleep. Did

80

you hurt yourself climbing the tree earlier? Are you cold?"

"Oh, no, it's fine," Ann said, stretching. "I had a bad dream, that's all."

Nicolas looked at the book lying open on the bed with a frown. "It was time for dinner ten minutes ago."

"I'm sorry, I didn't realize I had slept that long." Ann slid off of the bed, her feet landing softly on the floor.

Instead of keeping his distance, Nicolas stayed with Ann as they made their way to the parlor. The tea was already chilled and a single slice of buttered rye bread sat on each plate, the last of the loaf. Ann and Nicolas took their seats and had a sip of tea and a bite of bread each.

Usually that was when Ann would dive into a conversation, but instead she focused on eating. Meanwhile, Nicolas stared restlessly out of the window. He could still see the tracks left behind from the day's play.

The bread was gone. The sun would soon set on the seventh day. She had to leave, but he couldn't stop her words from echoing in his mind.

Were they happy when I disappeared?

She was nothing like him. She was nothing *to* him. She was a small, powerless, untidy human woman with no title, no home, and no memories, nothing of value to offer him. All he had to do was tell her that her time was up and send her away. Surely she would understand and cause him no trouble, and he would never see her again.

But it was that very thought that troubled him enough to cause an almost physical pain in his chest.

This simple human somehow understood him far better than any of his peers ever had. That was not to say that she *did* understand, but she had come closer than any other.

Have you always been alone?

He took a deep breath and steeled himself for the consequences of his decision.

"Ann," he said, for the first time. Her attention was on him immediately. "I would like to invite you to stay in the castle until you find your home."

Her eyes widened. "You would?"

"Yes." He added a short nod for emphasis. "But do not misunderstand. I still require privacy and quiet when I am working, and I would prefer that you not disturb me when I am in my study unless you are on the precipice of death. And no more of these negative thoughts. They are unbecoming. Someone must care for you."

"How do you know?"

"Because..." Nicolas struggled for an explanation. "Because you are nothing like me."

Ann looked first confused, then hurt. "How could you say something like that *right after* telling me not to put myself down?"

"I did not intend it to be taken that way," Nicolas said, and it was his turn to be confused. Why was she upset by what he had said? He had neither friends nor family. It therefore made sense to him that, because they were nothing alike, she ought to have family and friends somewhere.

Still, Ann's frown persisted. "People care about you, Your Majesty. They must. What about the King and Queen?"

"The King and Queen?" He rarely ever spoke to them, as much as he wanted to. Nicolas had the same reverence for Titania and Oberon that all members of their Court did. Sometimes that respect was all that stopped him from summoning a blizzard in the middle of spring or summer. There was hardly anything he wouldn't do for the smallest amount of acknowledgement from Oberon.

Ann must be confusing reality with her storybooks again, assuming that he was a part of their family. How he wished that were true! His title as a *Regional* Prince had nothing to do with relation to the King and Queen. He was fairly certain he had told her that.

The King and Queen. By letting Ann stay with him beyond the allotted week, he was actively defying them. Oberon was the first winter faerie, his King, his idol. Titania was his beloved Queen and the fairest ruler that had ever been or would ever be. How could he betray them this way?

He wondered again if this woman might not be some kind of enchantress. What was it about her that compelled him to do these things?

Because she wants to understand. Because she will not cower, he thought, and that was worth it.

"Okay, maybe not the King and Queen," Ann said. "But what about human women suffering from amnesia who got lost in the woods? I can think of at least one of those who cares about you."

"You mean yourself," Nicolas replied.

"Does that make it any less true?" Ann asked.

"I suppose not." He raised his teacup to hide his

smile. "And I *do* suppose, then, that you are cared for by a powerful frost faerie of high rank. Neither of us can claim that we are uncared for again."

Nicolas held his cup steady. Try as he might, he could not make his lips be flat again. Ann made no attempt, her usual cheerfulness returning as she munched on her bread. She was cared for, and it had been silly to think that she wasn't, even for a moment. Nicolas and Cecil had become dear friends in only a week, and she looked forward to seeing Tanya again someday soon, as well.

The idea of finding her home and recovering her memories felt a lot less daunting when she thought of the friends she had already made.

"Thank you for allowing me to stay, Your Majesty. I promise, I'll do everything I can to find my home soon," Ann said.

"I trust that you will."

Nicolas finished his bread and tea and said, "I will be working in my study for the rest of the night. Please find your own entertainment," before excusing himself from the table.

If Ann was going to stay longer in the ice castle, she would need a warm coat to keep her from freezing as the days became shorter and colder. When Nicolas returned to his study, he grabbed his pattern books and a bolt of pink wool fabric that Julius had once given him as a joke. He feared the wool wouldn't be warm enough on its own, so he grabbed the rabbit furs to add as liner. He flipped through the pattern book with one hand until he found the right design, while the other hand waved a new ice mannequin into being, recreating Ann's shape as best he could from memory.

He donned his reading glasses, then set to work cutting the pieces of fabric and placing them on the form. As he sewed, he planned the embellishments. Bows, he decided. A neck bow to accent the fur collar, a bow on the back to tighten the coat to her frame as she liked. And fur trim was a must to keep her hands and legs warmer. It would extend to just above her knees, if his memory was accurate.

Each passing stitch nearly made Nicolas smile. It wasn't painting or sculpting, but it put his mind at ease to take plain fabric, fur, and ribbon, and turn them into something more. He could hardly remember the last time he'd sewed anything of note; the tailcoat, maybe, just after the turn of the century.

The next few hours passed in a blur. By the end, Nicolas's fingers were sore, but he felt much better with a project to finally work on. He yawned and closed his book, for the hour was late. He placed his glasses aside, and went to bed to have a far better night's sleep than a traitor to the crown deserved.

5

THE TWOFOLD GIFT

THE RAIN CONTINUED FOR a few days more before finally coming to a stop, but the clouds remained. It was noticeably chillier than it had been only a week ago. Autumn was finally getting on track toward winter.

Ann did not interrupt Nicolas in his study again. He was pleased that she respected his privacy, and he imagined that she spent the rainy days reading her books or studying the maps in his library. She claimed to have already done so, but there was always a chance that she'd missed a detail that would guide her home. Now that the clouds had parted, she could visit the library in town to return her borrowed books and investigate the human town further for anything familiar.

Nicolas's mind wandered toward that subject often while he sewed her coat. He was sure Ann was not the awful person she worried she might have been, but he could not comprehend why her family would have left her in the woods—unless, of course, she had no family. He did not want to tell her his suspicions, lest she decide to stay with him permanently, but the only way her situation made sense to him was if she was an orphan.

Whether she had a family or not made no difference.

He was still breaking the law, and if Oberon discovered her presence, he could expect nothing less than a slow, painful death by wing amputation. Nicolas had never seen it done, and it had been centuries since an execution had occurred in such a manner, but the stories were enough to make him keep his wings tightly folded to his back. Cutting off a faerie's wings deprived them of their magic, their very souls. No being, magical or not, could survive for long without a soul, and the brief life faerie led after amputation was quite possibly worse than death. That was how the dark things that prowled the forest at night had come to be, and why good, sensible creatures stayed away from the cursed woods.

Ann had a good heart, but she was far from sensible. Another reason for the coat—it would carry threads of Nicolas's magic, and the threat of invoking his anger might keep some of the dangerous imps and spirits away.

He made the final stitch to attach the neck bow and took a step back to admire his work. Then he removed it from the mannequin, disintegrated the form into crystalline powder, and folded up the coat. He'd present it to Ann when she returned for tea, but how should he give it to her?

He could place it on her bed, but he didn't like entering her room without permission unless there was dire need. Sometimes he still heard her having bad dreams when he passed on his way to bed, but he did not know why they came or how to stop them. He would serve her chamomile and jasmine tea the morning after, and by the time she had her first sip she would have already forgotten ever having the nightmares. If only he could stop them from coming back!

The thought that Ann had been hurt made Nicolas tense. He had heard of this 'human attachment,' of course. Lesser faeries had often become enamored with their catches in centuries past, to the point of doing such ridiculous things as lavishing them with treasures from the Faerie Realms. Many refused to give up their captives when family and friends came riding to the rescue and ended up mortified at being outsmarted by mortals. It was for good reason that Oberon had outlawed the practice.

Such utter nonsense, Nicolas thought, running the coat between his fingers to get a sense of its thickness. Had he added enough insulating fur? Perhaps it needed more embroidery?

Time had gotten away from him, and before he could decide, he heard the castle doors open. Since Ann came and went so often, he had thinned them and usually left them unlocked during the daytime.

Nicolas checked his pocket watch. *He* was not late; rather, *she* was early. But he still had no tea or treats prepared.

"Hello?" echoed a voice far too deep to be hers. Nicolas recognized the Oceanic accent and fluttered his wings in annoyance before leaving his study to meet the intruder in the throne room.

"State your business," Nicolas demanded from the top of the stairs, glaring down at Jack while the other looked around the room with a stupefied expression.

"Oh, there you are!" Jack greeted him with a short wave. Nicolas scowled in response. "It's been more than two weeks since the Equinox Festival and we haven't heard from you."

"I am aware of how long it has been since I had to speak to you," Nicolas said flatly.

The glow in Jack's wings faded, and Nicolas noticed they weren't as bright as they had been at the Festival. The overcast weather must have dampened his spirits. Light fae never lasted long in the Northern Realm. After a century or two in the north, most Summer Rulers gave up their positions to take on jobs of lower prestige in warmer, sunnier realms. Jack had not been groomed for his position from birth like Nicolas had, and would likely pass on the crown as soon as he could.

"I was worried," Jack went on. "You haven't had any trouble?"

"Why should I?" Nicolas returned, aloof and unbothered. When Jack's serious expression deepened, he repeated, softer, "Why should I?"

Jack glanced around the room, looking for a safe place to rest his eyes. "I don't know if I should tell you this, but Drew had an audience with King Oberon and Queen Titania about your behavior after the Equinox Festival. I don't know what they decided, or if he was even able to speak to them, but I thought I should check on you all the same. Though, I suppose, if the King and Queen *had* decided to punish you, we'd all know, wouldn't we? It would be, um..." He shivered. "...A very public decision, right?"

Before Nicolas could process the weight of Jack's words and formulate a response, the light faerie added, "What have you got there?"

Nicolas felt a brief moment of confusion before realizing that he still held Ann's coat.

"A coat," he said plainly. "I understand that you have probably never seen one." Despite visiting the ice castle, Jack somehow saw fit to barely dress at all, wearing only sandals and a bright cloth tied around his waist.

"A pink one? I didn't think that was your color, mate," Jack said, flying up to get a closer look. Nicolas pulled back, but it was too late. "It's not your size, either. It looks like—" Jack's playful grin dropped into a frown as he gasped. "Oh, no."

Nicolas hid the coat behind his back. "Before you speak, let me explain."

"Human! A human!" Jack exclaimed, wings shining bright once more. "You have a *human*? Where is she? It is a 'she,' right?"

Nicolas wanted to yell at Jack to be quiet so he'd have time to think up an excuse, but it was hard to hear his own thoughts. Jack's voice punctuated every millisecond with questions about the human and reminders of how incredibly *illegal* it was for Nicolas to have her, and how *public* the execution would be, and did Nicolas have a replacement chosen in the first place because he should decide on one right away and, and, and—

"*Enough!*" Nicolas barked finally. "You are hardly one to speak on this issue. I have heard stories of light fae that attend human parties, and I know you are counted among them. Drew cannot speak against what I am doing, either, when he has gone as far as siring children with humans in the past." The *recent* past, at that. Drew carried quite a reputation with partners of every sort, and always had a few grown children hanging around.

"That's different. We always disguise ourselves,

90

and we don't ever let the humans come back home with us. We liven up their parties, have some fun of our own, then leave. It isn't as if they remember us once we're out of sight." A wistful look appeared in Jack's eyes. "We're outgrown, they're outlived. As for Drew—I don't speak for him or the floral fae. They have their nature, we have ours, and you have yours."

"Just what horrible thing do you think is in my nature?" Nicolas asked. "Do you think I have stolen some poor human girl away from her family and held her here against her will? She has no family, and no home, either. I am merely providing her shelter. She is free to leave whenever she wishes."

The worry did not fade from Jack's expression. "Are you sure? Do you swear, by King Oberon's crown and Queen Titania's wings, that you won't try to stop her from leaving?"

Nicolas scoffed at the ridiculous notion, but he spread his wings, bowed his head, and said solemnly, "I swear, by King Oberon's crown and Queen Titania's wings, that I will make no attempt to prevent her from leaving if that is her wish."

Jack did not look convinced, and though Nicolas spoke with conviction, he could guess why. Nicolas had heard the stories. A few lost treasures, an embarrassment here or there, was not the sole reason Oberon had made the law. There had been faeries, powerful ones at that, who went mad over their obsessions. They locked up their mortals and subjected them to horrible hexes if they tried to leave, sometimes going as far as killing them to prevent anyone, human or faerie, from stealing their precious companions. Even the humans were aware of this danger, and had learned to fear the advances of even the most benevolent faeries. Didn't Ann have a book on that very subject in her room?

"This is still dangerous," Jack said.

Nicolas did not disagree, which was why he had not argued against the oath. He could not do anything to keep her with him now.

"That is why it must remain a closely guarded secret. You cannot tell anyone—not Drew, not Julius, not a single other living soul," Nicolas said.

"I don't know," Jack replied, grinding his pointed teeth in thought. "If I don't tell anyone, and they find out about her, and they find out *I* knew about her, I'll be in as much trouble as you."

"Yes." Nicolas nodded. His stomach felt colder than usual. It didn't matter if Jack didn't personally want him dead. If he told anyone about Ann, that would be the end of it. Nicolas would be executed, and Ann would be out on her own, unless the King and Queen disposed of her, too. Either way, plenty of awful things could happen to a young human woman who had nowhere to call home and nobody to claim her as family.

"You must keep this secret," he insisted. "If not for *my* sake, then for hers. Do you know what happens to humans who live with faeries when they are discovered?"

Jack shook his head slowly, but the growing terror in his eyes and nervous shudder of his wings told Nicolas that he did not need to say anything else. All light fae had an infamous soft spot for humans. The kind-hearted and easygoing Summer Ruler wouldn't endanger an innocent life.

"I swear, by the first light of dawn, that I will not reveal your secret to anyone, and I will help you care for the human in any way I can."

Nicolas placed a hand over his mouth to hide his displeasure at the last part of that oath. "What do you mean?"

"Have you ever interacted with humans before?" Jack asked. "Significantly, I mean. For more than a few minutes."

"Of course not."

"Exactly." Jack folded his arms. "Humans are complicated, delicate creatures. They need socialization and physical contact, hugs and things, to prevent them from getting melancholy and dying. Their diets and environments have to be just so, or else they get sick and die. What have you been feeding her?"

"Tea and sweets. And bread. Mostly tea and sweets."

Jack shook his head. "That's no good. She needs fruits, veggies, and meat, too. Otherwise, sick and dead."

"She will have to find them elsewhere, then," Nicolas said. His kitchen was equipped for the singular purpose of baking; he didn't have meat or fruit or vegetables in his stock, and he didn't know how to prepare them.

"I can handle that, if you want," Jack said with a shrug. "I know my way around a grill."

Nicolas almost agreed, then thought better of allowing Jack to take over Ann's meals, especially if he intended to cook in the ice palace. He could just see Jack unraveling his carefully placed enchantments by accident and melting the castle down. "How often do humans need to eat this food?"

"At least twice a day, more if they're active," Jack answered.

"No, thank you," Nicolas replied. "I will figure out the meal situation, and the coat will keep her warm. She can socialize with other humans in town and hug them. That covers everything. Thank you for the information. You may leave now."

Before Nicolas could see Jack out, the door opened again, and Ann entered the room.

Jack's wings flickered and glowed softly when his eyes fell on her. Ann paused for a moment, one foot hovering over the threshold. A silent chill enveloped the entryway as Nicolas watched the two study each other.

Of course she was taken with him; humans were always more appreciative of warmth and light than they were of snow and long nights. And, admittedly, Jack was not difficult to spend any length of time looking at. Though Nicolas had never directly asked, he assumed that Ann appreciated both men and women. It was extremely common among faeries, including himself, and he saw no reason why she should be any different.

Ann shook herself out of her fascinated staring. She entered and let the door close behind her. Jack approached her, circling once. "Well, aren't you a small one, Sheila?"

"Actually, my name is Ann."

"Nice to meet you, Ann. I'm Jack! Err, I mean— my name is Jack Barnaby, Ruler of Summer, Regional Prince of the Light Faeries, etcetera, etcetera. But you can call me Jack."

"Oh!" Ann curtseyed. "Pleased to meet you! Are you one of His Majesty's friends?"

"'His Majesty?'" Jack snorted and looked over his shoulder at Nicolas, who was once again hiding his frown. "You make her call you 'His Majesty?' Why don't you just use your name?"

"That is quite enough," Nicolas said. "You have seen her. Now go."

Jack chuckled and tucked a lock of Ann's hair behind her ear. Nicolas cringed; surely *he* wouldn't have to touch her that way to prevent her from becoming depressed?

"It was nice meeting you, but it sounds like I've worn out my welcome. You'll see me again soon." To Nicolas, he added, "Remember, mate, I'm on *your* side! Don't forget your promise, and I won't forget mine. I will be checking in."

He left the castle without fanfare. Through the ice walls, Nicolas and Ann watched him spread his wings and easily clear the gate, as if to question why it was even there in the first place.

"He seems nice! I hope he visits again soon."

Nicolas somehow managed to sigh in both relief and frustration.

"What's that?" Ann asked, bringing him back to the moment. She was pointing at the pink fabric sticking out from behind Nicolas's back.

He brought it out to show her. "A coat. I made it for you."

"For me?" Ann beamed and held out a hand to receive it. After checking that her fingers weren't covered in dirt or tree bark, Nicolas offered it to her and she tried it on. The measurements were not quite exact, but they were close enough. Ann twirled and watched the coat flare around her wide hips. "I love it!"

"Are you warm?" Nicolas asked, and Ann nodded vigorously. "Good, then. It serves its purpose. You may leave it on while you are in the castle. I will not consider it rude, given your circumstances." He glanced at his pocket watch again and saw that they were late for tea. "Please wait in the parlor while I prepare our tea."

By the time the citrus tea, scones, and orange marmalade were ready and set at the parlor table, it was nearly ten minutes past the appropriate time. Nicolas would have to cut this tea short in order to get back on schedule. There had been plenty of spare time over the past few days to work on the coat, but now he needed to establish his winter plans. He'd have to send them to his administrators soon so they would know when and where snow storms were to take place.

His annoyance made him quiet and, as usual, starting the conversation fell to Ann. "It was a welcome surprise to meet one of your friends! I hope someday I'm able to introduce you to Cecil. I think you two might get along." It was difficult to gauge how Nicolas might react to the librarian, but Ann had hope that they would find common ground with their mutual love of literature.

"Perhaps," Nicolas responded flatly. He would never think to call Jack, or any other faerie for that matter, his friend. Ann might have integrated herself into his life, but her ideals were still strange to him.

"It never occurred to me that the other Princes would be close by," Ann said. "I thought they would all live far away."

"No. All of the Seasonal Rulers live in the center of the realm. You most likely saw their homes marked on the maps in the library," Nicolas answered.

Her eyes widened and their blue depths seemed to flash for a moment. "What are they like?"

"More annoying than Jack, to put it mildly," Nicolas said, raising the teacup to his mouth and holding it there. Drew and Julius were responsible for his entire predicament. If Julius had changed the seasons on time, there would have been no conflict, Drew would never have gone to Titania and Oberon, Jack would never have barged in, and Nicolas would not now be relying on Jack to keep his secret.

Ann gave him a curious look, but she wore her usual smile, so he thought little of it. With a laugh in her voice, she asked, "Do you have a hard time getting along with *every* other faerie?"

"It is not I who has a hard time with getting along," he said, an edge to his voice. "*They* are the ones who refuse to get along with *me*. If they tried harder to see things as I do, if they would just understand…"

"Your Majesty?" Ann asked, her smile gone.

Nicolas waved his hand. "Never mind all that. I have a request for you today."

"Oh?" Ann's eyes widened. "What can I do?"

"I require cookbooks," Nicolas explained. "My expertise in the kitchen lies with pastries and sweets. Jack informed me that humans need additional types of nourishment to survive. If you would pick up a few books from the library with recipes you'd like to eat, I will try to learn how to cook human food." He thought for a moment. "Please."

"It's getting dark earlier now, so I'd better get moving if I'm going to be home before sunset," Ann said. She bolted from the table, leaving Nicolas in a state of bemusement. He had no idea what he'd said that had made her react that way, and she hadn't even finished her tea. He shook his head. There was no dealing with an excitable human. Ann did enjoy food, after all.

Ann dropped by the castle library before she left to make sure she had her coordinates right. Examining the maps more closely, she could see where the other Princes' homes were. Jack's was the farthest away, being near the beach, but the Spring and Autumn Rulers lived in the forest, a comparatively short distance to the south of the ice palace.

She set out at a brisk pace, her steps filled with determination. Nicolas had offered his home to help her while she recovered her memory. It was time she did something to help him, too. She would break through the barrier that kept him isolated. Otherwise, she worried what he would do with himself after she eventually found her way in the world. Ann couldn't bear the thought of leaving him all alone in that empty tomb of a castle, not the way she'd found him.

She had a good idea of where she was going. The time she had spent scouring the woods for signs of passing humans had left her with excellent geographical knowledge. She had already memorized several of the landmarks that would be guiding her way.

Best of all, it wouldn't be too far out of her way to pop in on one of the other Princes before going to the library to get Nicolas's cookbooks.

She repeated the path that she had marked out in her mind as she followed it. *Walk along the river until it splits in two directions, then head south from the fork, walk between the two oaks whose branches have grown together and follow the slope down...*

The path led her toward where she had first woken up. She knew the area well. She'd searched it multiple times for a dropped license, or signs of friends or family that had come looking for her. She never found anything but dirt and leaves.

One more look couldn't hurt. She walked around the little hill and checked in the bushes and behind the tree trunks, startling a number of squirrels and birds as she went. She restrained the urge to chase them and charged up the hill again.

Maybe, just maybe, today would be the day.

Her foot sank into the ground at the top of the hill and she pulled back with a yelp. The rain had softened the earth and created a sinkhole. Ann tugged her foot free and wiped her muddy boot on the grass, to no avail. She'd have to make a proper attempt to clean it before she returned to the palace.

The scents of lavender, mint, and a dozen other herbs wafted through the air. She sniffed, tracing the familiar aroma to its source—the hole she'd opened. With careful steps, she drew nearer. Why would a hole smell like herbs and flowers?

It was the same as the scents from her dreams, before the burning stake made everything stink of ash and smoke.

The thought of her nightmare made her wrinkle her nose. Ann turned away from the hill to continue on the path to the Autumn Ruler's home. If she had gauged the distance correctly, it shouldn't be much farther. All she had to do was find the river again and follow it west.

As she walked the final stretch, she put the lingering thoughts of her nightmares out of her mind. They were only dreams, and they couldn't hurt her here.

She knew immediately when she found the Autumn Ruler's home. A white fence stuck out against the mixed reds and oranges of the forest around the cottage, which looked, in a word, *tilted*. The first story was good and flat, but each level built above it leaned one way or another. Pipes stuck out every which way, billowing cinnamon-scented smoke into the air. At the teetering top of the monstrosity sat a room with a three-pointed roof, almost like a crown for the cottage. Pumpkins big enough to use as furniture sprawled across the yard. Their vines had managed to break through a weak point in the fence, producing a trail of gourds into the forest beyond.

At first Ann was worried that the gate might be locked, but it opened easily when she tried it, and there didn't appear to be any enchantments guarding the house. She strolled up the path to the porch, making sure not to step on any of the stray tendrils creeping out from the pumpkin patch.

It was only once Ann approached the door and raised her fist to knock that she realized she hadn't brought a gift. She fished around in her bag for her wallet; a few gold coins might work. Whether or not her books of fairy tales were true, she was certain faeries of all sorts would appreciate gold.

Instead, her hands closed around soft yarn. She removed an unfinished scarf with a snowflake pattern from the bag. She was certain it hadn't been there before, but given that she could nearly hit her entire body into a bag small enough to bounce against her hip as she walked, she wasn't going to ask too many questions about it.

Satisfied, Ann knocked on the door.

Nothing happened. She had expected that the Autumn Ruler would be busy this season, so she stood patiently for a few moments before rapping her knuckles on the door again.

This time she heard shuffling within the cottage, but the door remained shut. Instead, a small panel in the wooden entrance slid open. Ann jumped back in surprise, but the panel closed again before she could glimpse the faerie beyond.

"Who are you?" A voice called to her, emanating from what appeared to be a phonograph speaker affixed above the door.

Ann looked up at the device, then searched for a similar speaker where she might answer back. Failing to find anything, she leaned toward the door's panel. "I'm Ann. Are you the Autumn Ruler?"

"...Why do you want to know?"

Ann couldn't imagine why he was acting so suspiciously, until she remembered that she hadn't offered him anything yet. "I brought a gift!" she said, holding up the scarf first to the phonograph speaker and then to the panel.

The door opened.

Ann was surprised to find she was ever so slightly taller than this faerie, though she hardly had to look down to see his freckled face and hazel eyes beneath his curly ginger hair. His eyes wouldn't stay focused on any one thing in particular, flicking back and forth between her, the scarf, and everywhere else. She offered the scarf to him. His large orange wings fluttered in agitation before he looked off to the side again.

Julius wasn't sure what to make of this. Ordinarily, his primary worry would be owing a human hospitality for a week while trying to manage his season, which was in full swing. However, she had known to address him as the Autumn Ruler, and she'd presented him a scarf with faerie designs woven into it.

He sniffed the air around her. The heady scent of

the forest clung to her, but the clean, crisp scent of frost fae cut through it.

"Where did you get that?" he asked, breaking the silence. It was no concern of his if some frost faerie had taken a human, but it *was* a concern if that faerie had sent her to try to negotiate some kind of deal.

"I found it in my bag," Ann said, and he gave her carry-case a glance. Probably enchanted, but she didn't seem like the sort who would have any talent with magic. Julius was still sure she was acting on someone else's behalf, and hesitant to accept something that would cause him to owe any faerie a favor.

"I don't want to stay here," she added when he made no move to take the scarf. "I'm happy where I am. I just thought it would be polite to bring a gift since I'm showing up unannounced, that's all."

Julius accepted the scarf, carefully holding between his thumb and pointer finger. The interwoven gold strands, the snowflake pattern—his apprehensive frown deepened. This was undoubtedly Nicolas's handiwork. In fact, Julius realized the pattern was familiar beyond containing the frost faerie's signature motifs. He himself had chosen the pattern the last time he'd been on civil terms with Nicolas.

Flooded with unhappy memories, the Autumn Ruler clenched his fists.

"Did Nicolas send you?" Julius demanded, almost throwing the wretched thing to the ground. "Is this his idea of negotiating? Sending a lackey to make little offerings? He can't even come to see me *himself*?"

Ann backed away with her hands up, careful not to fall off the porch. "No! I came on my own, for the sake of curiosity. I wanted to meet the other Princes—"

"Then why would you have *this*?" Julius snapped, giving the scarf a rough shake.

"I-I don't know. It came out of the bag, like I said," Ann stammered.

"I have half a mind to curse you right where you stand," Julius snarled. "See how Nicolas likes that! I could make your hair gray early. I could wilt one of your arms, or a leg, or rot your teeth out!"

Julius looked back at her, expecting to see a frightened face, or a fleeing figure already in the distance. But she remained where she was. Her eyes were wide with confusion and curiosity rather than horror.

"Why?" she asked.

"Because you...you..." Julius sighed and pulled at the scarf. The fibers stretched, but did not tear or unravel. How to put into words a century's worth of pain?

"Did His Majesty do something wrong?"

Julius snickered. She asked so *innocently*. "Yes. *His Majesty* did something wrong, and if I were in your position, I would steer clear of him." It was bizarre to him to even think of Nicolas housing a human willingly. Once the time limit ran out on Law of Hospitality, this poor girl would likely end up as an ice sculpture somewhere. "How long have you been with him now?"

"How long? I think..." She counted on her fingers, "Two weeks? Maybe a little more, or a little less."

All of Julius's thoughts and emotions came to a screeching halt.

Two weeks?

Defiance of the law, he thought. *Possible execution.*

104

Probable *execution. For a human? Nicolas, of all faeries, risking his life for a human?* Julius almost had to laugh. *Has he finally gone all the way off his rocker? What is the world coming to?*

"I apologize for lashing out," Julius said, clearing his throat. "I don't know what came over me. I was caught off guard, I suppose. So, you've been staying in Nicolas's palace for more than a week, you said?"

"That's right." Ann nodded. "But I don't feel like I fully understand him, and on top of having a chance to meet other faeries, I was hoping you might be able to give me a little more insight. Please…what did he do? Why does he stay locked away in his palace?"

"I could tell you," Julius said, gesturing to the porch swing before sitting down. Ann joined him, plopping down and making the chair rock. "I could tell you a lot of things. But first, I want to hear about your experience. How has he treated you?"

"Very well," Ann said. "As well as he can, I think. He has a hard time talking sometimes, and he doesn't always understand what I mean or when I'm joking. But he tries."

"And that coat—he made it for you?" It should have been obvious from the moment he'd laid eyes on her that she had ties to the Winter Ruler. Nicolas's magic clung to her, likely an attempt at a ward. Most faeries wouldn't waste their time with such efforts for a human they would only know for a week. Nicolas must be serious about keeping her, which further intrigued and baffled Julius.

"He gave it to me earlier today," she ruffled the fur cuffs with her gloved hands. "It's cute, isn't it?"

"Of course," Julius said through gritted teeth. "And why did he give that to you?"

"Well, if I'm going to live with him for a while, I'll need more than a sweater!" Ann said. "He's always asking if I'm warm enough. I wonder if he'll stop that now."

"And he makes you call him 'Majesty?'"

"It's better than calling him Prince Nicolas of the Frost Faeries, Ruler of the Season of Winter, Bringer of Chilly Weather, Maker of Sugar Cookies, Brewer of Tea, Hider of Feelings Behind Teacups, and so on."

Julius genuinely laughed at that. He could see himself liking Ann if he got to know her better. He could see Jack and Drew liking her, too. She was pretty enough to draw their eye, but not so pretty that they would have to fight off too many other suitors. Like most light and vernal floral fae, they only seemed to come into contact with humans when romance was involved. Julius didn't know why, but they had told him that in the next few decades or so, he would be old enough to understand.

But *Nicolas*, the cold-hearted tyrant who had threatened Julius, his season, and his subjects for the last hundred years? He couldn't believe Ann had anything special to offer someone like that. As far as Julius knew, Nicolas had no interest in love or thirst for human blood.

"Why?" he asked before he could stop himself. "Why does he treat you so nicely when he treats me like I'm worthless?"

Ann paused to collect her thoughts. She knew Nicolas could be abrasive, but she didn't think he was that bad. Then again, that might be because he didn't treat *her* badly. "I'm sorry—it hasn't been that way for me. I think it's..." How to explain? "I think it's because we're both alone."

"He's only alone because he *chooses* to be!" Julius snapped, rising to his feet as his wings flared out. "I was his friend once! Jack tries endlessly to get on his good side, but what are we to him? Rubbish! Nuisances! Why can he treat *you* with kindness, but not us?"

She faltered for only a moment before replying. "I don't think he sees it that way. I don't think he knows he has a choice." Now she stood, offering a hand to Julius. "I don't intend to stay with him forever. I'm going to find my home, and as much as I would like to think that Nicolas and I will still be friends when that happens, I won't see him as much anymore. Will you help me show him that it doesn't have to be this way?"

Julius looked at her open hand, and at the scarf in his. "You think I'd want to help him? After the way he's bullied and harassed me?"

Ann withdrew her hand as Julius went on. "You have no idea what you're getting into. But..." This was a golden opportunity. Nicolas had broken the law, and the human he'd done it for had come waltzing right into Julius's path. It was too perfect to be a coincidence. Perhaps fate was finally smiling on him, giving him a chance to confront Nicolas, and have a little fun while he was at it. "I'll think about it, but I'll do it my own way."

"I don't mean to tell you what to do," Ann said hastily. "And I still don't know what exactly Nicolas has done to wrong you, but if you don't want to —"

"I'll think about it," Julius repeated firmly. "However, there is something you could do. Did you know that Nicolas loves painting?"

Ann thought back to the time she had ventured into his study. She had seen an awful lot of blank and half-finished canvases in the room, but she hadn't paid special attention to them at the time. She had assumed that whatever Nicolas did in that room was of grave importance to ruling winter, and was therefore not for mortal eyes. For some reason, her only reaction had been to remark that he did not have any charcoal drawings.

"I have some spare paints I'm not using," Julius said. "I only ever dabbled in oil painting, anyway. Photography is my art. I would appreciate it if you would take my paints to him. I'm sure he'd make better use of them than I would. But, until I make my decision, I'd prefer you didn't mention they came from me."

"Okay!" Ann smiled, warm and genuine, and Julius almost felt bad enough to reconsider his brewing scheme. She was a sweet creature, and it was generally frowned upon for faeries of Titania and Oberon's Court to put such a harmless thing at risk. But, if all went well, she would come to no harm. And if it didn't… well, Nicolas would bear the brunt of that, and it was no concern to Julius.

He gave her the paints and sent her on her way. Whatever did or didn't happen, he had no further debt to pay.

Ann was being sneaky, or at least trying. As far as Nicolas knew, she had never lied to him before, and now he could see why. She was terrible at it. As soon as she'd gotten home, she'd had a huge grin plastered over her face. When he'd asked what had put her in such a good mood, she'd giggled and said, "Nothing!" When he'd asked why she had left tea in such a hurry, she'd giggled more, given him the cookbooks, and pranced off to her room without a word.

Now it was dinnertime, and she was staring at him from across the table with a mischievous little smirk and knowing twinkle in her eye. It was distracting, and he didn't care for it, especially given that his first attempt at cooking a human meal sat on the table. Jack had taken the liberty of sending him some meats, fruits, and vegetables. Nicolas had decided a warm dish would be best, even though it had lost its heat almost the moment it left the oven.

"Are you going to share whatever it is you have on your mind?" he asked again.

"After dinner," Ann replied.

Nicolas looked down at his plate. The beef pot roast might look succulent to a human, and the carrots and potatoes added a little color to the presentation, but to him it was a mass of unsweetened waste. "After dinner will never come if you do not eat," he pointed out, mostly to himself, and managed to take a bite to encourage her.

"Right!" Ann started shoveling the pot roast down her throat, clearing the plate in record time. He couldn't help but wonder if she had even tasted it, but was glad enough that she'd eaten it at all. He didn't think he could stomach more than two bites.

"Ann, please, tell me what has you so excited," he

said. He made a point of using her name; he had read in one of the old books in the library — *Caring for Your Human* — that humans liked the sound of their own name, and would respond more readily when it was used. In fact, he had spent much of the day studying that book, and had learned quite a lot about humans and how easily they died. He had concluded that Ann must be sturdier than most of her kind, especially as exposure to cold didn't cause her 'hypothermia,' 'frostbite,' or the dreaded 'sniffles.'

"Why tell you when I can *show* you?" Ann raced off to her room and returned with a dingy brown package. It hadn't been sealed well, and the crinkles and odd shape suggested that whatever was inside wasn't boxed. "Ta-da!"

"What inspired this?"

"I saw them in town and thought of you," Ann lied. She could tell him it was the Autumn Ruler's idea later.

Nicolas picked up the package and began to unwrap it carefully, shifting his plate aside so he'd have more room. Inside he found a set of paint brushes and tubes of paint.

"Do you like it?"

Nicolas sat motionless for a moment, looking over the gift. The paints were not in his usual palette. He typically dealt with white, black, blue, and sometimes a touch of lavender or dark green. The paints she had given him covered the range from red to light green, bright, warm colors that were out of place on the snowy landscapes he painted. At least she had included white. He was probably running low on it. He was *always* running low on it.

He set the items aside and made a hasty grab for his teacup, bringing it up to his lips to conceal his growing smile. The gift wasn't perfect, but it had been given with the intent of making him happy. It was the first gift he'd received from his human friend.

"Your Majesty?"

He looked back at her. She was smiling the way she usually did, and watching him carefully. He realized she was waiting for his reaction to the art supplies.

"I love it, thank you."

Ann made a sound of pure delight and Nicolas knew he would not be able to move his teacup any time soon.

"What will you paint first?"

Nicolas shook his head. "I do not know yet. When I do, you will be the first to see it."

She beamed so brightly that Nicolas could have mistaken her for a light faerie. He kept the teacup close and shook his head again, to himself. No, she would not be a light faerie. In his mind he imagined her wings would have the long tails of the royal family. She would be one of Oberon and Titania's own.

That must be a good omen, and a sign that he was doing the right thing.

6

THE FRAYED SCARF

Nicolas watched the sky with mild interest from his place next to the parlor window. Thin, wispy clouds cloaked the sun, but not completely; there was enough light to indicate it was morning, and there would be enough to show when it was midday, then afternoon, and finally sunset. Then the children would emerge from their homes in ridiculous costumes, light squashes on fire from the inside, and harass the good, sensible people of the world for treats.

The faerie rolled his eyes. What a foolish holiday.

He had never cared for the autumn celebration, acknowledging them only to be polite or to count down the days until winter could begin in earnest. Try as they might, harvest festivals never fully masked the resentment of the cold season that spurred them on, the humans making a show of squirreling away their food and making preparations for the dark, dead months ahead. Modern times had only made the celebration more grotesque and garish.

If he thickened the clouds just a touch, Nicolas could

summon the first storm of an early winter and bring a prompt end to the sugar-fueled revelry. The world would be better off for it.

Ann entered the parlor, took one look outside, and smiled. "Oh, good. I was worried it would rain today, but it looks like this might blow over!"

"Hardly," Nicolas muttered.

She took her seat and sipped her tea, recoiling slightly once it touched her tongue. "Rose?"

"And what is the matter with rose?" Nicolas asked. "I thought you liked rose." As did most human women, according to *Caring for Your Human*, though Ann would have to do without the flowers themselves. Nicolas could not grow flowers. Even if he hadn't lived in an ice castle eternally surrounded by snow, his touch would freeze the bulbs when he tried to plant them, even with gloves on. Ann occasionally brought him flowers from the woods, and they all invariably froze and shattered at his touch as surely as they would wilt in Julius's.

"I do like it! But with today being Halloween and all, I was expecting something more…pumpkin-y. Cinnamon or cider, at least."

He hid his frown behind the teacup, breathing in its fragrance to soothe himself.

"You don't like Halloween?"

"Not even slightly," Nicolas said.

"Why not? It sounds like so much fun." Ann removed a book from her bag titled *Holidays Around the World*. "There's candy and costumes and scary stories and—"

"I know what Halloween is, and I do not care for it," Nicolas said before she could launch into an explanation

113

about the importance of carving vegetables, and why the phrase, "Trick or treat," was used to steal candy from complete strangers. "I only concern myself with the winter holidays, which are far superior."

Ann gave him *the look*. He had grown accustomed to it over the past month, but he still couldn't pinpoint what it meant. She was smiling, so he assumed she was happy or amused, but her eyebrows were arranged just so. He didn't think she was laughing *at* him, yet he couldn't help but feel something about him was making her conceal a chortle.

She finished her tea and the slice of lemon cake Nicolas had set out—one of the required servings of fruit that the book insisted she needed—before speaking again. "Alright, stay here and miss out on all the fun, then. I was waiting to see if you were going to do anything tonight, and now that I know you aren't, I think I'll go spend the day with Cecil. There must be tons of ghost stories to read in the library. And maybe if I'm in costume, the townspeople will give me some candy!"

As she stood, Nicolas grabbed her hand. She could be fast, and he wanted to make sure she paid attention. Between two pairs of gloves, his and hers, he trusted her skin would not freeze, but he didn't hold tight. There was always a chance he could hurt her, no matter how sturdy she seemed.

"Wait. Tonight is a full moon. Should you lose track of time and debate whether or not you will have enough light to make it back to the castle, stay in town. It is not worth the risk, especially tonight. Do not go into the forest after dark. Do you understand me?"

The Unseelie Court would be out in force tonight,

more ruthless and reckless than any other time of the year, up to the nastiest of their tricks. Some lured humans toward water and drowned them for sport. Some toyed with human senses, charming mortals so thoroughly that they would starve before a banquet. Even well-meaning fae like Leshes could mistake Ann for an enemy in their lands and cause her to become lost in the woods forever. Despite her wearing the coat, he could not be sure that she would be safe on such a night.

Ann gave his hand a small squeeze before slipping her fingers out of his grasp. "I'll be careful," she said with a softer smile. "I've been reading lots of books. I know what to look out for."

"Things in the real world are not as they are in fairy tales," Nicolas warned.

"I've noticed," she laughed. Then, brisk as the winter wind, she was down the hall and out of his sight. If he chose to follow her, she'd be in the courtyard before he could make it to the bottom of the stairs. He had once thought of getting her a pair of ice skates and dismissed them as unnecessary, since she slid around just fine with her boots.

Nicolas looked outside in time to see the pink of her coat disappear into the woods. She rarely ever took it off, and he was glad of it, certain she would freeze otherwise.

He glanced again at the clouds. She was right; the wind was already beginning to disperse them. It would be a clear night—all the better to enjoy the nocturnal festivities under the light of the full moon. The forest would be swarming with Unseelie fae, werewolves, vampires, and other nasty creatures after sundown, but for now they slept, and Ann was safe.

Nicolas sat at the parlor window and thought hard. At this time of the year he might get away with a blizzard to put Julius in his place, but Ann was so excited. This would be her first Halloween. At least, the first that she would remember. He didn't want to spoil her fun, or do anything that might put her in harm's way. Perhaps he would hold off a while, and bring the snow down once the festivities were close to an end and she was sheltered for the night. Surely that was not an unreasonable level of spite.

If Julius complained, he could always claim he simply hadn't noticed it was Halloween. Such a frivolous holiday was beneath his notice, anyway. He wouldn't remember it at all, if not for one dreadful night…

His hands clenched at the mere thought of that memory, almost hard enough to break the handle off his teacup. He set it down, no longer caring to finish his tea or cake.

A blizzard would come. Later than originally intended, perhaps, but it *would* come.

Until then, Nicolas was determined to treat this day as any other.

He picked up *Caring for Your Human* and flipped through it. Over the past few days he had read every single word and examined every picture. The book was in disrepair, with several pages barely held in place between the cracked, worn covers, so he had to handle it carefully as he turned the pages again.

"'Humans need to eat five servings of bread, four servings of fruits and vegetables, two servings of dairy, two servings of meat, and may have one oily or sugary treat per day,'" he repeated under his breath. Ann was small, so he only gave her half that amount: a sweet pastry and a fruity or floral tea for breakfast; fruits, bread, sweets, and cheese at teatime; and servings of bread, vegetables, cheese, and meat at dinner. He allowed the extra sweets because she had proved she could handle more than one daily serving, and he liked them. Preparing so much food was sometimes tiring, but at least most of it could be served cold.

"'Humans need plenty of sleep at night...'" He skipped that section, moving to another page. "'It is not known why humans dream. It was once thought that dreams were some form of dormant magic left over from Oberon and Titania's Gift of Enchantment to the human sages. However, this theory was abandoned when one of Princess Hanako's humans reported dreaming of swallowing a large purple alligator whole for seemingly no reason. Asking a human will yield no answers, as their dreams are as mysterious to them as to the fae and likely mean nothing.'"

Nicolas had a hard time believing Ann's dreams meant nothing when he heard her whimper and cry at night. He was unable to help her in those moments. He knew the dreams were not dangerous to her in any tangible way. She seemed to sleep well enough, and was never bleary-eyed or in bad health when she joined him for breakfast.

Still, he wished he knew what caused the dreams so he could make them stop, but that might be a bad idea if there were pieces of her lost memory in them.

He did not like the idea of Ann having any sort of past that could cause her to experience night terrors.

Shaking his head, he progressed to a different section, trying to ignore that awful, gnawing feeling he got when he thought too much about such things.

"'Humans need stimulation to stave off boredom, which can cause them to become unhappy and lead to destructive behaviors. Humans should be provided with playthings or activities.'" That, like most things in this book, didn't cause him any worry. Ann kept herself busy with her search for her home, and spending time playing in the forest chasing after animals or reading books with her human friend in the town.

However, he did worry what would happen when the weather turned and she had to stay in the castle. He didn't know what kinds of activities Ann could do, unless he felt like enchanting animals out of snow for her to chase. The idea of her racing across the icy floors did not please him. Despite her skill in moving around the palace, there was always the small chance she might slip and hurt herself.

Especially with her recklessness. He sometimes wondered what thoughts went through her mind. Climbing trees was one thing — he had seen her do that with ease — but she also jumped out of them. She chased after any animal she saw, wherever they went, without realizing those animals could turn and attack her to defend their hoards and holes. She had also told him about an activity she called 'squirrel jumping,' which involved racing along one branch, launching herself from its end, and catching another branch some considerable distance away. *Without wings.*

He skipped to the next passage. "'Humans have a finite amount of blood. If they lose too much of it, they will get sick; any more beyond that point, and they will die. Do not let your human bleed, and if they do, dress their wound immediately and move them to a quiet place to rest. Monitor them closely until their condition improves.'"

Sometimes he worried that Ann would injure herself in the forest, so much that he was occasionally tempted to go with her. He trusted that if she did get hurt, she would immediately return to him or go to the town for treatment, but still he found worry creeping into his mind whenever she was out of the palace. It made him grateful for the rainy days when she would stay inside, in danger of nothing but boredom.

With those unhappy thoughts lingering in his head, he closed the book and looked for something else to do.

Ever since Ann had given him the paints, he had felt a renewed urge to create more snowy landscapes on canvas. She might have given him the wrong colors, but he felt inspired again, and that was gift enough. He had already painted a dark night sky over banks of snow, and today he nearly smiled at the thought of finishing that piece. The snow banks were just white splotches, in need of blue shadows and perhaps a dark tree or two sprouting from their depths. Maybe he would add a red bird to one of the trees this time; then he would show it to Ann and challenge her to catch it, just to see what she would do.

He would have been content to spend the whole day painting, but a loud knock echoed through the palace and brought Nicolas out of his artistic reverie. He headed downstairs to let Ann back in. Or maybe it was Jack, come to celebrate Halloween with him.

119

The light faerie had returned to the castle with annoying frequency, and he filled Ann's head with summery thoughts of sandy beaches, lazing in warm sunlight, and days that lasted almost until midnight. She was eager to experience summer, but she always remembered to add that she couldn't wait for winter, too.

Nicolas paused at the top of the stairs. Ann and Jack knew the door was open. They would not knock, because they knew they did not need to, and the noise would disrupt him — not that Jack had ever cared about that, but he appeared to take a sort of pride in the fact that he could enter at will.

With each step down the stairs, Nicolas stiffened his shoulders and hardened his face a bit more. Whoever had arrived at his door was not welcome to visit.

Nicolas decided to open the doors with his hands, taking a firm hold of the handles and pushing them open. *I am in charge here*, he reminded himself. He had been master of this castle for nearly two centuries, and he would not tolerate intrusion without an appropriate gift.

Outside stood Julius, his rust-colored hair an eyesore against the snowy backdrop of the courtyard. In his hand was a large bag — less a bag, really, and more a hulking sack.

Nicolas started to close the doors, only to have the Autumn Ruler wedge his boot between them. "Hold it. We have business to discuss."

"What business?" Nicolas growled.

"Business that I won't discuss outside. Invite me in," Julius responded, though his smug expression wavered with the hint of an uncertain frown. The castle was Nicolas's domain, after all, and while Julius was at his most powerful this season, Nicolas was certainly not weak.

When it looked as if Nicolas might pull the door shut regardless of Julius's foot being in the way, or maybe *because* of it, the smaller faerie reached into his bag and pulled out a half-finished scarf. "Do you remember this?"

Nicolas faltered for a moment, then opened one of the doors just enough to admit Julius. He squeezed into the palace, his oversized bag barely making it through the narrow entrance.

Julius looked around as he walked, taking his time and possibly making an escape plan just in case Nicolas's mood became frostier. "It's been a while since I've been here. It looks almost the same as back then." Not almost. Exactly. Nicolas hadn't changed a thing in a hundred years, not that Julius had expected any different. He had always known the Winter Ruler hated change. He assumed that came with the territory of his season. Winter froze things and preserved them. Oberon himself had ruled a desolate, unchanging world for a million years before Queen Titania had brought the first spring with her birth, and Nicolas couldn't be too much different from his sovereign.

"There is no need to improve upon perfection," Nicolas said flatly. "Now tell me why you have that scarf, and what this business is, so you can leave. I do so hope that you have not added thievery to your list of heinous hobbies."

"It's an interesting story. One you must already know part of," Julius answered slowly. "A human woman gave the scarf to me in exchange for an audience. She was nice. Naive maybe, but sweet. And she had a rather unusual proposition."

The flutter of Nicolas's wings was the only indicator that he was bothered by those words. "How strange. I did not know autumnal fae kept much company with humans. Perhaps Drew's bad habits are rubbing off on you."

"'Strange' is exactly what I thought." Julius examined the throne, ignoring the scathing remarks about the Eldest. Nicolas was trying to get a rise out of him, and by doing so, he revealed he had a reason to be defensive. Julius would not relinquish control of the situation to respond to a juvenile comment directed at his erstwhile caretaker. "A human with in-depth knowledge of the Princes and Princesses that rule the seasons is quite *strange* indeed. That would lead me to think she was living with a rather high-ranking faerie. *You*, specifically. That is a severe offense for someone in your position." Nicolas gritted his teeth in the most satisfying way as Julius ran his fingers over the throne's ornamentation. "So maybe, in light of that, you could apologize to me and drop whatever grievance you have."

"All you've accomplished is ensuring that it will continue, you brat." Nicolas's voice rose. "I had considered showing you mercy, but no longer. You deserve every moment of suffering you receive!"

"That's too bad. I guess I'll just *have* to tell Oberon about, oh, what was her name? Ann, right?" Nicolas's steely façade dropped for only a moment, but Julius caught it. "I'm not bluffing. I know all about her. A Prince defying the will of Oberon doesn't look good, does it? Add the fact that the Prince in question has a history of unbalancing nature and overstepping his boundaries, and has already been reported for it to the King and Queen once this year, and it would be nothing short of a miracle if that Prince *didn't* get his wings ripped off. And there's no telling what they'd do to the *human*."

Nicolas's wings snapped shut before he could stop them.

If *Caring for Your Human* made one thing abundantly clear, it was the delicate nature of human emotion. Being separated from their friends for too long, grieving for a dead friend, going too long without affection and friendly conversation — all of these things could kill Ann. The King and Queen could cause her death without intending her any harm. He had reached the conclusion that Ann was more capable of withstanding physical conditions than most humans, but she was still vulnerable to human emotion as much as any other.

It made him think of the way she had looked weeks ago in the tree. Even before he had read that such strong negative emotions were dangerous to her health, he had not ever wanted her to look that way again.

"But it doesn't have to be that way," Julius hastily added, his hands open and palms facing upward in supplication. "If things are different from now on, that is…"

"I will not allow you to blackmail me." Yet, Nicolas couldn't see much choice otherwise, unless he could find some way to make the King and Queen disbelieve Julius, or threaten the younger Prince into keeping quiet. Neither option seemed likely.

"I wouldn't call it blackmail," Julius replied. "I don't plan on abusing this information. I'm not as ruthless as you, and I don't want you, or her, to come to harm. All I want is for you to stop treating me the way you do. And *one* other, simple request."

"Demanding beast."

"It's just a small favor," Julius insisted. "Nothing bad."

Nicolas sighed. "What is it?"

Julius thought of wording his request to make it sound fancier and more appealing to Nicolas, but he decided a straightforward approach was best. "It's Halloween. I want you to take me trick-or-treating."

Nicolas stared in bemusement. "No. That is absolutely out of the question. You are too old to indulge in such childishness."

"Gosh, I guess I have *no choice*, then. I hope you've got all your affairs in order, picked who you want to be the next Winter Ruler and all that. Or maybe Oberon and Titania will do it for you, since your pick probably can't be trusted, with you being a traitor to the Court and all. Who do you think they'll choose?"

Nicolas's hand twitched and the temperature dropped significantly. Julius trembled, but instead of ducking for cover, he stood firm and held out his hand. "Do we have a deal? *Please*?"

With a snarl, Nicolas took his hand and gave it a rough shake. "Fine. But I get to choose my costume."

"That's fair. And while we're setting conditions, don't think you're just going to take me to a house or two. I expect at least two hours of solid candy time, as soon as the sun goes down. Now hurry and choose a costume. And you can't dress as a king, a prince, or a winter faerie."

There went ideas one, two, and three.

Nicolas massaged his temples. "Give me some time to think. It will be an hour until sundown."

"I'll stay here until you're ready, then. I brought my costume, and I remember the way to the kitchen. I trust you still keep sweets around? I'll have to sample some to make sure you aren't losing your baking skills."

Before Julius could walk away, Nicolas grabbed his sleeve. "You will stay where I can see you and answer my questions. You said the human came to you with an unusual proposition. What was it?"

Julius took his time formulating a response, further angering the older faerie. "I think I had better hold onto that information for a while, until I see how this turns out."

"Fine. Keep your secrets," Nicolas snapped. He released the autumn faerie's sleeve and made his way to his dressing room. Julius followed without hesitation. He nearly took to the air to avoid slipping on the ice, but decided against it in case Nicolas decided *that* was a threat, too.

Nicolas rifled through his trunks of old clothes, quietly seething. This was the most idiotic, embarrassing situation he'd been faced with in a century, and he didn't know how he would make it through the evening without dying of shame. His image, his name, all reduced to jokes by this insect!

Julius's voice cut through his cloud of angry thoughts.

"That cape and vest go well together," Julius said,

pointing them out. He reached into his bag. "I've got some jewelry you could add to make it into a vampire costume."

Nicolas grimaced at the idea of dressing as a blood-sucker, but he had nothing better; his wardrobe did not lend itself to costumes. At least as a vampire, he could maintain his elegance in the face of this humiliation. Even if it was Julius's suggestion.

Without a word, he changed into the outfit, switching out his shirt for one he hadn't worn in decades that was a touch lacier, and trading his tie for the matching cravat. Julius gave him a brooch to tack onto the cravat and a chain adorned with tiny metal bats for the cape. The fake fangs wouldn't fit in his mouth due to his own long canines, but those alone got the point across.

The frost faerie felt ridiculous, but Julius looked him over and nodded in approval.

"And what, pray tell, is *your* costume?" Nicolas asked.

"You'll see it soon. Now—" Julius produced a map from the bag and unfolded it. Nicolas considered suggesting that he get an enchanted bag like Ann's instead of hauling that great ugly thing around, but decided the less he spoke of her, the better. "We can't go to the town nearby because of the iron gates, but I've been scoping out some of the other cities in the area."

Nicolas glanced at the map. Ann had not mentioned visiting towns other than the iron-gated one by the woods. She may have family somewhere else, in another human settlement. It shouldn't be too hard to identify them; all he had to do was go to the right house. Then he could bring her news of her home and family, she would be happy, and he would no longer have to worry for her safety or his own. He would not be happy to see her go, but safety was more important.

"Very well. I will escort you to this town to obtain candy."

Julius smiled. "It'll be fun. Like the old days."

"I hardly wish to remember the 'old days,'" Nicolas scoffed. That took the smile right off Julius's face.

"I don't even know why I bothered," the younger faerie said. "You being kind enough to the human woman for her to ask *that* of me must have been a fluke. I thought maybe you had changed, and you might be nice to me for once."

"Why should I, when you have come here to make threats?" Nicolas asked.

"You made the threat first!" Julius returned, but with a shake of his head and wings, he let it go. "I'm going to get dressed."

Nicolas had a moment of peace to examine himself in the mirror as Julius left to change his clothes. The vampire outfit was not horrible, but it was so outdated that it was hard not to be a little self-conscious. The last time Nicolas had worn these clothes had been a century ago, when vampires had been all the rage in the human world thanks to some book. He was pretty sure the offending tome was buried in his library somewhere.

Julius took what felt like an endless amount of time to get into his costume. He must have put a considerable amount of effort into it, being the Ruler of Autumn.

It nonetheless infuriated Nicolas. If he had not sworn himself to this charade, he would have thrown the autumn faerie out of the nearest window when he saw Julius's costume.

Unlike his usual warm-hued clothes, Julius now wore gray and silver. Even his hands and face had been splotched with makeup to turn his skin sickly white. His clothes looked nice enough, almost matching Nicolas — a pair of slacks, dress shoes, a button-up shirt, and a vest. Chains of varying thicknesses were wrapped around his chest and arms, and a fake weighted ball was chained to his ankle. The ball was hollow, and he held it in his hands to serve as a way of carrying the collected candy.

Of all things, he had chosen to dress as a ghost.

"What do you think?" Julius asked. "I wasn't able to make my eyes turn bloodshot, but I don't think anyone will notice in the dark."

"What do I think? As if you do not already know." Nicolas barely contained a snarl. "It is nearly sundown. You have two hours, starting now."

"Starting when we get to town."

"Starting *now*," Nicolas repeated more forcefully, and he spread his wings before Julius could challenge him. They did not bother going down to the courtyard. Nicolas's bedroom connected to a wide balcony, and it was just as easy to take flight from there. Once they were in the air, Nicolas summoned the North Wind to carry them swiftly to their destination, landing on its outskirts so they wouldn't be spotted by any gifted human children before they could don human glamours.

The town was alive with candlelit pumpkins and children running around the streets in groups while parents walked behind. The sounds of laughter and merriment filled the air, punctuated by a chorus of shrill voices shouting, "Trick-or-treat!" Nearly all the costumes were made of household items or cheap taffeta, and Nicolas was able to at least take a little pride in the fact that he and Julius looked by far the best.

That pride vanished when he remembered that he was comparing himself to *children*.

Julius wasn't daunted. "Come on—we'll start on this bit of sidewalk and cross to the other side of the street when we reach a dead end. Here, take this." He shoved a coffin-shaped box into Nicolas's hands.

"What is it?"

"Aren't you going to collect candy, too? No, let me rephrase that. You're collecting candy, too. That's the most fun part of the night."

Fun. Ann would think this was fun, wouldn't she?

I will look for her family, but I will not lower myself this far! Nicolas thought. "Absolutely not. I agreed to escort you, and that was all."

"Come *on*," Julius sighed. "Lighten up for once. It won't kill you."

"Anything to get you to cease your whining," Nicolas muttered. It wasn't as if anyone would recognize him. At least this way he would get a better look at the people opening the doors; Ann's facial structure and coloring were firm in his mind. He would know her relatives immediately, and take note of their house so he could describe it to her later.

Nicolas followed Julius up to the porch of the first house, where an elderly man sat in a rocking chair with a bowl of wrapped candies.

"Trick-or-treat!" Julius chanted enthusiastically.

"Great costume!" the man said, placing two candies into the ball weight. He looked to Nicolas expectantly, as did Julius.

"What?" Nicolas asked. Julius nodded his head toward the candy dish, eyebrows raised slightly. The realization dawned. "No."

"You'll look more foolish if you *don't* say it."

Nicolas took a deep breath. He would kill Julius for this later, once Ann and he were safe. He was certain that he could make the Autumn Ruler's death look like an accident. Skating on a layer of ice that was too thin, perhaps…

As quietly and quickly as possible he mumbled, "Trick-or-treat."

The old man deposited one candy into the coffin box with a kind smile.

"Thank you," Julius said. Nicolas was already walking to the next house. Would the mortification never end?

Nicolas kept them moving between houses at a hurried pace. He only needed a glance at each person who answered. He barely even looked at the candy accumulating in his box.

None of the humans looked at all like Ann. Some had a feature or two in common with her, but never enough to make him believe it was more than coincidence. He didn't get the feeling that any of these people were related to her. None of them struck him as distraught, as someone who had recently lost a child or sister should be.

Many people commented on their outfits. Some asked Nicolas if he was too old for Halloween, and others gave him a look that said the same thing. A chilly breeze kicked up in his wake, but his face still felt hot.

"Let's stop for a while," Julius said once they reached the end of one side of the road, having detoured into every inlet and side street along the way. He sat down on the curb. "We're making great time, and this thing's getting a little heavy. It's time for a candy break."

Nicolas took a handful of sweets out of the coffin box. Under the light of the street lamp he could read the colorful labels, but they might as well have been written in a foreign language. He didn't know what any of them were.

"That's a good one," Julius said. "It's chocolate and almonds."

"It cannot be better than my chocolate," Nicolas sniffed. "How long will this candy break last? We need to keep going. You can eat while we walk."

"What's got you so eager all of the sudden?" Julius asked. His eyes were wide, the same way Ann's sometimes were. The comparison unsettled Nicolas. Julius, conniving and clever and *backstabbing*, was nothing like his human friend.

"As if I would tell you anything."

Julius rolled his eyes. "It can't be *that* important. And I never would have told Oberon your secret, anyway. I don't want to hurt you."

"How was I to know that?" Nicolas replied. "You sounded serious. You *were* serious. You only say that you would have kept my secret so you can believe you are in the right and I am the villain. You are as much a trickster as you ever were."

"We used to be friends," Julius said quietly.

"Used to be. And who is to blame for that change?" Nicolas glared at Julius, and Julius glared back.

Eventually, Julius lowered his head and stared into the candy bucket in his lap.

"This was a dumb idea," he sighed. "You can go home, if you want."

"So now you intend to be rid of me. Typical."

Julius stood up, toppling the ball chain and scattering candy everywhere. "You always say that, yet you act like you'd be happy if you never left your castle! Do you want to be included or not? What is your *problem*?"

"My 'problem' is that the only time I am invited to anything is when I'm being mocked," Nicolas shot back. "Don't try to pretend that you had any other intention. You made this request because you knew it would embarrass me, and because you had the threats necessary to make me do whatever you wanted."

"What about the Equinox celebration? Did we invite you to that to make fun of you, too?" Julius pointed out. "We didn't *plan* for what happened then. You did that all yourself."

"Don't change the subject."

"I'm not changing the subject, I'm stating facts! While we're talking about this, why not go back to the start?" Julius wiped his face with his sleeve, smearing his white makeup. "Why don't we go all the way to the beginning, when you started ignoring me and calling me names and treating me like I'm lower than the dirt beneath your shoes? You even stopped knitting my scarf when you were halfway finished! Was that because I embarrassed you? Did I wrong you somehow?"

"Yes!" Nicolas realized he had shouted and glanced around to make sure no one had noticed. A few people looked over before awkwardly turning their children away from that side of the street, taking them to other houses instead.

"What was it, then? What did I do to deserve this?" Julius went on.

Nicolas heard the same crack in Julius's voice that had been in Ann's voice on the day she'd confessed her fears. The smaller faerie wiped his face again—not to get the makeup off, but because he was trying to scrub away tears before they could fully form.

The frost faerie shook his head. This was an act, surely.

"You say that like you don't know, yet you dressed like that," Nicolas said, keeping his voice quiet to avoid causing a scene.

Julius looked over his costume. "What's wrong with it?"

"Don't play dumb with me. You know what you did. It's the whole reason why you dragged me out here tonight!"

Julius stared at him. Nicolas tried to read his face for signs of understanding, but he couldn't make a guess at what the younger faerie might be thinking. He never could—not with Julius, not with anyone.

Nicolas frowned. "Fine. I will 'jog your memory,' as they say. You've used Halloween to torment me before. Think back on it."

It took Julius a minute to respond. "The haunted house? But that was one hundred years ago!"

"Does it matter how long ago it was?" You took me there, knowing that I—" Nicolas lowered his voice further. "Knowing that I cannot stand the presence of ghosts. Knowing what was in that wretched place."

"I thought it was vampires you hated most," Julius said.

"I do not like that they drink blood, but otherwise vampires are *tolerable* creatures," Nicolas corrected him. "Ghosts, however, are irredeemable. You knew this, and yet you took me to the mansion under false pretenses and proceeded to abandon me."

"False pretenses? I didn't know it was really haunted!" Julius replied. "The splitting up part was just a silly joke about how humans write ghost stories. I didn't intend for us to lose each other! I had thought you would have been able to pick up on my magic and locate me no matter where I was. I didn't know there was *other* magic in the place until we were already inside!"

"Lies."

"I'm not lying!" Julius's lip trembled and he covered his face with his sleeves. "I'm *not*!"

Nicolas's expression softened. Perhaps this wasn't a farce. "Why should it matter to you if we're no longer friends?"

"Because I liked being friends. Or at least I liked being able to talk to you without feeling like you hate me," Julius sniffed.

"Hate you?" Nicolas paused. Did he hate Julius? When he was angry, when he felt that he was being made a laughingstock, the answer was a definite yes—but at those times, he hated everyone. Julius had once been his friend, like Ann was now. Could he ever say that he hated her, even if she embarrassed him?

"The way you act..." Julius continued. "You treat my season like it's worthless. You treat *me* like *I'm* worthless. Just because I accidentally scared you? Just because of *that*?"

The frost faerie frowned. He wanted to claim there was some deeper offense, something inexcusable, but there wasn't. "I do not necessarily *hate* you. I only want to begin my season as soon as possible, and you prevent me from doing that."

"I did that when we were friends, too. It's nothing personal, it's just nature," Julius pointed out. "It's alright. You don't have to try to fix it, if that's what you're doing. I don't think it can be fixed now. Knowing you threw away our friendship over something like that, without even talking to me…I don't know if I still want to try to fix this."

Julius leaned down and retrieved the spilled candy. "I need to think for a while. You can go. I won't revoke my promise; your secret is safe. I swear it on King Oberon's crown and Queen Titania's wings, in honor of the friend I *used* to have."

Nicolas debated staying, but Julius's expression was withdrawn. Storm clouds were beginning to form in the sky. He emptied the coffin box into the ball chain and whisked himself away on the North Wind.

The moment he walked through the castle doors, not caring that he was still dressed as a vampire, he called out, "Ann, I wish to speak with you." There was no answer, no noise from upstairs indicating that she was getting out of bed to come see him. He frowned, then remembered that Ann was out for the night with her librarian friend.

He went to the kitchen and made himself a cup of tea before placing a few candies in a box with the bat chain and brooch. In his study, he drafted a note that read:

Dear Julius, Thank you for lending me your costume accessories. Perhaps in some future year I could use them again. Happy Halloween. Sincerely, Prince Nicolas Rasmussen.

His hand stalled, but he forced out the last line.

P.S. – I apologize for my behavior then and now. I did not know you meant no harm. I would have acted differently otherwise, and will act differently from here on out.

Nicolas opened the window and summoned a messenger. "Take this to Prince Julius's home, tonight."
The tiny sprite nodded, took the box, and vanished.

7

THE GHOST STORY

ANN MADE QUICK STRIDES across the snow. It was getting deeper, reaching up to her calves as she bounded to the courtyard gate. She hadn't caught Nicolas in the act of making a storm, but he must have been conjuring snow while she slept.

She didn't understand his reluctance to celebrate Halloween. She didn't understand his reluctance for most things.

With a shrug, she plunged into the forest. It was a nice day, and she intended to enjoy it.

The breeze swirled the leaves around her feet and into the air. Every so often she caught a flash of red or orange moving against the wind, which she assumed were tiny autumn fae readying the forest for Halloween. As much as she would like to see how they celebrated the holiday, she would keep her promise to Nicolas and not stay out after dark.

Ann charged through another whirl of yellow leaves. One of them skittered away from the others, circling back around to land on her head. She shook it off and chased it to the ground, pouncing into a pile of fallen leaves. A few flashes of light flew over her, then darted away.

"Sorry if you were organizing that," she said to any autumn fae that might still be around. She sat up and dusted stray leaves off her coat.

Looking around, the woods felt familiar. The alignment of the trunks and the dark green of the ferns reminded her of something distant. For a moment she got excited as the memory surfaced, only to sigh when she realized she was sitting on the hill where she'd woken up. She wasn't remembering something from her life before that.

Ann groaned in disappointment and fell back onto the leaf pile, staring at the shifting canopy overhead.

The pile moved under her. It sank down, and she struggled to get up before it collapsed entirely. The leaves disappeared into the earth and Ann stared at the place where they had been, heart pounding. The hole had gotten bigger, and the herbal scent was stronger.

It's familiar, she thought, and her heart skipped a beat.

Carefully, she crawled toward the hole, staring into it. She couldn't see much, or tell how deep it was. It could be a used rabbit warren, but she got the idea that it hadn't been dug out by animals. It was too symmetrical, too planned.

Ann put her hands on either side of the hole and lowered her torso in. As expected, her entire upper body fit. The air inside the hole was colder, and she could feel it stirring around her. From her new vantage point, she saw the hole widened significantly below. She pushed herself back out and turned around, entering legs-first and dropping down into the dark.

The heels of her boot struck something hard, and she almost toppled over. She could still reach up and stick her arms into the tunnel up to her elbows. If she jumped, she could probably grip the edges of the hole again. She moved away from the entrance, light streaming down from above to illuminate a floor of leaves and what appeared to be a table.

An earthy aroma wafted through the air. It was comforting, even more so than the rich scent of Nicolas's tea and cookies. Ann crouched, touching the wood of the table with her hands and feeling the grain of it. The few leaves that had followed her in fluttered to the ground, and with them came something more solid than the brittle autumn foliage: a piece of paper. She jerked her fingers back when they brushed over the unexpected texture, knocking it off the table and onto the ground. She shuffled through the shadows and found it. It bore words in dark ink, but the cavern was too dark to read the letters clearly.

What was a paper doing in a hole in the woods? What was a *table* doing in a hole in the woods?

Ann examined the room once more, but found nothing except dirt and leaves. She clambered up on the table, paper in her mouth, and jumped with her arms spread. She hooked one of her hands over the lip of the hole and wriggled her way up. She accidentally crinkled the paper as she moved, but it was still intact when she got out.

She stood and walked away from the hole. She hadn't minded being underground, but she much preferred being able to see the world around her, and being able to read the letter. The script was fancier than what she was used to reading in books, but still legible.

Halloween, 1982 —

My dear,

I can only hope this letter reaches you, and that you are unharmed. You cannot imagine my surprise to find that you had disappeared in my absence.

If you are reading this, and you have found your way back, come to this hill on the next full moon. When I know that it is you, I shall reveal myself and collect you. Until then, you must know these things:

1. The town is dangerous to you. Do not go there unless you absolutely must.

2. The only vice humans are prone to more than violence is greed. I have left you with my enchanted bag and coin purse; when in a pinch, scatter gold coins on the ground and run.

3. Likewise, your bag will hold whatever you need to carry no matter how large or heavy, and when you seek inside it, it will always give you the thing you need most.

4. I had to leave my enchanted boots behind and could not find them again. If you have them, do not rely on them too much. They are old and unpredictable. If you click your heels together three times, and the boots feel like cooperating, each step will take you seven leagues. Click your heels three times again to deactivate the spell.

5. Do NOT walk over water.

6. Do NOT touch fire.

With hope, I will see you when the full moon rises again.

Sincerely yours,
Anais

Ann read the letter twice, then three times, then three times more. It wasn't addressed to anyone by name, but she couldn't imagine that it *wasn't* for her. How many other people had a bag that was bigger on the inside and always seemed to give her just the right thing at the right moment? As for the boots, she'd rather not risk checking. She didn't know offhand how far seven leagues was, and she liked her walks just fine. The last part about not touching fire seemed a tad unnecessary, but she'd heed that advice, too.

"Anais." No last name, but it was more information than she'd had. It didn't bring much to mind, though. All it did was spark a sense of Ann's usual nightmares.

Cecil might know more. At the very least, he could check for the name.

Ann tucked the letter into her bag with care and

started off for the town with renewed purpose. She had been looking forward to Halloween already, but now there were answers to find, too.

The town was sparsely decorated for the holiday. She supposed that to be expected, given how few permanent residents there were. Some had placed Jack-o-Lanterns near their doors, a few of which were already lit. The store was having a sale on candles, but beyond that, it had done nothing to celebrate. In fact, Ann conceded, the sale might be completely coincidental.

When Ann entered the library, she found Cecil poring over an old book, curling his hair between his fingers and sticking his tongue out between his teeth as he usually did when he was deep in thought. He wore a button-up blouse, a cobweb-patterned skirt, and spider earrings.

Spooky! she thought with a smile. She wasn't necessarily afraid of spiders, but she always paused when she saw one. She used to catch them, but that had stopped promptly after she'd returned to the palace once and informed Nicolas that she'd been bitten. He had demanded that she stop catching spiders, quizzed her endlessly on how much blood she'd lost and if she felt light-headed or ill, and made her stay in bed until dinnertime.

Ann stood in front of Cecil for a few minutes before he looked up.

"Oh! Ann, you startled me! I didn't hear you come in with all the noise out there."

"Noise? What noise?" Ann said, tilting her head.

"In the square. It's always busy on Halloween. Lots of…visitors."

That only made Ann more confused, and Cecil did not seem keen to elaborate, so she changed the subject. "What are you reading?" she asked, leaning on the desk to look at the book. The pages were old and worn, but they looked sturdy.

"*Dracula*," Cecil said, marking his page before closing the book. "It's a classic. I'll loan it to you someday, if you're interested."

Ann beamed. She had made leaps and bounds in her reading, advancing from fairy tales and children's books to the works of Alexandre Dumas and short stories by Nathaniel Hawthorne. She would have liked to spend some time talking about her latest literary adventures, but thoughts of the letter dominated her mind.

"Have you found any clues about people who might know me?" she asked, finding her enthusiasm fade with each word. The more time passed, the more she was convinced her family was dead, or she had been unlikable and alone.

"Ah, well, no," Cecil said, adjusting his glasses. "I'm sorry, Ann. All I can really do is ask around town, and no one can recall seeing you prior to a month ago when you first turned up. If I just had a name to go off of, maybe I could do more."

"How about 'Anais?'"

Cecil somehow frowned with his entire body. "Where did you hear that name?"

Ann pulled the letter out of her bag and showed it to him. "I found this earlier. I think it was written for me."

"Written for you?"

"How many other people regularly take walks in

the woods? I can tell you from experience, it's a number you can count on one hand. And look!" She pointed. "It's signed from someone named 'Anais.' There isn't a last name, but one name is better than none."

"I suppose it is." Cecil removed his glasses and rubbed the bridge of his nose. "But that name carries some pretty heavy baggage around here."

"Sounds like a story," Ann said excitedly.

"It isn't a story I like to tell."

"Please?" Ann asked, her hands clasped around the letter. "It's the only lead we have."

Cecil sighed and motioned for her to follow him. "I suppose it's one way to start the scary stories." He led her to one of the book forts, this one decorated with orange lights and fake cobwebs and spiders. A bowl of candy sat on the table. Cecil grabbed it before they ducked under the table, settling themselves on the bats-and-spiders blanket.

For once, he didn't grab a book from the lining, instead offering Ann a piece of candy before removing his glasses again. He folded them carefully, turning them over in his hands a few times, before closing his eyes. His eyebrows pinched together in concentration.

"About a hundred years ago, when this town was big enough to have a name, a woman came from the forest. She would not say where she was from, or why she'd chosen to visit, only her name: Anais. As much as I would like to say that the townspeople respected her privacy and were hospitable, they only allowed her to stay because they feared she was a faerie who would curse them if they were rude. She rented the house at the end of the road, and the people stayed away…until a curious child looked into her window one night.

"What he saw has never been shared. He fell ill almost immediately afterward, and within a week he was dead. Of course the townspeople thought his death was her fault, but they were too afraid to confront her. They thought as long as they stayed away and kept their kids inside, they'd be safe.

"However, the situation only worsened. A fever spread through the town and took more lives. Each time someone got sick, their family would find a collection of plants at their doors. And once that ominous bouquet appeared, death was certain.

"When almost half the town was sick, the mayor, my grandfather, finally gathered all the able-bodied people he could to do something about it. They knocked on Anais's door once—" he struck his knuckles on the hard book covers, "—and said, 'Come out and speak for yourself, and lift the curse on the town, or you will be burned at the stake.' There was no reply. They knocked twice—" he tapped the books twice, "—and said, 'We know you leave flowers that mark women and children for death. Explain yourself and give us the cure, and we will leave you in peace.' And still there was no reply."

Cecil opened his eyes and leaned in. Ann did, too. Her heart was beating fast, and she had to make an effort to calm her breathing.

He struck the books three times. "They knocked again, and this time they said, 'Half the town is on their deathbeds, and the other half is here to make sure you share their fate. If they live, you will live.' Finally there was a reply. The door opened, and the witch spoke.

"'You may burn me to ashes if it pleases you, but they will still die.' Then she threw more of the same mysterious plants over the crowd. Some people screamed and covered their eyes. Others fled. My grandfather and a few other men grabbed Anais. They marched her straight to the town square, where they already had the stake set up, just in case.

"They tied her up and burned her right then and there. But some say she escaped into the woods, her cloak on fire over her. And as she ran, she turned and said, 'Half fall ill and half fall down; and half in half a century shall be your town.'"

Cecil fell silent. When Ann could no longer stand to wait, she asked, "What happened next? What does this have to do with the letter?"

"The woman might have gone into the woods," Cecil said. "The town never heard from her again, whether she really survived or not. As for the curse—the town is less than half as big as it used to be, and it's been well over fifty years since this all happened. The old town square was lost, along with other parts of town. It's somewhere in the woods now."

"Did the sick people ever get better?"

"I don't know. Some did, probably. We do have records of a strange illness spreading through town in the late eighteen-hundreds, right around the time the name 'Anais' appeared in the town guestbook. However, it was nowhere near as deadly as the story says it was. People quarantined to slow the spread, and with proper treatment and rest, most patients recovered." He ran a hand through his hair. "It couldn't be the same person who left this letter. Even assuming she didn't die from her burns, it's been a century, and she was a grown woman then. She would have died of old age decades ago. *If* the story is true at all." He popped a hard candy into his mouth. "Whoever left you the letter probably knows about the town lore, which strikes me as odd. It's possible they avoided signing in at town hall, but someone else should have seen a new person around."

"It's still more of a clue than I've had," Ann said, looking over the letter again. She decided not to mention her nightmares of being burned, though the story was uncanny in its resemblance to them. She would puzzle that out later, by herself.

Cecil placed a hand on hers. "I know, Ann." He gave her a smile. "In the meantime, maybe there's something happier we could focus on." He took her hand in his as he showed her to the back room behind the front counter.

Ann was immediately met with loud mewing, and

three white-and-orange furred heads poked over the rim of the cardboard box in the corner. Beside it sat two dishes, one empty, the other full of water.

"Oh, how cute!" Ann squeaked, dropping to her knees to lift one of the purring kittens up to her shoulder. Its whiskers tickled her ear.

"Their mother brought them here a little over a month ago. She hasn't turned up since then, so unfortunately I don't think she's coming back. I hope a fox didn't get her." He glanced toward the door with a sigh. "I would have shown them to you sooner, but it kept slipping my mind." Cecil offered a sheepish smile in apology. "As far as I can tell, they're just over two months old, two girls and a boy. I'd normally ask if you could take one of them, especially since they're warming up to you so fast, but I'm *pretty* sure that won't be possible."

"Not until I find *my* home." Ann nodded. She took a closer look at the kittens. Two of them, including the one she held, were mostly white with a few orange spots; the other was mostly black, and splotched with orange and white. "What are their names?"

"You're holding Marmalade. The others are Marshmallow and—"

"Molasses?"

"George." Cecil rolled his eyes. "Graham named her."

Ann felt like that was supposed to be some sort of joke, but she didn't quite get it. She went right on petting Marmalade, and decided not to think too hard on it. "Am I ever going to get to meet Graham?"

"Maybe someday. He tends to be shy, and a little

reclusive. Not unlike your forest friend, hm?" Cecil winked.

"Oh?" Ann blinked. She hadn't considered that Graham might be magical — but, then again, there was no reason to think he wasn't. According to Nicolas there were all kinds of magical beings in the world, not just faeries.

"Now that you're acquainted, there's something I'd like your help with," Cecil continued, and Ann immediately nodded. "I picked up some dewormer yesterday from the vet in the next town over, but I haven't been able to give it to them. They aren't exactly willing patients. Graham's allergic, so he hasn't been much help. Every time he came into the room he'd start sneezing so hard that he couldn't even keep his eyes open. If you could just hold them steady one at a time, I'm sure I could handle the rest."

"Sure!" Ann picked up George, holding her securely by the scruff while Cecil grabbed the dewormer. Within minutes, all the kittens were lapping up the water to get the bitterness of the medicine off their tongues.

"You did that so easily! Maybe you used to have a cat," Cecil suggested.

"Maybe!" The kittens crowded around Ann to get their share of scratches under the chin and behind the ears. Marmalade crawled into her lap and George sat on her knee. "It's a shame I can't take one, but I'd never be able to choose which!"

"I'll find someone. Even dog people love kittens." Cecil reached over to pet Marshmallow. "They'll need a little more socializing first, anyway. They do alright with me, but I suspect that's because I was friends with their mom."

"And she just abandoned them?" Ann asked, a note of personal offense in her voice.

"She was a smart cat. I don't think she would have left them here if she hadn't intended to come back, hence my comment about the fox. She wasn't *my* cat; she was a stray from the woods. I just left food out for her and she let me pet her. She never would come inside, which was just as well, because if she did I probably wouldn't have let her go." Cecil looked out the window at the trees. "I hope she's alright, little Cookie-cat."

"Come again?"

"Oh, it's just something I used to say. I named her Cookie, because she was so small and she had this little splotch of orange and black on her back that looked a bit like a cookie. So I'd call her my little Cookie-cat."

Ann was so used to listening to Cecil describe things when he read that she could clearly picture the cat in her mind, a small calico with round, golden eyes. In her mind, Cookie dropped the last of the kittens at the back door of the library and walked away into the woods with a wave of her tail that said, "See you soon," before disappearing into the foliage, never to be seen again. Was she retrieving a fourth kitten when she was interrupted by a predator, or had she forgotten about her babies and her human friend?

Moreover, Ann couldn't quite figure out why she cared so much what a stray cat did with her kittens. Perhaps she saw too much of her current situation in them.

George reared onto her hind legs to bat at Ann's hair. Ann picked up the kitten with a smile. "Don't you go messing up my hair even worse, or I'll never hear the end of it."

Cecil watched, glad to see her smile again, before clapping his hands. The sudden noise scattered the kittens. "Oops, sorry! It was just a gesture, kittens. Right then…we had Halloween festivities to get to, didn't we?"

"We did." Ann knew she couldn't take the kittens to the castle with her, but she gladly scooped them up in her arms so she could spend more time petting and playing with them in the library. "Spooky stories and candy time?"

"Spooky stories and candy time."

Sleeping that night was nearly impossible.

Cecil had added two sleeping bags to the pile of blankets and was snoring softly next to a stack of classic horror and gothic novels from the turn of the century. Ann had her back to him, facing a row of books. It was too dark to read their titles now, but she'd memorized them not too long ago.

The sleeping arrangements weren't as cozy as her bed in the castle, but the sleeping bag was comfortable and warm enough. Especially with three kittens snuggled on top of her hip, purring themselves to sleep.

She wasn't being kept awake by all the sugar she'd ingested or the scary stories that made every shadow and sound a dozen times more menacing, either.

Her mind was racing. Whenever she closed her eyes

for more than a minute, she saw either the cat or the letter. She couldn't stop thinking about them.

She *knew* they were somehow connected. Her memory hadn't returned, but she could feel something important hovering at the edges of her mind, urging her to put it together. A stray cat from the woods, a letter found in a hole and signed with the name of a local legend—were her lost memories trying to tell her that Cookie belonged to whomever had left the letter behind? Maybe she had owned a cat. Maybe Cookie was *her* cat.

And Cookie had gone missing around the same time that Ann had woken up in the forest. Had Cookie gone back to the woods to find her, only to discover Ann was gone?

Did that mean she'd lived in the woods before losing her memory? But Nicolas had told her no humans lived there. It was too dangerous for people, and the number of warning signs she saw around the town reinforced that message pretty loudly.

Then again, Nicolas rarely left his castle. How much did he know about what went on in the forest? Maybe someone did live there, or had tried to once, in a hidden hole in the ground…

A woman with a cloak as red as fire, maybe?

And how did her nightmares tie into Cecil's story about Anais? Were they inspired by lost memories of the story, or forgotten pieces of her life?

Maybe the scary stories had affected her, after all. She couldn't shake the image of a gnarled old witch standing over her with a knife, and she didn't know why she imagined the witch so clearly with a weapon.

Ann squeezed her eyes shut.

It felt like she only closed them for a moment, but when she opened them again, Cecil was pulling aside the blanket wall and light was streaming through the windows beyond.

"Ack, sugar headache," he moaned. "Good morning, all the same."

"Good morning." Ann rubbed her eyes.

"You don't look like you slept too well. Did I snore?"

"No, just restless thoughts," Ann replied. "Will you take another look at the signature on the letter? See if it matches any handwriting? The person who signed it might have used an alias, but the handwriting should be the same."

"Of course, I'll do all that I can. Is it alright for me to hang onto the letter, then?"

Ann frowned. "I guess you can, for a little while. I want to show it to my other friend too, when you're done with it."

"Naturally. I didn't intend to keep it forever."

She crawled out from under the table and stood up, brushing the kittens and a few candy crumbs off of herself. They squeaked at her indignantly before batting at her boots. She set them aside to put them on, and they occupied themselves with tugging on the laces. "I'd better get going. Thank you for everything, Cecil—I had a ton of fun! We'll have to do it again next year, if I'm still around."

"We'll have to do it again next year even if you move to a different country," Cecil said.

The townspeople were already smashing their Jack-o-Lanterns and clearing the atmospheric cobwebs from their windows and porches. They stared at Ann as she passed, but she kept her gaze fixed firmly ahead on the town gate. She wondered if they thought she was a witch and walked a little faster, not slowing until she passed the hill with the hole.

It would be midday before she reached the castle. Her mind drifted to the letter, and what it had said about her boots. Magic.

Cecil had said that Anais, if she really was a witch, couldn't have survived after being burned like that. She had been chased out of town a hundred years ago. But how much did Cecil know about witches? As much as Nicolas knew about humans?

She had thought that finding a clue to her identity would make her *less* frustrated, not *more*.

Ann decided against trying to activate the boots' magic, since she still didn't know how far a league was, and didn't want to risk overshooting the castle and ending up in the mountains. She did her best to focus on her surroundings and not think too hard about the potential clues to her past. Not for the first time, she wondered if she really wanted to know.

Once the palace came into view, she started running and didn't stop until she made it to the doors. They opened easily.

Inside, Nicolas was seated on his throne. He stood up the moment she entered and strode toward her.

"Ann. I want to talk to you."

"Great, because I've got a lot to…" She broke off when she saw his face. It wasn't strange for him to frown — that was his default expression — but this frown was different. Rather than being a flat, stoic line meant to conceal his emotions, it dragged his whole face down and made his eyes glossy. "What's wrong?"

"I may have…" He faltered. "It is a long story, and I fear that you will not like me by the end of it."

Ann took a breath and let it out slowly. She had so much to say, but that could wait until he wasn't so upset. After all, it wasn't as if she had the letter to show him. She would hold off on that, and on wondering who Anais might be, until she got it back and could share it fully.

"I'm listening."

8

THE WOMAN IN THE RED CLOAK

NICOLAS STARED DOWN AT HIS WINTER PLANS, pen in hand.

November marked the beginning of the frosty season. While still technically autumn, during this time he was allowed to command his faeries to create small flurries and spread layers of frost. Anything more than that required the Autumn Ruler's permission, and though the hints of winter made Nicolas itch for a proper blizzard, he refrained from contacting Julius. It had been a week since Halloween, and the younger faerie had not written back to him. It would be rude to ask for a favor before he knew his apology had been accepted.

He crossed out a previously scheduled snowstorm as a show of good will. Ordinarily he would already have distributed the plans with a multitude of storms planned, regardless of Julius's feelings, but he kept finding reasons to change them.

If he did not send them out soon, he would have messenger sprites showing up at his door to receive their masters' orders, and that would risk one of them seeing Ann. Thankfully none of them had arrived while she was in the castle, but with the cold season coming, it

was bound to happen if Nicolas didn't submit the orders for winter. Then they would be too busy to come to the palace unannounced and catch her coming or going.

Most of his administrators were loyal enough, but he knew of a handful who would gladly reveal his secret in the hopes that they might be awarded his crown. And none of them would dare defy the King and Queen. He was still somewhat shocked that Jack and Julius — especially Julius — had agreed to keep his secret safe.

He wrote in the first blizzard of the year for late November, and added a few smaller flurries before that. This would certainly not be his most spectacular winter, but it would do. Adding the final edit to the copies of the plans, he opened the window to summon his messengers from the snow banks in the courtyard. When he leaned outside, he found himself face-to-grin with Jack, who was hovering in the air.

Nicolas leapt back, a hand over his pounding heart. "Do not do that!"

"Sorry, mate. You were so absorbed in your work that I didn't have the heart to knock and distract you. Those are your plans for this winter?"

"Obviously," Nicolas sniffed. "All that is left to do is send them on, and the cold season can begin. If you would *kindly* get out of my window."

Jack fluttered into the study. "Not a problem."

Nicolas narrowed his eyes, waved his hand to conjure messenger sprites from the chill, and handed the tiny winged creatures each a copy of the plans as they arrived. "Hurry," he told them before turning to deal with Jack. "And just what are you doing here? You know Ann is usually gone during the daylight hours, and I am in no need of human food supplies yet."

Thankfully, Ann hadn't avoided him after hearing about what had transpired between him and Julius. She had not been pleased to hear what had happened, despite Nicolas's omission of the fact that it was largely her fault he had been blackmailed. She had frowned at him, which he had not enjoyed, but in the end she had conceded that it was not her conflict. She'd told him she was glad that he was trying to make amends and dropped the subject, which was a relief.

Still, he couldn't help but wonder if she thought of him differently now that she knew how he'd acted toward the Autumn Ruler. More worrisome was the fact that he still didn't know what sort of proposition she'd offered Julius. He didn't feel comfortable asking her directly. He wasn't entirely sure he wanted to know.

"I have a few reasons, actually. The first is this." Jack handed Nicolas a small pumpkin-shaped parcel. "From Julius. We were talking about what went down on Halloween."

"How often do you talk about me behind my back?" Nicolas asked, placing the box on the table.

"Not a lot. He wanted to get my opinion on what he should do. I think he would have gone to Drew if he could, but Drew's probably having a hard time getting out of bed without falling asleep on his feet this time of season. It'll be nice when he starts perking up again. Which reminds me, reason number two—how's the party planning going?"

"Party?" Nicolas stared at him in confusion.

"*Yule!*" Jack exclaimed. "You know, the celebration of the start of winter? End of autumn? The day we all get to hang out together?"

"Oh. Yule." Nicolas hadn't given it much thought; it was over a month away, and it paled in comparison to the importance of finalizing the weather patterns for the season. He rarely ever did anything spectacular for Yule. As much as he hated to admit it, even Julius's fairly humble Equinox celebration had been more extravagant than what Nicolas typically did for his season's holiday. He didn't like to share his home in general, let alone with noisy, reveling faeries. His appreciation for winter far surpassed any of theirs, after all, and he kept those under his command too busy at the dawn of the season for extended partying.

Jack's eyes widened. "You haven't been planning? I thought you would be really excited for it. Especially this year, since the King and Queen are celebrating in the Northern Realm."

Nicolas's already pale skin turned white.

"The King and Queen were due to celebrate each of the seasonal holidays in the Eastern Realm this century," he said.

"They changed their minds, then. It's all anyone's been talking about, but I, uh...I guess you wouldn't have heard." Jack laughed a little. "You need to get out more."

The King and Queen would be celebrating Yule in the Northern Realm. The King and Queen would be *in his home.* And he had not even begun planning. He couldn't bring himself to be upset or enraged over the fact that this was likely Drew and Julius's fault. There was too much to do.

"I need to get started immediately," he muttered,

grabbing a few blank pieces of paper and making sure his pen was full of ink. He would have to spend the rest of the day working on these plans, and did not want to interrupt his train of thought to find another pen.

"That's more like it." Jack nodded with a smile. "Of course, this celebration will be huge, and I'm happy to help in any way I can!"

"*Huge?* It must be *perfect*. But I fail to see how you could help. Frost and light fae tend to have dissimilar tastes," Nicolas pointed out.

"I could help with Ann."

Nicolas froze once again.

"She *will* be at Yule, won't she? If she's still living here, it wouldn't be fair to exclude her while everyone else is having a good time. It'll be hard to hide her, but I'm sure I could find an acceptable excuse."

Nicolas *had* read that humans could suffer emotional damage if they were excluded from social gatherings. He didn't want Ann to be hurt in any way, least of all by his own actions. This was far too important to allow Jack to handle alone, but he appreciated the offer.

"Thank you for reminding me. I will figure out how to keep Ann's human status a secret," Nicolas said, and hoped he was telling the truth.

"Let me know what you decide so we can get our stories straight," Jack said, slipping back out of the window. "I'll leave you to work for now, but I will be back later to help. And if you need a break, feel free to come to my place. There's plenty of room in the sand castle if you shrink down a little!"

"I will think about it after I have everything settled. Perhaps in spring," Nicolas said, waving a brief farewell as Jack disappeared into a stream of sunshine.

Alone again, Nicolas snatched a few more pieces of paper and all but slammed them onto his desk. He had less than two months to plan a celebration worthy of the King and Queen, *and* find a way to conceal Ann from them. He could always ask her to leave the castle for the celebration—she had that librarian friend in town—but that ran the risk of harming her. He never wanted her to look at him the same way Julius had on Halloween. He would *never* make her cry like that. She was the only friend he had left, since he'd ruined things with Julius.

The banquet would have to include human food. Would that alert the other fae to the fact that there was a human among them? Perhaps he could spin the story to sound like he had found her within a week of Yule, and was within the acceptable limits of necessary hospitality.

But could he lie directly to the King and Queen?

No, that would never work. Firstly, because they would detect his dishonesty immediately, and secondly, because *they were the King and Queen.* Some faeries would give one of their own wings just for a chance to see the royal family, and the fact that Nicolas had been afforded more chances than most did not dull his admiration for the rulers of the realms.

Nicolas started working on the menu. Caring for his human friend and receiving new ingredients from Jack had opened up a whole new culinary world to him. Though he had been reluctant to accept the changes, he now found the new recipes to be a welcome challenge. The idea of being in the kitchen helped ease some of his nerves.

He might just be able to pull this off if he themed it

correctly. Humans had a celebration around that time. Christmas, wasn't it? Lots of sweets, a gift exchange, silver, gold, red, and green colors, or perhaps just silver and gold.

He could pull this off.

He *had* to pull this off, or else his wings would be ripped from his back by the end of the night.

His hand knocked against the pumpkin parcel as he scrambled to write everything down. He had forgotten all about Julius's reply, though he held no hope for redemption.

Setting aside his planning papers, Nicolas slowly opened the package. It was a cute little thing; the container was orange, and it opened at the top with a green ribbon bow that comprised the stem and leaves of the pumpkin.

Nicolas delicately removed the folded paper inside. A few pieces of candy remained at the bottom of the pumpkin.

He looked away when he unfolded the letter, until he was sure that he was ready to see its contents.

The image on the paper was faded, and stained a rustic tan. Two faces looked back at him: his own and Julius's. Though their expressions were stoic and serious, as was the custom of the time, he remembered both of them had been excited to try out the fairly new human invention that captured a still image on special paper. Julius had been so enthusiastic that Nicolas had let him keep the photograph without a fuss.

Nicolas remembered Julius talking about it afterwards, equating it to one of his paintings and saying that someday photography might become a respected art form. "Just imagine—I could shoot photographs of landscapes and things, and you could paint them!" He wondered if Julius had indeed pursued artistic photography as a hobby. He had never asked, and had never developed an interest in it himself. He vaguely recalled Drew mentioning that Julius had gone abroad for a season or two to study something in the West, so perhaps he had done so after all.

Did sending the photograph back mean he no longer wanted to remember the time they had spent together as friends?

Nicolas turned the photograph over to see the writing on the back.

Dear Nicolas,

I'm still not sure how to feel about what you said. What you did hurt, and it has hurt for a long time. I don't know if I should forgive you or not, but Jack said that I should give you a chance. I'll see you at Yule and maybe by then I'll know.

Sincerely, Julius.

Nicolas set the pumpkin and the photograph to the side of his desk, arranging them so that the picture sat upright against the box. One more reason to make sure this year's Yule was the most spectacular celebration he'd ever hosted.

He added pumpkin pie to the menu. A little out of place at a Christmas table, perhaps, but he figured most faeries could overlook that.

A few more items made their way onto the menu, all the staples he had read about that came to mind. Ham, turkey, and lamb for the meat, salads and dressings and fruits in abundance, cookies, pies, cakes, and candies. He would be cooking for a month to prepare every-thing. At least most of it was sweets.

Nicolas set aside the menu and grabbed a new paper. He sketched a quick outline of a woman's figure, then flattened the chest a bit and widened the curve of the hips. If Ann was to accompany him to the ball—and there was no other choice, as it would be the easiest method of keeping an eye on her and making sure none of the other faeries discovered his secret—she would need a magnificent gown. He took fashion magazines from the bookshelf and pored over them, trying to find the perfect cut for her shape. He would add a fur shawl to hide her lack of natural wings, so the neckline didn't matter much, but that would put even more emphasis on the skirt. It had to be just right, and he needed to decide on the design soon to have enough time to sew it. The coat had been easy; he could stitch a coat in his sleep, but a dress was another matter.

He set to work, whistling a Christmas tune he had heard centuries ago when Princess Bethilde had allowed him to accompany her on a sleigh ride through a human town. She had already aged beyond her prime then, and had needed him to drive the sleigh, commanding the speed and direction of her silver reindeer.

It had been so long ago that he could scarcely recall the specifics, but what stood out most in his mind was how delighted the children had been when gentle flakes of snow drifted from the sky in Princess Bethilde's wake. They'd formed balls of it to throw at each other and made shapes in the fresh powder.

"Remember this," she had told him. "Remember

that the most important part of our magic is the love we have for it."

"Of course, Your Highness," he had replied absently as he guided the reindeer. They responded to him with almost no effort, being made of frost magic themselves. "I love the snow and frost. I will never forget that."

The memory filled him with a new and invigorating urge to create, the likes of which he hadn't experienced in decades. This was going to be nerve-wracking, and his future held many long, sleepless nights for sure. But with the right mindset, it might be his chance to make everyone finally understand the beauty of winter.

Ann shook as a water droplet fell on her head. She looked skyward to see if it had started raining again. The clouds were still scattered, but the trees were dotted with leftover rain. The drop must have come from one of the overhanging branches.

She circled the hill for the hundredth time that morning. She had found no follow-up letter, no further instructions, and no signs that anyone other than her had been there recently.

There was plenty of time until the next full moon, and Ann kept shifting between dreading the deadline and feeling like it couldn't come fast enough. How was she supposed to prove that she was herself when she had no idea what Anais was expecting? True, Ann might remember the truth as soon as she saw her mysterious letter-writer, but with all the faeries and other magical beings in the forest, it might take more for Ann to convince her.

It was too much of a coincidence that two people had gone missing in the same area at the same time, but if Ann couldn't make Anais believe that she was her lost — *sister, daughter, granddaughter, niece?* — then the other woman might very well leave her behind.

Walking around the hill didn't help Ann recover any memories, as she had hoped it would. She searched her mind until it almost hurt, only succeeding in making herself more and more anxious.

Ann had thought up countless ways to start a conversation, but none of them felt right.

"I hope I'm who you're looking for, but I don't know for sure because I don't know who I am. Sorry."

"Are you actually a witch from this local town legend? Does that make me a witch, too? Just for curiosity's sake, would a faerie be able to tell the difference between a witch and a human and would he respond differently to a witch, hypothetically speaking?"

"I don't know who I am, but I really hope that I'm your family, except I'm not sure if I really want that or not because I don't know who you are, or who I am, and we could potentially be mean, awful people who everyone avoids because of how mean and awful we are."

It was all *terrible.*

Ann sat near the hole and glanced into it, as if she thought that would make things clearer. All she saw was the mysterious dark. The sound of moist leaves being pressed under sure feet drew her attention away from it.

"Today is a lovely day for a walk, is it not?"

166

Ann smiled at the red-cloaked woman who sat down beside her. "Tanya! It's been so long since I've seen you. How have you been?"

"I have been well. And yourself?" Tanya smiled, gesturing to Ann's coat. "I believe it is safe to assume you are faring better than when we first met."

"I am!"

Tanya placed her basket between them and unwrapped the cloth covering the food inside. "I enjoy this weather, and thought I would have a picnic in the woods. Before I left my home, I had the strangest sensation that I should pack enough food for two." She removed a knife from the basket and cut two slices off the loaf of bread, then placed a piece of cheese on one and offered it to Ann.

Ann rubbed her hands on her pants to clean them before accepting the bread. "Thank you. I was just starting to get hungry, too!"

While Ann savored every bite of the bread and cheese, Tanya continued to pull food from the basket: a thermos of apple cider, the rest of the bread and cheese, a small jar of apricot preserves, and chocolate cookies dusted with powdered sugar. Ann watched carefully, examining Tanya more than the food. In the daylight, Ann could clearly see that she was a bit younger than she sounded, probably not much older than Ann herself.

"I prefer simpler flavors," Tanya explained when she had arranged the full spread. "Sweet, but not too sweet."

Ann beamed when Tanya handed her a small mug of cider. Something about the woman made her feel like she should be quiet and listen closely until spoken to, though not out of intimidation or fear. She couldn't quite place the feeling, but she didn't dislike it—though she knew that as soon as she did speak, her words would rush forward like a river that had been dammed.

"How was your Halloween?" Ann asked once she felt she could.

"Busy," Tanya answered. "There is always much to do on Halloween, many places to go and people to see, and I have my children to tend to as well. I had hardly a moment of rest, though I would not complain of it. I had fun. And yourself?"

"I spent the night at the library in town reading scary stories with my friend, Cecil. And playing with kittens! There's three over there now, and they're just the cutest little things." Ann sipped the cider, but it was still too hot. Tanya must have a good thermos. "You have children? How many?"

"Many," Tanya laughed.

Ann had to wonder how old Tanya was, in that case. One or two she could easily imagine, but how many was 'many?' Four, five, more than that? Maybe Tanya was in her later thirties, after all.

"And what of your living situation? Have you found your home?"

Ann faltered over her words. "Not yet, but I think I have a pretty good clue. I found a letter here a few days ago, and Cecil is going to look into it to see what he can discover about who might have written it. He told me a story about that, actually. Kind of."

She was struck with an idea. What if *Tanya* had written the letter? It seemed a little strange that she would show up at the hill right after Ann had unearthed the letter. "Tanya, have you ever heard of a woman named Anais?"

"I have." There wasn't any hesitation in her voice, and she didn't widen or narrow her eyes like Ann had expected she might, if the story meant anything to her.

"My friend said she was a witch who lived here a hundred years ago. Do you believe that?"

Tanya chuckled and blew on her cider to cool it. "My dear, when you have lived the kind of life I lead, you begin to believe a great number of things. I can believe rather easily that there may have been a witch by that name living here at one point or another."

Of course she believes in witches, Ann thought. It had been a foolish question. *She knows about faeries. It only makes sense that she knows about other magical beings, too.*

"Do you think she might have written the letter?"

"What do *you* think?" Tanya returned.

Ann tried a sip of her own cider again. Still too hot. She had gotten used to Nicolas's touch perfectly chilling the tea in the palace.

"I think it's possible, if she was really a witch, but if she wasn't, then it must be someone else using her name because they don't want their identity to be known. And that's a whole other can of worms. But whoever wrote the letter wants me to meet her, and I don't know what to say when I finally do."

"Why not tell her what you have done since you arrived in the forest?" Tanya suggested.

"And what if what I've done doesn't match up with what she's expecting?"

"Dear," Tanya said in a stern voice, "you cannot live your life asking 'what if' at every turn."

"But—"

"*If*," Tanya cut in, and Ann fell silent. "If it should turn out that this person does not wish to provide a home for you, I would gladly offer you mine."

"You would?" Ann gasped. It seemed too good to be true! "I couldn't possibly…that would be asking far too much!"

"I have the resources and experience necessary to care for you, and I would like to," Tanya answered. Her tone was so reassuring and resolute that it was difficult for Ann to disagree. "You will find that I am an excellent judge of character."

"Don't get me wrong, I'm grateful for the offer," Ann said, her words falling out in rapid succession, "but I'm still getting to know you. If this 'Anais' person isn't really my family, or doesn't want to bring me home, I think I would like to stay where I am now. I'm happy there. Not that I wouldn't be happy with you, I'm sure that I would, but—"

Tanya chuckled again. "I understand, my dear, but this does not change my decision. I am sure we will come to know each other well in the near future. You have a home with my family and me, should you ever need or want it. I will consider you one of my children, no matter where you may choose to live."

For a moment Ann wondered if that was how Tanya had gotten to have 'many' children at her seemingly young age. Did she make a habit of taking in wandering, lost souls? How often did that happen? Still, Ann's chest swelled with pride, like being one of Tanya's children was something to aspire to.

"I am glad to hear you are happy where you live

now," Tanya continued. "Tell me, are you treated well there?"

Ann nodded with enthusiasm. "Very well. I have a warm, comfortable bed to sleep in, and delicious food every day. And we talk a lot. We didn't at first, but now we have conversations over tea all the time, about all sorts of things, like the weather and books and art. Well, not all at once. We usually just talk about one thing for a long time. But it's nice!"

Typically, that one thing was one of Nicolas's interests, but Ann didn't mind. She found his passion enthralling, and they both liked discussing books and art. She was just as happy to listen to a forty minute dissertation on why snow was superior to hail, and how Nicolas only summoned hail when he was in a particularly downtrodden mood, as she was to tell Nicolas all about the latest book she'd read.

"What of the faerie?" Tanya asked, sitting back and smoothing her skirt. "What do you think of him?"

Ann had to consider that question. Putting Nicolas into words wasn't the easiest task.

"A little odd," she said. "Even though he acts grumpy, he's actually caring. But he's distant at times. At first I thought that maybe all faeries were like that, and I didn't mind. I still don't, now that I know otherwise. He is the way he is, and I like him, and that's all there is to it for me. But beyond that, he's smart, and interesting to talk to, and kind." Not that he would ever describe himself that way. "Kinder than he realizes."

Though not always, Ann thought. What had happened with Julius couldn't be ignored, but she wanted to believe he could be better than that. She believed he was *trying* to be better than that.

Tanya hummed in approval. "He sounds like a... suitable caretaker."

"Caretaker?" Ann paused for a moment. "I wouldn't use that word. He does take care of me, but I take care of him, too. We're friends."

"Even better." The woman's smile widened. "I am truly happy for you, my dear. Here, try one of the cookies next, I am rather proud of how they came out."

They continued to eat and talk. Hours seemed to pass by in mere moments, until the sun was nearly setting in the sky.

The more they spoke, the more Ann was certain Tanya had not written the letter. Tanya wasn't the type of person to beat around the bush like that; if she had recognized Ann when they met, or at any other time, she would have told her directly and brought Ann home.

Ann also became more certain that the person who had written the letter couldn't compare to Tanya's gentle voice or quiet understanding. She found herself thinking more about the red-cloaked woman's offer. Any place where Tanya was sounded like an ideal home. If Ann went with her, she would have siblings, too. An entire family. Tanya only made passing remarks regarding her husband, and though they were mostly teasing, Ann could tell she loved him dearly.

Hadn't Nicolas said that she was only to stay in his castle until she found somewhere else to live? If not, he had certainly implied it. But that had been a month ago, and now they were more than acquaintances. They were friends. *Best* friends. Ann liked to think he would miss her if she left. She knew she would miss him.

As the sun rose higher and all too quickly began to set, Ann found herself feeling disappointed as she waved goodbye to Tanya. She was sure she would see the other woman again, but parting still filled her with longing. Why couldn't Tanya have been her mother?

She is, if you want her to bet, Ann reminded herself.

Perhaps she would accept the offer. It would be something to discuss with Nicolas, along with Anais's letter, when she got it back from Cecil. There was still plenty of time until the next full moon.

Ann followed the familiar path back to Nicolas's castle. Her head was so stuffed full of thoughts that she didn't know how she would ever sort them out. Yet, if she had Nicolas, she knew she could manage. As long as she could call him her friend, she would have a home.

9

THE FALLING STARS

THE PASSING DAYS DID NOT make the right choice any clearer to Ann. The more time she spent thinking about where to go and what to do, the more confused she became. She knew, deep in her heart, that she was not who she should be. Anais's letter offered an explanation for who she was; Tanya's invitation offered a chance to become part of a family, whatever that might mean or look like. Somehow, Ann felt she could not choose both simultaneously.

And then there was Nicolas, and the ice palace. She enjoyed her life as it was, loved spending time with her friend and learning about the world of faeries through his admittedly cynical explanations. Yet, if she stayed, she too would become frozen in time, unchanging. Was that what she wanted? She couldn't say for sure.

Ann was thankful for the rush of Yule preparations. The options weighed heavily on her in the late evening hours that she spent alone in her room, chasing her into restless sleep. Her days, on the other hand, were filled with activity that kept those thoughts far away from her mind.

Nicolas had been brief in his explanation as he

hurried to solidify plans, but she knew it was a massively important party for the King and Queen and all of winter. He had asked for her help with gathering things from the forest, and she was happy to do what she could to pay back all he'd done for her.

She crossed her legs around the branch on which she sat, staying close to the trunk, and began to saw away at the limb with a knife made of frost magic. Meters below her was a pile of fresh-cut spruce boughs, enough for ten wreaths. Added with the others she'd gathered earlier, she would be close to the amount of supplies needed for the fifty wreaths Nicolas had requested.

For the past two weeks, Ann, Nicolas, and Jack had been consumed by a seemingly endless list of tasks. Jack was more or less in charge of food preparations, though Nicolas rarely let him enter the kitchen unsupervised. As such, Nicolas's daily activities had followed a straight, narrow line between the kitchen and his study as he hastily assembled everything he needed to make Yule a success.

Ann's duties kept her out of the castle, which suited her just fine. Her coat kept her warm, and she enjoyed being in the forest and watching it change day by day. More than half the leaves had fallen, and from her perch in the spruce, she could see the skyward-pointing branches of the deciduous trees to the south. Sometimes she could spot a wisp of chimney smoke from Julius's cottage when it was chilly enough.

There was always frost on the ground nowadays, and occasionally Ann glimpsed something white or silvery flit away out of the corner of her eye. She was sure these flashes were Nicolas's messengers, or else a minor frost faerie coating a few leaves in ice. Just a week before, it had started snowing when she had been working outside, and her only disappointment was that Nicolas hadn't been there to see her react with joy. Even if he never looked like he was impressed by anything, she was sure it would have done him some good to watch her catch a few falling flakes.

The branch cracked and fell to the ground, bouncing against the pile.

Ann swung her legs around and dropped to the next branch down. One more hop brought her to the ground. She enjoyed the rush of wind past her ears and the rising sensation of near-weightlessness in her belly as she descended. She'd have to continue her work to get enough clippings for the last few wreaths later. Her arms were getting sore, and she wanted to see how the other preparations were coming along.

She opened her bag and shoved the cut branches inside, all of them miraculously fitting inside. Anais's letter had claimed it was enchanted, and all of Ann's experiences told her that was true—which again cast confusion over whether or not this Anais was the same as the one in Cecil's story. Could there be more than one witch named Anais in the area? How many witches were there in the world?

Thinking about Cecil made her remember the piece of paper that was tucked away in her back pocket, where it had been for nearly a week. She could still clearly recall every word of that exchange…

There were people out in the town that day. Ann assumed they were enjoying the break in the rain while it lasted. She kept her head down as they watched her pass on her way to the library, their eyes narrowed in suspicion. She heard one of them mutter something that sounded a lot like, "Witch," and walked faster, skirting what remained of the town square.

She knew the current square was not the same as the one that would have existed in Anais's time, but it made her uncomfortable to walk through open space in the town. Too easy for people to circle and trap her.

A chorus of mews greeted her as she stepped into the library. The kittens were growing fast, and refused to stay contained in the office behind the desk anymore. Though Cecil complained of them getting into everything and knocking books from shelves, he looked like he was in high spirits when he came to the front of the library, his button-up shirt noticeably covered in cat hair.

"Ann! How nice to see you," he said, giving her the gap-toothed smile that she'd grown so fond of.

"Hi, Cecil." Ann smiled back, catching George as the kitten leapt into her arms, and wincing as the other two began trying to climb her pant leg with their sharp little claws.

"Stop that, you two… Anyway, I'll bet you're here to return White Fang. *How did you like it?"*

"It was interesting," she answered, setting George down and leaning over to pet all three kittens and stop them from scratching up her legs. She had thought she wouldn't like the book much because it was about a dog, but it was more about the wild, and she liked that just fine. "I'm also here about the letter, if you've found anything?"

His grin dropped. "I'm sorry, Ann. I've looked through our guest books all the way through the past decade, and I still haven't found handwriting that matches your letter. Whoever wrote it avoided coming to town, or perhaps changed their handwriting if they did write in the guest book. This person doesn't want anyone but you finding them." He shifted his weight from one foot to the other. "I don't know if I trust it. If you do meet this person, please be careful and take your friend from the forest with you. Please?"

"I'll be careful," Ann promised. Cecil opened a record book from behind the desk and traded her the letter for the worn copy of White Fang. *She tried to perk up, and gave him another smile. "I'm also here for some Christmas ribbon!"*

"Christmas? But we're only halfway through November!" Cecil gaped.

Ann removed the list of decorations from her pocket. "I need to get started now if I'm going to get all of this stuff! It's for —" She stopped herself. How could she ask Cecil for help with supplies for a party, then tell him he wasn't invited? It wouldn't be fair at all, but she didn't want to lie to him, either.

Cecil offered to take the list, waving his hand to dismiss her worries. "This isn't your handwriting, so I'm guessing this is from your forest friend."

Ann fidgeted with the hems of her sleeves. "It is. It's, uh…" She sighed. "It's for a party."

He gave her hair a good-natured ruffle. "You don't need to look so worried. I know better than to show up unannounced to a faerie party."

"You know about them?" Ann gasped. While she had never deliberately covered up the fact that her 'forest friend' was not human, she had never gone as far as telling Cecil what he really was. She had been certain he'd think she was crazy…or a witch.

"You don't grow up here not knowing about the fae. Besides, Graham and I have plans of our own, and I almost never go out anymore."

"Why not?" Ann asked.

"Too much gloom and doom," Cecil said, nodding toward the front door of the library. "Everyone out there is always so dreary, milling about in the streets with nowhere to go. It's a much happier existence in here, with my boyfriend and my books."

Still, she averted her gaze from his face. She would find a way to make the inadvertent exclusion up to him later.

"There is a lot on this list," Cecil went on, adjusting his glasses as he scanned the paper. "How many meters of ribbon?!"

"Yeah — he's the type to go over the top for this sort of thing, and he's receiving some very important guests this year, so he wants to make sure everything looks just right," Ann explained. "I'll have to hold off on checking out any new books. I don't think I'm going to have time to read for a while!"

Cecil shook his head with a chortle. "How will you go on?"

"It's a tragic sacrifice, but it must be made," Ann said, looking at the letter.

Of course, Nicolas had been too busy for Ann to ask him to sit down and look over the letter with her. It had stayed in her pocket from the moment Cecil had returned it to her that day.

Nor had she been proactive in her attempts to get his attention.

If she didn't have time to read books from the library, then neither she nor Nicolas had time to delve into the kind of detail the letter required. And they were only going to get busier and busier as Yule approached. Sacrifices had to be made somewhere, and if they had to wait to talk about the letter, Ann was willing to wait, if only to live a little longer in the moment.

This was who she was, right now. Nicolas's friend, Cecil's friend, Jack's friend, Tanya's potential daughter, and Julius's…acquaintance, or something like that. She had avoided going to see him again under the assumption that he was also overworked with his season, and she didn't want him to think Nicolas had sent her to resolve their dispute. They needed to work that out, and she had no place in it. She never would have involved herself if she had known the details.

Ann's steps grew heavy as she continued her walk back to the castle. She wanted to think the magic of the satchel was wearing thin, and it was the weight of the branches that was dragging her down, but she knew that wasn't true. Thoughts about the letter were always heavy.

What would Nicolas say once he read it? He was difficult to understand sometimes, and reacted to certain things in odd ways.

He would be happy for her, she told herself. She finally had a clue to her identity. Tea would go long as they discussed who Anais might be, mother or sister or aunt or grandmother. Ann doubted he would have heard the local town legend, so he wouldn't display the misgivings toward the letter's author as Cecil, and even Ann herself.

Now if she could just catch him in the right mood.

Nicolas leaned back in his seat and looked over the papers stacked atop his desk. Four pages of menu items, two pages of decorations, six pages each for his and Ann's attire, three pages for the invitations and their presentation, six pages front and back devoted to the guest list, dozens of pages of instructions, and hundreds of invitations to be written up and mailed out.

Ordinarily he would have a small army of helpers. His messenger sprites would still deliver the invitations, at least, but he himself would have to do most of the cooking, decorating, sewing, cleaning, and writing. He couldn't risk any of the other frost fae discovering Ann without her disguise, and the non-sentient helpers he could summon with magic were barely useful for such delicate tasks. They could hold fabric in place or flip a page in a cookbook, but they were overall not of great assistance. The messengers Nicolas conjured were far more capable, but they were also *only* messengers. Asking them to do more would be suspicious, and probably unsuccessful.

At least Jack and Ann had been helpful. Ann had collected nearly everything he needed for the decorations, and Jack brought fresh fruit and vegetables daily to store in the kitchen freezer. The freezer was as far into the kitchen as Nicolas was willing to let him go, lest his enthusiasm cause the oven to overheat and burn whatever Nicolas was cooking.

He picked up the menu papers again. Hundreds of visitors required refreshments into the thousands. Anything that was to be served cold could be made ahead of time. With a Christmas theme, that meant lots of cookies and candies, which Nicolas didn't mind in the slightest. But how was he to prepare all the hams, turkeys, beef roasts, and lamb chops the day of the party?

Perhaps if he could get Ann into her dress early, he could summon help from the lesser fae who would have nothing else to do that day, in exchange for allowing their attendance at a party where the King and Queen were present.

A knock at the door brought him out of his thoughts. With a sigh, he willed it to open. "Ann, I have told you that I am too busy to talk. You can leave the supplies at the door."

"I know," Ann said, stepping inside sheepishly. He could tell by the way she kept her arms close to her body that she wasn't comfortable being in his study. He didn't want her to get too cozy in his place of work, of course, but it bothered him that she would show such hesitation when he allowed her in. "I've barely seen you for days."

"And you may never see me again if I cannot finish my work," Nicolas retorted, instantly regretting it when he saw how Ann flinched. "I am under a lot of stress at the moment. I apologize that I have not been present for tea. You have found the food I left out for you, I take it?"

Ann gave him *the look*. "You're hopeless. I came here because I miss *you*, not because I'm hungry."

"You miss me?" Would she become ill from that?

"Yes, I miss you. It's this new thing where if someone cares about another person, they'll be sad if they don't see them for a long time. What are you up to in here, anyway? You're keeping all your own preparations such a secret," Ann responded.

She sounded somewhat disappointed. Nicolas had

183

read that while humans sometimes liked to keep secrets, they rarely enjoyed having secrets kept from them, especially between friends. It was one of the many paradoxes that defined human nature. "I would have told you eventually, I was just waiting for the right time," he answered, pulling the sketch of her dress out of the pile and handing it to her. "This is what I have been working on lately."

Ann looked over the design, silent for a moment until she squealed, "Oh my goodness, it's beautiful! Are—are those *wings*?"

"Yes." Nicolas took the paper back and set it aside, grabbing the measuring tape from his box of sewing supplies. "This is a faerie-only celebration. As such, you will have to disguise yourself as a faerie. I can make you a fake pair of wings to wear with your dress. The capelet will cover where they connect to your back. So long as you keep it on, no one should be able to see that they are not attached. Of course, it matches my suit. I assume that you will be attending as my personal guest. You were always welcome, since you live here, and I do not want any harm to come to you. However, this is an important night for me, and it would please me to invite you as my formal, *platonic* date."

He made certain to emphasize 'platonic' so she would not get the wrong idea about his intentions. If *Caring for Your Human* had taught him one thing, it was that misunderstandings due to unclear communication was the leading cause of emotion-based trauma for humans.

"Your date? But I'm not, I mean…" Ann's voice trailed off into mumbles too low for Nicolas's pointed ears. Even if he intended them to go as friends, she'd still been caught off guard.

"Not what?"

"Beautiful. I mean, I'm not *ugly*, but there's a difference between faeries and humans, isn't there? You're so beautiful and graceful, and I'm not."

Truth be told, Ann sometimes had trouble taking her eyes off him. Her storybooks told her that was a common mortal reaction to magical beings, but she tried to avoid staring because she knew it might bother him. Jack, on the other hand, seemed to relish the attention he got from her, and showed off his wings a bit more than necessary when they were alone.

"I thought we agreed that you would not say such things in my presence," Nicolas said sharply. While it was true that she was not as fair as one of the aptly named fair folk, she was moderately attractive by human standards, and Nicolas had seldom seen squirrels climb trees with her ease and confidence.

Ann shrugged in reply.

Nicolas frowned. "We can say that you are learning to disguise yourself as a human and do not want to break the illusion. Unusual, but not unheard of for young adults."

"Faeries can disguise themselves as humans?"

Nicolas nodded. The light around him shifted briefly and his wings disappeared. In the blink of an eye he was transformed, still handsome, but no longer was he otherworldly in his perfection. It may have been the result of the way he carried himself, but he even looked shorter. His hair darkened to a slightly more golden blonde, and his skin bore a few blemishes. Only the slight point to his ears remained to hint that he was something other than an ordinary mortal man.

"Impressive," Ann said.

"There are many things faeries can do that I have not told you, and you will not find them in your story-books. This is a fairly simple trick," Nicolas explained, shedding the glamor and returning to his normal appearance. "But it provides us with a way to explain this unattractiveness you think you possess. Now stand up straight and hold still while I measure you."

Ann stood as tall as she could while he circled her, still pondering the wings he had drawn. When he was done measuring, she commented, "The wings on the design look different from yours."

"Of course. All faeries have different patterns—"

"No, the shape," Ann said, pointing to the sketch. "Your wings have three points each, so they make a snowflake when they're spread out. I know the patterns are unique, but I thought all frost fae would have snow-flake-shaped wings. These are different."

"Ah, well, that," Nicolas stammered, a faint shade of red rising in his cheeks. "You are not wrong. Frost fae do have six-pointed wings. However, I did not design your wings to be those of a frost faerie."

"Oh?"

"Designing wings for you was a…unique challenge. They have to match your soul. Do you understand how hard it is to make a drawing of someone's soul?"

Ann was going to tell him she liked the wings he'd drawn, but he kept going before she could.

"I tried to draw your wings as those of a frost faerie, but nothing looked right. If you were a faerie, you would

186

not be a frost faerie. You are too warm."

"Too bad," Ann laughed.

"A true shame," Nicolas agreed. "This design was based on the wing shape of the royal family. All who see them will know immediately what kind of person you are, and I had to be exact." He pointed to a swirl. "This represents how playful you are," he moved his finger to the almost feathery touches near the edges. "And how kind."

He went on, speaking rapidly about the meanings of the different symbols together and coupled with the royal wing shape, almost frantic. "Speaking generally, the greater the number and size of the markings in a faerie's wings, the stronger their magic. Thicker marks denote *more* of that feature. You can see just the smallest touches near the edges — these round shapes — that mark your interest in intellectual pursuits, meaning reading. It is not what I think of most when I think of you, so it is fainter, but still there."

Ann touched his hand to bring him back to the conversation with her. "Nicolas, I think they're perfect. But won't the shape draw attention, if that's how the King and Queen's wings are?"

"I considered that, but I could not get them right any other way," Nicolas said. Ann noticed many smudge marks, indicating how many times the wings had been erased and redrawn. "If you were a faerie, you could be nothing less than a princess." He cleared his throat. "Now, I have a lot of work to do. If I push myself, I can finish this dress within a week. Stand still so I can finish the measurements, please."

"But what do your wing patterns mean?" Ann

asked. "I'm curious now!"

Nicolas paused. He was glad Ann couldn't see his face, since she took standing still to also mean facing forward. He answered carefully. "They mark me for my power. Mine is the strongest magic to be born into a frost faerie for nearly one thousand years."

"Isn't that a good thing?" Ann asked.

"I suppose," he answered brusquely. Bitterness entered his thoughts. If the broad spear point markings on his wings were anything to go by, his icy magic was the only part of him that was worth anything. No one particularly enjoyed it, but he had nothing else to offer. "I have taken the measurements I need."

Ann watched him as he jotted down the numbers next to the drawing of her dress. "When was the last time you took a break?" she asked.

"I slept for five hours last night. That is enough of a break."

"No, it's not," Ann said, rolling her eyes again. "You look unhappy. You can't expect yourself to put together a party worthy of the King and Queen if you aren't able to put your all into it. I'm sure Jack and I can figure out how to assemble the wreaths based on your instructions and examples. So while you *aren't* doing that, would you please relax for an hour or two?"

"Relax? I—" Nicolas paused when he caught Ann's gaze. Perhaps he ought to add a mark for power on her wings. Maybe the fact that they were shaped like royal wings was proof enough that she could be intimidating sometimes. "I will."

"Thank you," Ann said. To show her appreciation, she left the study so he could start straightaway.

Nicolas looked around the room. How to relax? He checked his pocket watch. He didn't feel sleepy, and he was never one for naps in the middle of the afternoon. That was a light faerie custom they called 'sunbathing.' There was no room for napping in his schedule.

The study was a neat mess. Everything he usually spent his time on had been rearranged to make room for the Yule plans. Sewing eased his nerves, but he was certain if Ann returned to find him working on her dress, she wouldn't qualify that as 'relaxing.'

One of the nearly finished paintings in the corner of the room caught his eye. He hadn't painted in a while, and the soothing motion of the brush strokes was sure to count as 'relaxing.' He unfolded his easel and set up the canvas, examining the piece to see where he could improve it.

The scene was a winter dawn. Fresh, powder-white snow glistened in the blue light spilling across the horizon. The sky was mostly a blend of dark blue and black, making it difficult to tell if the scene was dawn or dusk, especially given how easy it would be to mistake the falling snow for stars. Nicolas grabbed his palette and reached for his tubes of paint, pausing when he saw the bright colors that Ann had given him.

He hesitated only a moment before grabbing the red and white and mixing them together into the same pink as her coat. He dabbed a spot onto the canvas, positioning it carefully between the trees. He added a little pink to the dawn light, then a little more red into the blues, making a rosier sunrise over the snow. The black sky lightened to a dark blue, and blended into hues of violet near the middle.

Most of the snowflakes had been painted over, melted away by the sunlight, but two remained near the top. Nicolas exchanged his brush for one with a finer tip and added little white streaks to these snowflakes, turning them from falling snow into falling stars — ordinary into extraordinary, a chance encounter, a moment that could be missed with the blink of an eye captured on canvas. A split-second decision to look at something a little longer and change things forever.

Once he was satisfied, he left it to dry. He had to admit, he felt much better now, the world righting itself through his brush. But what to do with it? It was too far from his usual style to keep in the study.

Christmas usually included the giving of gifts; perhaps this painting would make a good present for Ann. *Caring for Your Human* did say that humans enjoyed sentimental gifts over practical ones.

And Ann herself was, if anything, far more senti-mental than practical.

If Nicolas had been in the habit of keeping mirrors in his study, he would have noticed the wide smile that lifted the light of those stars into his eyes.

Downstairs, Ann listened with rapt attention while Jack spoke of the various holidays he had celebrated over the years.

"Of course, we celebrate Yule differently in the Oceanic Realm," Jack said as he laced a garland of rib-bon through the trimmed branches. "For starters, we have it earlier in the year, because our winter starts in June. We usually do stuff like this—the tree, the pres-ents, and all—in the summertime. Everything's flip-flopped up here! And the Winter Ruler down there is a real charmer, always good at hosting a party, so you can imagine my surprise when I got here and heard that Yule is barely celebrated in the Northern Realm. I thought it'd be even more over the top, since this is where frost fae are usually at their strongest."

Ann secured a bow to the wreath. "Really? You mean this isn't normal? I know he's doing a little extra for the King and Queen, but I assumed Yule was always something like this."

"Actually, *this* is normal," Jack said, "Parties and celebrations and dances, *that's* normal. But Nicolas…"

"Isn't," Ann finished.

"Don't let him hear you say it, though," Jack

191

laughed. "I've never met a more ornery faerie, especially for a frost faerie. They're usually a fun bunch. Get on great with light fae. My best friend back home was the Winter Ruler. I wasn't anywhere near as important back home as I am here, so that tells you how much he liked socializing! He actually helped me get this position, but, well…" He sighed. "Nothing against the Northern Realm or anything, but most light fae don't want to work here unless it's in the southern regions. It's cloudy all the time this far north. *Total* mood killer!"

"Then the frost fae don't mind it being drier in the south?"

"As long as it gets cold, that's all they need. I'm sure they like snow, too, but they don't *need* it the way light fae *need* sunshine. It's what we draw our strength from. It's nice and warm and bright and *not* dark and *not* cloudy and *not* rainy. I don't understand how these northern faeries can deal with flying when the air is so icy," Jack groaned.

"It's hard to be away from home, isn't it?" Ann asked.

Jack offered a gentler smile. "Yeah, it is. But we do alright, don't we? Me with the clouds and not having my friends around, you with not having your family. But I have to admit, it is nice to see how light fae here are born, when the sunlight breaks through the clouds and you can see the rays coming down…beautiful."

A wave of golden yellow light washed over his wings. Ann braced herself for the warmth that always followed and made her nose and ears feel toasty. It was fascinating how different frost and light fae were from each other. It had been a long time since Nicolas's natural cold had made her uncomfortable, and she barely noticed it anymore, but she couldn't deny being drawn to the sunny warmth Jack exuded every time he felt the smallest amount of joy.

As if catching her train of thought, Jack said, "Personally, I always enjoy spending my time with humans, but that's just the difference between me and jolly old Nicolas. I love humans, he doesn't. Or rather, he thinks they don't like him." He looked at Ann. "Then again, he seems to think no one likes him. Except for you."

Ann focused on tying her next bow.

"I've been trying to figure that out. How is it that decades of me and Drew reaching out to him doesn't do a thing, but you turn up out of the blue and he starts turning into a better person?" He leaned in, looking at her more closely. "What did you do?"

"I haven't done anything," Ann protested. "How could I make him change into someone else, when I don't even know who I am?"

"Whoa there—I didn't mean anything negative. The opposite, actually." Jack set down his wreath and placed a hand on her shoulder. The smell of pine and sap calmed her a little, or perhaps he was using some form of magic. "Whatever you have or haven't done, I'm grateful for it. You didn't know Nicolas before, and I barely did myself so maybe I can't talk, but from what I've heard he was…well, with his strength, it could have been bad if he didn't change his tune."

Ann could believe that. Sometimes when he talked about snow and ice over their teas, she got the idea that he still was a potential terror. It was a little frightening to think what he could do with all that power. And yet, despite that, she had faith that he wouldn't abuse it. He was better than that. He could make better choices.

"He told me about Julius," Ann added quietly, as if to prove it.

Jack's eyes widened. "What did he say?"

"That's…not really for me to share." She remembered how distraught he'd been that night, how he'd practically begged her not to hate him for what he'd done. She couldn't reveal that vulnerable of a moment with someone else, not without his permission. Ann looked back up to Jack. "Still, Yule means so much to him, and I'm nervous that I'm going to embarrass him and he'll never speak to me again. I can't wait a hundred years for him to change his mind and realize he handled it the wrong way!"

For a moment Jack looked like she had slapped him.

"Well, you aren't wrong…"

After an awkward moment, she realized her mistake. Jack had probably known many humans over the course of his long life. He must have had friends hundreds of years ago that weren't alive anymore.

Before she could apologize, he patted her head. When his hand moved and she saw his face again, his usual amicable smile had returned.

"If he does that, it won't be your fault, and I'll give him a fresh one right in the face." Jack pumped a fist into the air and patted his bicep. "But like I said, if not you, then *something* is changing him. I don't think you have to worry."

"What do you think it is, other than me?" Ann asked.

"Hmm…" Jack's wings lit up when he answered with a laugh, "Me!"

The two shared a chuckle, then returned to their wreath making. They were silent for a time, until Jack spoke up again. "Ann?"

"Hm?" Ann didn't look over, trying hard to match the bow to the model Nicolas had drawn out for them to follow.

"What you said earlier, about not knowing who you are? I don't think that's true." She turned to give him a bewildered stare, only to find his eyes already on hers. She had never noticed them before—orange and yellow, flickering and glimmering like tiny stars. "You don't know who you *were,* but you definitely know who you *are.*"

Ann opened and closed her mouth a few times, trying to form a response. In the end all she could do was turn back to her wreath-making.

That night, Ann dreamed again. It took her a moment to realize it, because she wasn't tied to a burning stake, but was instead in her room at the ice palace. It wasn't until she went down to the throne room and saw two Nicolases that she knew she wasn't in reality.

One Nicolas sat tall and regal in his throne, chin lifted and eyes glowering across the room. His wings were spread, and Ann noticed a telltale shimmer around their patterns. The other Nicolas was on his hands and knees on the floor, sorting through pieces of ice.

The Nicolas on the throne made Ann nervous, so she approached the one on the floor. "Your Majesty, what are you doing?"

"Should one not face the person to whom one is speaking?" the Nicolas on the throne said. His voice was as cold and sharp as the winter wind.

"Uh…yes, Your Majesty," Ann said, looking to the one on the throne. "But I wanted to speak to the *other* you."

"Then address him," the Nicolas on the throne said.

Ann turned to the faerie on the floor, confused for a moment before realizing what he meant. "Nicolas?"

"Not now, Ann," he said. "I am too busy to talk."

She took a few steps closer and saw that the ice pieces were cut into specific shapes to form a puzzle. Nicolas had managed to fit a few together, but Ann had no idea what the puzzle was supposed to look like. There seemed to be far too many pieces.

"But Nicolas, it's *ice*. You can use your magic to arrange the pieces how they're supposed to be," Ann said, scooting a piece closer to his hand with the toe of her boot.

The Nicolas on the floor didn't respond, and the Nicolas on the throne remained as cold and distant as ever.

"You have to help him," Jack said, now standing beside Ann.

"How?" she asked.

Jack shook his head. "You have to help him. You're the only one who can."

"But *how?*" she repeated, and Jack continued to shake his head, his wings glowing brighter and brighter until she felt their warmth on her face. They flickered and crackled until they were a fire, and in a flash, she was back on the stake.

The crowd was shouting at her again, calling her a witch, demanding she bring back their lost children or die to ease the town's suffering. There were more familiar faces this time. Jack stood beside her. His wings added to the heat of the flames while he spoke casually about his old home and friends. Julius was roasting a marshmallow on the fire. Tanya lingered near the edge of the gathering, her scarlet cloak half-concealing her face, which wore an unreadable expression. In the distance were the two Nicolases, one still on the throne, the other still trying to solve the puzzle.

"Cut me down!" Ann shouted to Jack, then Tanya, then the crowd. "Cut me down, I have to help him so he can…" So he could what? Stop being who he was?

I don't want to change him. I want to understand *him,*

Ann thought.

A new voice rose above the din, and though Ann couldn't see the speaker, she instinctively knew the voice belonged to Anais. It was so eerily similar to her own—angrier, yet somehow calmer.

"He betrayed you. *He betrayed you.*"

10

THE YULE FESTIVAL

THE NEXT FEW WEEKS were a whirl of ribbons, ornaments, present boxes, invitations, and—in the few rare moments that the three had any kind of a break—tea and cookies. Jack didn't care much for the tea, but he wolfed down as many of the treats as Ann did.

The throne room was transformed. The icy walls were now decorated with wreaths connected by silver and gold ribbon. Tall, color-coordinated piles of present boxes lined the space beneath the wreaths. Some of the boxes contained small gifts of candy or simple jewelry, while others, on Jack's suggestion, were weighed down with pieces of coal. Streamers wove through the air, using the chandelier as a centerpoint. Nicolas's throne had been moved and replaced with two gilded seats, complete with a holiday red carpet leading from them to the front door. One of the thrones' frames had been made to look like blooming flowers, while the other resembled carved antlers.

Jack and Ann carried food from the kitchen to the banquet table, which was already set with a lovely red and green table runner and a gorgeous silver snowflake centerpiece that would reflect the festivities to come.

Ann was doing her best to stave off her appetite for the party, but being tasked with handling the food made it impossibly difficult. Neither she nor Jack had been able to resist sneaking snacks from various trays.

"Did you manage to get a date?" Ann asked, placing a tray of fruit between the cheeses and meats, next to a bowl of yogurt dip.

"No," Jack answered with a shrug and a shake of his head. "I prefer to go solo at these things. Dates are kind of in-name-only, anyway, so why bother? I'm not here to climb the social ladder. There's nowhere higher for me to go!"

That made sense. After all, Nicolas had asked her purely as a formality, but it still made her happy that he wanted to share such an important night with her. "*I'll save a dance for you, then,*" Ann offered.

"Aww, thanks!" Jack ruffled her hair.

Nicolas emerged from his study in a rush. He descended the stairs with a long scroll that trailed behind him, despite his attempt to bundle it up. "These are the names of everyone who responded to the invitations. The King and Queen are at the top of the list, of course. Are there enough treats? Present boxes?"

Jack put up his hands before Nicolas could get carried away. "Don't you start worrying. All the food and decorations are set, and we still have hours before the guests start showing up."

"Yes, but we need to get Ann into her dress before they arrive, which may take some time. And you need to change into your Yule attire, which I see you did not bring with you."

"How much time could it take?" Ann asked. "It's a

dress, not a suit of armor."

"It is not *just* a dress. It is a dress, makeup, hair, wings, and all of it has to be—"

"Perfect, I know. And we've had so many fittings and dress rehearsals that you could probably do all of that in your sleep," Ann said, keeping her tone gentle. "Everything is going to be fine, and everyone is going to have a lot of fun. You've done a great job putting this together. We all have."

"I know." Nicolas checked his pocket watch, then took a deep breath. "I am perfectly calm and at ease. I will be fine."

Jack patted his arm. "We'll get back to the food. Does it look okay so far?"

Nicolas inspected the spread, adjusting the placement of a star-shaped sugar cookie that had been too close to another one. "Yes. You are both doing wonderfully. Thank you."

It took several more trips to bring out all the delicacies that Nicolas and Jack had prepared for the pre-dinner refreshments. Ann and Jack had to work together to bring out the massive ice-sculpted punch bowl.

Once the party began, Nicolas's summoned attendants would handle the food so Ann and Jack could enjoy the celebration as guests, and Ann couldn't have been more relieved. Trekking endlessly between the kitchen and the table had her feeling like she'd just walked all the way to town. Plus, there would be an even greater selection of foods for dinner and dessert, not to mention all the plates that would have to be refilled throughout the evening.

"That's everything," Jack said once they centered

the punch bowl among the refreshments. "I had better head home and change. See you at the party for that dance!"

"See you later!" Ann replied, watching as Jack stepped into the courtyard and flew away, leaving a circle of melted snow in his wake.

With nothing else to do, Ann went to check on Nicolas. She wasn't sure what he was doing to get ready, aside from pacing in his study a lot. When she interrupted his hurried steps and finger-twining, he nearly knocked a chair over.

"Your Majesty," she said, briefly brushing his fingers with hers. He flinched, but then stilled his hand to let her give it a small, reassuring squeeze. "The first course is out, the decorations are set, and Jack has gone home to get ready for this evening."

Nicolas drew his hand away slowly and took another deep breath. This time it seemed as though the weight of the world lifted off of his shoulders. "We should get you into your dress, then. As my personal date, you will be greeting the guests with me as they arrive."

"'Thank you for joining us this evening. We welcome you to take anything you desire from the table, to dance, and to try your luck at finding one of the hidden gifts in the present boxes. Please enjoy your time here,'" Ann recited, adding a small curtsy at the end. This earned her a smile from Nicolas that he forgot to cover.

"Perfect. But not for the King and Queen—"

"—they'll be announced separately when they arrive, and no one is to speak until they make their official greeting," Ann said. "I remember."

Nicolas's smile widened. "Good. Excellent. Now, the dress."

She'd worn a mock-up dress plenty of times to practice ballroom dancing in a long skirt, and to see how the fake wings would look concealed underneath the shawl. None of that had quite prepared Ann for the real thing.

Nicolas had sewn hundreds of tiny crystals into the skirt, which had at least half a dozen overlapping layers of fabric. She hoped the extra weight wouldn't throw her off, but after walking around the room so Nicolas could see if it needed to be hemmed any more, she felt comfortable in it.

Next, he attached her wings. They hooked into specially designed straps on the back of the dress, which were then covered by the fur shawl. Ann wasn't sure what the wings were made of. They looked as delicate as ice and glass, but weighed almost nothing and didn't feel too cold. Clearly magic had been involved, for they looked almost exactly as they had in Nicolas's pictures.

A pair of fine opera gloves completed the outfit, and for some reason, Ann was particularly taken with them above all else. The feeling of the silk on her fingers was somehow so...*significant*. For a moment she thought she might be recovering a memory, but she shoved it away. She didn't want to think about her mysterious past during the Yule celebration.

The only challenge after that was sitting still while Nicolas did her hair and makeup. He managed to tame her mane into a loose bun, twisting her bangs out of her face and pinning them back, though one rebellious lock insisted on handing down in the middle of her forehead. A strand of pearls was woven into her hair and tied together with a gold flower pin.

The makeup was easier, at least. A light dusting of powder to even her complexion, a hint of blush and pale eyeshadow, and the slightest amount of stain on her lips to make them a brighter pink.

Nicolas paused to examine her completed visage. In a way, applying the makeup had been a lot like painting, and that had been the most enjoyable part of her preparations for him. She didn't look all that different. She had always been reasonably attractive for a human. He hoped she would be able to see that for herself.

"I have to get dressed now," he said, not giving himself too much time to ponder her appearance. "If you would please leave my dressing room…"

"I can't wait to see what you came up with for yourself!" Ann said as she stepped carefully across the floor, the small heels of her glassy shoes clicking against the ice. "I'll make sure everything stays exactly how it was when you last saw it, and keep an eye out for early guests. I know exactly what to say to them."

"Good. Yes, do those things. I will be down shortly," Nicolas assured her.

Ann carefully gathered up her skirts so she didn't accidentally tread on the fabric as she exited Nicolas's quarters. Once she was gone, Nicolas retrieved his suit from where he had stashed it beneath his desk. After all, he couldn't have Ann seeing him in his regalia before the party began, let alone in any state of undress.

He couldn't help but worry. There would be so many faeries at the celebration, and his experiences in crowds had never been positive. Dealing with people had always been like trying to solve a puzzle where all the pieces were identical and impossible to figure out—but with Ann's help, he might be able to fit together enough pieces to understand what the whole was supposed to look like.

The guests arrived in droves as soon as the sun went down. Ann felt more like she was attending a fashion show than a royal ball.

The floral fae were easily distinguishable because their clothes were mainly plants that had grown around their bodies, most of which were blooming vibrant flowers. One autumn faerie proudly wore a collar of branches that sprouted a plump, red apple every few minutes. However, Julius had hardly any plant life on him, preferring brown pinstripe pants, a matching vest, and a humble crown of gilded autumn leaves. The modesty of his clothes stood out among the rest, singling him out in a way he seemed to enjoy as he greeted the faeries of his own season and complimented them on a season well managed.

The light fae were dressed for warm weather, yet they looked completely comfortable in the ice castle. Most of their outfits consisted of jewelry and brightly colored strips of fabric around their hips and chests. Jack was the most adorned out of all of them, with a grassy cape that extended to his lower back and a woven belt that held up rows of beads over the fabric tied around his waist. He was at complete ease in the castle after spending so much time there during the preparations.

The other light fae followed his lead, their wings lending a warm glow to the festivities.

The frost fae all wore simultaneously gorgeous and outlandish clothes. On one end of the dress spectrum, some appeared with high collars and long sleeves that extended nearly to the floor; on the other end, some showed up in hardly anything at all. One was adorned only in thousands of tiny crystals that clung to her skin, while another wore a coat made entirely of live ermines that raced around her frame. The men mostly wore suits, but the designs varied, and some were quite vividly embroidered with silver, white, and blue metallic threads.

Nicolas was conservatively dressed when compared to everyone else: slacks, dress shoes, a shirt, and a fancier vest than usual. He had added a long cape to the ensemble in place of his regular tailcoat, richly embroidered with snowflake patterns, and a crown that featured a snowflake-shaped jewel. The cape had crystals sewn into it to match Ann's dress.

Compared to the women at the party, Ann's dress was almost prudish, though she supposed that was functional; the less she showed of herself, the less the others might catch on that she was human. She didn't love it any less.

The two stood at the open doors, greeting guests and taking their invitations as they arrived. Ann did her best to act like a faerie, but from the looks they gave her, she had to wonder if makeup alone was enough to hide the lack of elegance in her features that came along with her humanity. No disguise could cover that up.

When they had collected the last of the invitations,

Nicolas snapped his fingers. All the folded papers dissolved into a fine powder that merged with the floor.

"Everyone is here, save for the King and Queen," Nicolas said. "You may go and enjoy the celebration now. Thank you for your assistance."

From the way he kept wringing his hands, she could tell he was still nervous. That probably wouldn't stop until the King and Queen arrived, which meant there wasn't anything Ann could do to ease his anxiety. He didn't look like he could be distracted with a dance. "Okay. I'll be right over there if you need me."

Ann headed for the dance floor, and Nicolas went to the food table to check on the arrangement. He could still see Ann from where he stood, and Jack was close enough to keep an eye on her. That was enough for now.

The servant faeries were keeping everything in order. Food barely left the plates before it was replenished. Nicolas made sure his guests were enjoying the refreshments before taking a few things for himself.

He was doing his best, but the size of the crowd was overwhelming. There hadn't been a gathering of faeries this large in the ice palace since Bethilde had reigned. Back then he had stayed at her side the entire time, only breaking away from her to steal admiring looks at Oberon. He had spent so much of that time daydreaming about being closer to the King that he hardly remembered most of it, aside from the fact that everyone seemed to enjoy Bethilde's parties.

He could hear cheerful voices and laughter, including Ann's as she found Jack and his group of friends. Of that small gathering, Julius was the only other person Nicolas recognized. He had a camera strapped around his neck, and he grouped them all together for a photograph.

"I'm really glad you decided to have a full celebration this year."

Nicolas tilted his head to see Drew standing beside him, a small plate of finger sandwiches in one hand and a half-empty glass of rose wine in the other. He looked particularly well rested, despite experiencing a season's worth of magic fatigue. The crown of lively winter flowers blooming around his head gave off a sweet fragrance.

The frost faerie nodded and turned his attention back to the food. A stalk of celery had accidentally been knocked into the carrots. He corrected that.

"Wouldn't you rather be out there with the dancers? There are some experts on the floor right now," Drew said.

"If I preferred that, I would be there already," Nicolas answered curtly.

"I heard that you and Julius—"

"Who *hasn't* heard?"

"Don't be embarrassed. I think it's an excellent thing for both of you. Neither of you have been the same since your falling out, though I suppose with Julius that could simply be due to his age," Drew laughed. "Really, Nicolas. I'm glad you're letting people see you again. You've spent so much time alone here, everyone was worried."

Ordinarily Nicolas would have gone on a tirade about exactly whose fault it was that he chose to stay in his castle rather than interact with the other faeries, but he saw in Drew's expression the same sincerity he saw in Ann's. The elder faerie meant what he said. Drew was happy to see him, and some part of Nicolas was happy to see the floral faerie without being scolded for some misdemeanor, too.

He turned to watch the dancers. Jack and Ann were twirling their way across the dance floor with the bare minimum of coordination, of course. Jack spun her around so her back was to him, then they twisted to face each other again. Others, faeries that Nicolas didn't recognize, were dancing in perfect step with the waltz music.

A frost faerie with a trim beard and mustache cut in then, asking Jack to dance. The joy on Jack's face was almost tangible from across the room. It was certainly visible as his wings flashed so brightly that they spread light all the way up to the chandelier, which reflected it across the dancers. Jack greeted the frost faerie with a hug so warm that Nicolas was concerned the other might melt.

"You invited Tosya?" Drew asked.

"I thought it would be a nice surprise for Jack, as a reward for his efforts in helping to put the party together," Nicolas explained. It wasn't normal for seasonal rulers to invite those outside of their realm to their celebrations, but this was a special occasion. And it was worth it to see Jack so happy that he was practically illuminating the room by himself as he and his partner waltzed together.

That left Ann chattering with a female faerie who had short, tousled red hair. It didn't take long for them to start laughing as if they had known each other for years.

Of course Ann has no trouble making friends, Nicolas thought. *She can make friends with anyone. Even me.*

"You're keeping an eye on that girl," Drew noted, a more amused smile forming on his lips. "Is she your date?"

Nicolas's face felt a little hot. Did he see what she was? "Yes. She is a dear friend."

"Then why don't you go and dance with her?"

"It would look ridiculous. She is half my height and my legs are much longer than hers. The movements would be awkward," Nicolas reasoned. They had practiced dance steps to get around that, but the music wasn't quite right for the slower pace those particular moves required. "Besides, she is having fun with the others, and I would rather watch."

"Nonsense. But if you aren't going to dance with her, then you could at least dance with me," Drew said, finishing the last drop of wine and setting his plate down to be handled by one of the servants. He took Nicolas's hand and pulled him out onto the dance floor.

Nicolas pulled away. "I do not—" He stopped himself. He was already halfway there, Drew being more forceful than he looked. If he turned back now, it would be an even greater embarrassment. An act of cowardice. If Ann were at his side, she'd encourage him to go for it. What was one dance, one moment?

Thankfully, the music changed from a brisk waltz to something more traditional that didn't require close contact. The rest of the crowd was joining in, so there was less of a focus on Nicolas and Drew. It was less dancing *with* each other and more dancing *near* each other, but Drew looked satisfied that he'd managed to drag Nicolas onto the floor for a few minutes.

Nicolas glanced over to check on Ann, and saw that Julius and the redheaded light faerie were trying to teach Ann the steps. He could have cursed himself. He had gotten so caught up in teaching her classical dances that he hadn't bothered to teach her the dances almost all faeries knew from their youth. He could have tried to pass her off as a newly born frost faerie as an excuse, but he had already declared her his date.

At least she looked like she was having fun learning. She was certainly smiling a lot, which he hoped was a good sign.

The music changed after a few minutes, and the dancing fae found their partners. Drew nodded to Nicolas before walking away to talk to a group of frost faeries who were glancing flirtatiously at him.

Ann left her new friends and approached Nicolas. "It's a slow song. Do you want to dance?"

The Winter Ruler looked around the room again at the smiling faces, all of them similar to Ann's, no hostility or judgment. He couldn't match a single one of them to any of the names he had written down, and he realized just how long it had been since he had seen most of his subjects in person. Was Drew right? Were they glad to be in his presence again?

He redirected his focus to Ann. He couldn't let her down, so he held out his hand to her.

Despite all their practice, dancing with her would be a challenge. She couldn't reach his shoulder even on tip-toe, and he couldn't reach her waist without bending down, so instead they put their hands together. Then, just as they'd practiced, Nicolas led her through the steps. She matched each movement with grace, the skirt of her dress twirling and gathering to create a snowy illusion, as he'd hoped it would.

Ann was light, but he never lost the pressure of her hands against his, never over- or underestimated how forceful he should be with the turns or spins. She responded to his every motion as if she knew what he was thinking as he thought it.

At the end of the dance he kissed the back of her hand, as was the custom. Then he returned to the safety of the banquet table while she rejoined the crowd of dancers to find another partner.

He was surprised to find Julius standing near the banquet table, idly munching on a piece of pumpkin pie.

"That was meant to go with the dessert spread. How did you get it?" Nicolas asked.

"I made a request to the kitchen. I didn't think there would actually *be* pumpkin pie, but they brought it out, so I figured I should eat some," Julius answered evenly. "Nice party. Did Jack convince you to do this?"

"It did not take *much* convincing." Nicolas shifted his cape. "Are you enjoying yourself?"

"More than I did on Halloween, if that's what you're asking," Julius responded. He took another bite of pie so he didn't have to say anything else.

"I am pleased that you are having fun. How is the pie? It has been…a while since I last made it," Nicolas said.

"Could use maybe a little more allspice," Julius answered, taking another bite and working it over slowly. "Tastes like you tried to substitute it with cinnamon. But I like cinnamon, so it doesn't bother me."

"I recall. You used to eat cinnamon candies until your eyes watered from the spice."

"You remember that?" Julius asked.

Nicolas nodded. "I never cared much for cinnamon, myself. In pie, however..." He grabbed a plate and served himself a slice of pumpkin pie, taking a bite. Immediately he realized what Julius meant about the cinnamon not quite balancing out the lack of allspice. He hadn't had the time to taste-test everything.

"Your eyes aren't watering," Julius pointed out. When Nicolas gave him a questioning look he added, "You seemed worried about the taste."

"Not that. The King and Queen..."

"Oh, *that*," Julius said. He chanced a look at Ann, who was dancing with the red-haired faerie and a few other girls. "It's not *obvious* that she's not a faerie. I don't think anyone is looking too hard. And I haven't told anyone, not even Drew. Which was really hard, by the way. I've never kept a secret from Drew before." One of the girl faeries whispered something to Ann and she blushed scarlet, then gave a flustered laugh. "You know, you could keep a much better eye on her if you would stop hanging by the food and go talk to her, before someone steals your date?" Julius finished his slice of pie and stacked his plate on top of another, and Nicolas realized that he had already eaten more than one slice. "But first, we have a job to do."

Julius cupped his hands together, and with a small burst of golden light the seasonal leaf appeared. Its edges were still tinged white from Nicolas's outburst at the Autumnal Equinox, and Nicolas's wings fluttered with shame.

Nicolas led Julius across the room to the base of the two thrones. The orchestra faded out, and the gathered faeries' attention turned to Nicolas and Julius. For a moment, Nicolas sensed apprehension from the crowd as those who had been present at the Equinox Festival remembered their previous public interaction.

The ceremony was a simple one, owing to the fact that it was one of the oldest faerie rituals. Simple things tended to survive the changing tides of time more easily than complicated ones.

Julius bowed to Nicolas, offering up the leaf.

"The season of autumn has come to an end; we await the coming of winter and the season of reflection."

Nicolas accepted the leaf, and Julius raised his head. With a wave of his hand, Nicolas removed the touches of frost from the leaf and placed it, still golden, on the ice pedestal between the two thrones.

"One more hour of autumn would not be horrible," Nicolas said.

Julius smiled and spread his wings with elation. A sigh of relief lifted the crowd's spirits, and as the music rose once more they danced more joyously than ever. The feud was over, all threats vanquished, and they could enjoy the festivities without fear of conflict.

Before Nicolas let Julius return to the party, he quietly asked, "What was the proposition that Ann made to you? Surely you can tell me now."

"It isn't so easily put into words. Essentially, this," Julius answered, waving a hand toward the dancers, the food, the whole festival. "She wanted me to help you realize that you can have this, or something like that. How did she phrase it…? You have a choice in whether you're alone or not."

While Nicolas reflected on that, Julius disappeared into the crowd. Ann had nudged a piece of the puzzle into place, after all.

Having lost Jack and Julius as dance partners, Ann joined the group of light and floral faerie women who had become her friends over the past few minutes. She had no idea how much time had passed, and had read that faerie parties often had that effect on humans. It somehow felt like she'd been chatting and dancing with them for both hours and only a few moments.

The redhead, Zoe, was already treating her like a sister and keeping the others ladies at bay when they flirted with Ann. She looped an arm around Ann's shoulders, which the smaller woman subtly adjusted so the faerie couldn't feel her wing attachments under the furs. Warmth radiated from Zoe's wings and skin the same way it did from Jack's.

Ann thought again about Tanya's offer. She had said that she had a lot of children. Would it feel like this if Ann were to meet them?

Zoe waved to a tall faerie. Ann could tell he was a royal because of the shape of his wings, as were the faeries gathered around him. "That's my husband, the Crowned Prince," she said to Ann. "Married into royalty! Not bad, huh? Unfortunately he's a mess at big social gatherings. Right now he's probably just making sure everything is in place for the arrival of the King and

Queen."

"I know the type," Ann laughed. She tried to place his position in the hierarchy that Nicolas had explained to her during their lessons on greeting guests. As Crowned Prince, he would be Oberon and Titania's oldest son and future successor, the most powerful position after theirs. However, his features were round, mostly unintimidating, and somehow familiar.

A strawberry-blonde floral faerie approached Zoe's husband and struck up a conversation.

"And there goes Drew. He might rule spring, but his real talent is being a social butterfly, if you ask me," Zoe said, her tone good-natured.

"*That's* the Spring Ruler?" Ann asked, standing on tiptoe to get a better view. He looked younger than she'd expected, but then again, he did rule over the season of birth and new beginnings. It made sense that he would have a more youthful appearance, and the fawn-like freckles on his face and shoulders only added to that. He looked like a charmer, especially with his gap-toothed smile.

"You live up here and you didn't know that? I thought he'd be high profile enough to get your notice," Zoe commented. "Then again, I've never seen you at any of the family gatherings. How are *you* related to the royal family?"

Ann felt her heart stop. She tried to come up with a plausible answer, but Zoe shook her head and whispered, "Just kidding. I've spent enough time around humans to know one when I see one." She leaned in. "I don't know if anyone else noticed, but I doubt anyone will say anything. No one minds a human or two at a party. Just try to keep your head low when the King and Queen arrive, alright? Deniability, and all that."

"Oh, uh, yes. Thank you," Ann stammered.

Zoe giggled, grabbed Ann's hands, and twirled her back onto the dance floor as Julius approached. Once the two were close to him, Zoe let go of one of Ann's hands and grabbed one of Julius's, connecting all three of them in a circle.

More and more faeries joined in until they formed a circle almost as big as the ballroom floor. Even Nicolas got caught in the whirling dance, his long legs clunking stiffly along with the others as they turned in time to the jubilant music. Then, all at once, the faeries turned so they were facing away from the center of the circle. Ann barely managed to keep up, but she was better prepared when the circle turned inward again.

Suddenly, the music halted. The circle stopped dead in its tracks.

Trumpets sounded at the castle entrance. All the faeries turned to face the doors, bowing immediately, forming a perfect ring of humility.

Nicolas glanced across the room to find Ann again. She had thankfully followed the lead of the others around her, but was closer to the door than he would have liked. He had no time to reach her and offer assistance with receiving the King and Queen. He would have to trust that their rehearsals would be enough.

The faeries lowered their heads almost to the floor as the doors opened to admit Oberon and Titania. Nicolas had to fight to keep his head down.

Ann did not lower her head quite in time.

She saw Oberon first, which was only natural due to

his striking stature. He was as tall as Nicolas, perhaps even taller—it was hard to say when taking his crown into account. His hair was silver, straight, and tied back into a ponytail. His fur cape trailed behind him as he moved to the center of the room, held up by tiny sprites. His wings were massive and fully spread. They looked as if a piece of the night sky had come down to the earth, dark and spotted with silver.

The woman next to him couldn't have been more different. She was much shorter and had far rounder features. Her dress, though beautiful, was by no means the most extravagant in the room with its plain white base and embroidered accents. The red details matched her wings, a little piece of dawn. The only signifier of her position was the sparkling tiara rising out of her blond hair.

Most important, however, were her wise, kind blue eyes and gentle smile. Ann recognized those immediately.

The trumpets ceased their fanfare. Zoe's husband stood behind the King and Queen and said loudly, in a much-practiced tone, "Announcing the arrival of His and Her Royal Majesties, the Rulers of the Faerie Realm, Bringers and Keepers of Magic, King Oberon and Queen Titania."

"Tanya!" Ann called, unable to contain her excitement. She jumped to her feet, and all the faeries stared at her. Oberon frowned, but the queen gave a small wave.

Oberon cleared his throat. Ann kneeled again, keeping her face down to hide how red it was turning.

"Good evening to you, my loyal subjects. We gather again at the changing of the seasons to remember that each and every one of us plays a pivotal part in the balance of both the magical and mortal worlds. Only we faeries truly hold the key to harmony between these two realms, no matter what the witches say—"

"Which is to say, of course, that we are happy to celebrate the passing of another wonderful autumn, and we look forward to a merry winter," Titania cut in. "And happier still to take this opportunity to introduce the latest addition to our family."

Titania paused for a moment, then cleared her throat. One of the faeries near Ann nudged her, and she looked up to see that the Queen's eyes were on her. She had one hand extended, beckoning her forward. Despite how embarrassed and alarmed Ann was, she couldn't help but rise to her feet and walk toward the royal faerie.

"I'm sorry!" Ann blurted as she drew near the King and Queen. "I didn't—"

"My dear," Titania said, cutting her off with a gentle pat and a soft smile. "Stand and be recognized."

Ann was confused for a moment, but as she stood in the center of the room with the royal family, she realized the weight of what Tanya had said when she had sat down with her for a picnic in the woods weeks ago. She had given her the option of living with her, but had plainly stated that she viewed Ann as a daughter.

No matter what Ann chose, she had been adopted by the faerie queen.

She was a member of the royal family.

"It is our great pleasure to introduce our newest daughter, Princess Ann."

11

FLIGHT OF THE PRINCESS

Zoe and a small group of imposing faeries joined Titania, Oberon, the Crowned Prince, and Ann in the center of the room.

"Welcome to the family, little sister-in-law!" Zoe said, giving Ann a tight hug. A few of the others introduced themselves more formally as her new sisters, nieces, and nephews. Her head was still reeling from the news, and she knew she wouldn't be able to match the faces to the names unless they reintroduced themselves later.

"And now, without further ado, let the celebration resume," Titania added, as calmly and casually as if she had announced the addition of a dog or cat to the family, instead of a princess who would be expected to take a place in the Court.

Or would she? Ann had no idea what being a faerie princess meant. Nicolas took his position so seriously, and he wasn't a part of the royal family. Surely she would be expected to carry out duties as one of Titania and Oberon's children. But what could she do?

I don't have any magic! Ann thought frantically. *I can't make flowers bloom or conjure storms or any of that!*

The lower-ranking faeries were slow to rise to their feet, most of them still in awe of the presence of the King and Queen. Ann couldn't blame them.

Three of Nicolas's helpers approached to take Oberon's cape, and he looked much less intimidating without its bulk around his shoulders. This seemed to be the sign that it *really was okay* to go back to partying. Zoe looped an arm around her husband's elbow and dragged him away to spend time with her, his official duties done for the evening.

Ann looked for Nicolas in the crowd, and she wasn't sure what to make of his expression when she spotted him. He was trying to hide his emotions behind his usual cold façade, but he didn't have a hand or teacup over his mouth to cover his trembling frown. He blinked repeatedly, as if in disbelief, which Ann understood completely. His wings were drawn in so close that she couldn't see them behind his back.

None of that could be a good sign.

The royal faeries finished welcoming Ann into their family and melded into the crowd of dancers, leaving her alone with the King and Queen. She ought to say something to them, given that they were her new parents, but all the words stuck in her throat. Instead, Ann mumbled something to excuse herself and made her way across the floor to Nicolas, who was now forcing himself not to blink.

"Nicolas? Are you alright?" Ann asked.

He laced his fingers together and began the trek across the throne room to the safe haven of the banquet table. "Yes. Perfectly alright. Why do you ask — Your Highness?"

"You don't have to call me 'Your Highness,' just 'Ann' is fine," Ann said with a laugh that fell flat when she saw he didn't share her lightheartedness. "I don't *feel* like much of a princess. It's all so sudden."

A long silence stretched between them, and the longer it lasted, the heavier it became. Ann felt like a weight was slowly pressing onto her chest. She recalled her nightmares of Nicolas being far away while she was left to the mercy of a ruthless crowd.

He betrayed you. Who? Ann couldn't remember, but it felt so important now, like this had happened before. A revelation gone wrong.

"I'm the same woman I ever was," she blurted. She felt as if the weight was now compressing and closing around her heart with a tight, painful squeeze. "I'm still your friend."

"The same?" Nicolas stared at her. "You are *royalty*."

Ann gestured to her wings. "Isn't that also the same?" She couldn't even try to smile. "This is a lot to take in for me, too. It would be much easier if I had a friend to help me."

"How do I *help* with this?" Nicolas asked, a quiver in his voice. His mind was racing too quickly for him to keep up with his thoughts. "This is not getting decorations, or cooking a meal, or carrying a heavy object. This is far beyond any of that. And you...you *knew*. You knew the Queen, this whole time, and you didn't tell me? I thought friends told each other important things like that."

"I didn't know she was the Queen! She always appeared to me as a human. I thought that's what she was." A strange human, admittedly. A potentially magical human who didn't have any fear of the supposedly dangerous-after-dark forest. But wasn't Ann one of those, too? She had never fit in with the townspeople, aside from Cecil, who was eccentric himself.

"The bread loaf," Nicolas realized. "She gave it to you. She knew you were living here all along."

"That is correct." The two jumped when Titania appeared beside them at the table. Oberon stood behind her, holding a plate of cookies.

Nicolas's mind briefly leapt to the proposition Ann had made to Julius — did that have something to do with this? Had they been in league with the Queen the entire time, every move calculated to lead to this moment, to force him to make up with Julius?

Was his friendship with Ann a lie?

No! he thought, and it was the only word his whirling brain could hold onto. His chest burned, and he felt ill. What was happening to him?

Nicolas recovered himself and sank into a bow. "My King, my Queen, thank you for coming."

Ann wasn't sure if she was supposed to bow or not. Oberon looked down at her and she decided that she had better do so, to make up for her outburst earlier. She knew Titania was a kind woman and cared for her, but she had never met Oberon, and couldn't say the same for him.

She noticed that Oberon had a ponytail just like Nicolas's, only longer and straighter. And he carried himself much the same way Nicolas did. They bore the same neutral expression, dressed similarly, and both exuded a wintery presence. Ann inwardly winced; none of that could be a coincidence.

When Nicolas raised his head again, Titania continued. "I assume you have questions."

"I would never question you, my Queen. Your word is absolute—"

"Child." Titania raised a hand and placed it gently at the crook of his elbow. "I know you have questions. Both of you. I had better explain myself outright, since you do not know how to put them into words.

"I was informed about your behavioral problems a few months ago by your elder faerie, and came to investigate the matter myself. You are powerful, Nicolas. It is important that your power be used for good and to maintain balance, not for selfish personal gain."

Nicolas's face flushed. Titania continued. "By fortune or fate, I happened upon this young woman in the woods. In her I saw an innocent, pure heart, the likes of which I am always drawn to. And with that, I saw potential.

"It occurred to me that perhaps what you needed was not punishment, but understanding. If this girl could slip past your defenses, perhaps she could help you. So I gave her a loaf of bread to take to you, knowing that it would require you to show her hospitality for seven days, and began watching. I was not disappointed. There were no more misplaced storms, no shows of force against the other faeries. Both of you flourished in each other's company.

"I chose a key moment to reveal myself to Ann again, as a final test. I offered her a place in my home and she chose to stay with you instead. She called you her friend, and I knew that my faith in you was well earned."

Nicolas wasn't sure how to take that. Should he be happy that Ann had chosen him, or dismayed that his friendship with Ann had been nothing more than a test set up by the Queen?

Did that mean it wasn't real?

No!

"And you, Ann," Titania went on. "I had not initially intended to make you a part of our family, but as I watched you, I came to cherish you as my own. You are a warm and loving person, and we are happy to have you in our family. However, what we talked about in the forest that day still stands. You may be an official princess now, but you are free to live wherever you wish."

"I can't decide yet," Ann said hastily, almost a shout. "Can I hold off on making a decision, at least until I recover my memories?" She paused. "Or, will that change things too much? What if I find out I have a family? What will that mean for me being your daughter, or your princess, or—"

Titania hushed her, fixing Ann's hair, brushing the loose strands hanging in the middle of her face aside. "No matter where you go, you are ours, my dear."

Nicolas was still reeling. She wasn't staying with him, after all? He should be relieved, but his heart clenched again in the most painful way. "What of the law?"

"Protecting a royal princess is a far different matter from harboring a regular human," Oberon answered. "And as your previous harboring of a regular human was arranged and overseen by Titania, I will grant you and any conspirators full pardon. Perhaps honors, even.

We shall see."

The frost faerie barely managed to stammer out a quick, "Thank you, Sire."

Oberon nodded in dismissal. "Now then, I should like to enjoy these cookies with my wife. If you will pardon us." The two made their way to the thrones of honor. Faeries cleared a path for them, returning to their revelry only when the King and Queen were seated.

Nicolas felt like all the air had been forced out of his lungs, and was now pressing on him from all directions. There were so many people there. Everyone he knew had witnessed the revelation that he had been unknowingly living with a princess, that she had been sent by the Queen to keep an eye on him, that he had required supervision and testing from the royal family, and that she might not even be staying with him after all that. Not that he was worthy of it, of her—she was royalty now.

Blood rushed to his face so quickly that he thought he might faint. He took a seat at the table and grabbed a glass of punch.

Ann sat down opposite him. Pain, frustration, concern, embarrassment, and relief all chased each other across his face, and there was no way to know which was dominant at any given moment.

"Your Majes—I mean...Nicolas?" She could almost see his attitude toward her changing, and she would give anything to stop it.

"Please, go and dance," Nicolas said quietly.

"With you?" Ann offered.

"Perhaps in a little while. I feel under the weather."

Ann gave him a hug that he didn't return, then set

off to find Jack. She wanted to get acquainted with the frost faerie that he was clinging to.

Jack couldn't have been more eager to introduce them. "Ann! Congrats on becoming a princess, first of all, but this—" he cast an admiring look over his shoulder at the other, "—this is Tosya, my closest friend from the Oceanic Realm. I told you about him before, Ruler of Winter there, and all that? I can't believe he's really *here!*"

Tosya laughed, and immediately Ann knew he was nothing like Nicolas, despite sharing his position. His laugh was warm, like his eyes. "It's nice to meet you, Princess," he said with a small bow. "I'm glad Jack has someone to look out for him up here."

"I wouldn't say that I've been doing anything like that," Ann said, blushing a little as Tosya took her hand and kissed it.

"She's modest," Jack said to Tosya. "Give yourself some credit! I've had loads of fun hanging out here, setting up the party. And just *wait* until summer comes. I'm going to have to plan the most awesome summer ever so we can have more chances to hang out like this!"

Ann smiled, but she couldn't even think about summer. She could barely think about the end of the party. Instead, her thoughts were consumed by, 'I can't believe I'm a princess now,' and, 'What will happen if I find Anais?' and, 'What am I going to tell Cecil?'

Finally her thoughts came to rest on the letter waiting upstairs in her room, and the ever-nearing full moon. It was only two days away.

After the party I'll tell Nicolas, she thought. *No more secrets. That should improve his mood. And mine, for that matter.*

She did her best to forget the letter after that. It was almost impossible, despite Zoe, Jack, Julius, and a few other faeries—some of whom were her siblings now—guiding her in dances and making jokes with her and telling her about the royal family and what she might be expected to do. As an adopted human princess, and the lowest in rank, her duties would be functionally non-existent. It was likely nothing would change, and she would be allowed to continue living as she had been. If she had no other home, she'd be welcome to live in the royal palace, if Jack didn't steal her away to his own home.

Dinner was announced, but there was no formal meal. One spread of food was cleared and replaced with another. Two hours later, that was cleared away for the dessert spread. Ann sampled everything she could get her hands on, watching Nicolas from the corner of her eye. He sat at the table but didn't eat much of anything, or say more than a few words to anyone.

By the time the sun was rising, she sat down and tried to have another talk with him.

"The King and Queen seem like they're having a good time," she offered. At least Tanya—Titania—was. Many faeries approached the Queen with respectful bows, and she spoke to them softly. A few of her more spirited children, Ann's new sisters, managed to get her and Oberon onto the dance floor. Oberon's level of enjoyment was harder to gauge, but he wasn't resisting the urge to scowl like Nicolas did when he was annoyed, so she assumed the stoic King was content.

Nicolas nodded. "I am glad."

"Do you want to talk to them?"

"I have nothing worthy to say."

"We could go dance," Ann offered. "Might cheer you up a little."

"If you wish, Your Highness." He rose and danced with her, and with some others, but Ann could tell his heart wasn't in it. He was going through the motions so he could be left alone when he was done.

Her chest clenched every time she saw his face. He was absolutely miserable, and she couldn't stand the thought that she'd caused his unhappiness. Even though it wasn't her fault, she suspected he couldn't look at her without being embarrassed.

Ann thought about the letter again.

If her presence now made him so unhappy, maybe it would be better to stay with Anais when she found her.

The rest of the party, despite lasting into the following evening, passed in an unmemorable blur for Nicolas. Drew dragged him onto the dance floor again, and so did Ann and Jack. He followed along with their movements, but barely made eye contact or said anything. Julius suggested they get together to try out a new recipe he'd found for peanut brittle, and maybe talk about painting and photography and other art forms before spring. Nicolas muttered something like an agreement and nodded in a non-committal way.

Many faeries praised him for his work, and how

diligently he took care of his season, or told him how they enjoyed the clever Christmas theme. Those were the ones who'd found the hidden presents and now displayed them proudly, bits of icy jewelry worn on their wrists or necks. The frost fae nodded to him with respect and told him how eager they were to get the season's work underway, and apologized for pressuring him about the schedule while he had been arduously caring for the new princess.

He couldn't remember what he had replied in those moments, but it must have been satisfactory enough.

Now the party was over, and night had fallen again.

Ann started to unhook one of the ribbon streamers, but Nicolas called to her, "Leave it. We can handle that in the morning." Or perhaps the afternoon. His head was pounding from all the activity. He reminded himself that she was not someone he could speak to in that manner anymore and added, "If it pleases you, Your Highness."

"Oh, uh…"

"Did you have plans tomorrow morning?" Was it possible that she was already planning to leave for the royal palace? Or to go and spend time with her new friends? Nicolas had never begrudged her that before; he'd never given a single thought to her seeing the librarian, and his jealousy over her chats with Jack had nothing to do with Jack, and everything to do with humanity's preference for summer over winter. He had mastered hiding that envy, shoved it so far away from his conscience that he never shared it with her.

But now Ann had no more need for Nicolas. She was a royal princess. She had *outranked* him within less than a year of being a part of his world, without any magic and barely any knowledge of how Oberon and Titania's Court worked.

It twisted something inside him, something that clawed against his ribs and tried to climb out his throat in the form of cruel words, but he refused to let it. For the time being, Ann was still there, just not his special secret anymore. No longer would her presence bind him to treat Jack and Julius well, though he would do that anyway. They might oftentimes be strange to him, as Ann was—but if he could learn to enjoy her presence, then he could learn to enjoy theirs too.

"Yes. Tomorrow is the full moon," Ann said. Her response was unusually calculated.

"Why is that of special significance?" Nicolas asked. He was too exhausted to think.

Ann fiddled with the bow on her shawl. "I have something to show you. I've had it for a while, actually. I've been waiting until the right moment to tell you, and I think that moment has come."

He waited while she raced upstairs, still as quick as ever despite the heels on her feet. She was gone longer than he expected, and when she returned she had changed into her nightgown and slippers. A worn piece of paper was clutched in her hand. He assumed the paper was what she wanted to show him, since he had obviously seen her nightgown before.

"I found this letter in the woods on Halloween," Ann explained, handing it over. Her eyes were bright, as they were when she talked about how high she had climbed in a tree, or a new favorite book she had checked out from the library. "It was in a hole in the ground, near where I woke up. I think it was left for me by my family so I could find them—her—again. This is the *only* clue I've found. I had Cecil examine it to see if the handwriting or name belonged to anyone in town, but he said it didn't."

She decided to omit the part about the town legend. She knew Nicolas didn't like ghosts, so it followed that he wouldn't like ghost stories, and therefore wouldn't like witch stories, either.

Nicolas read the letter through several times. "And you say you found this in the woods? On Halloween?" Over a month ago. She had been keeping this a secret from him for over a month, nearly two.

"Yes. Like I said, Cecil was helping me try to figure out who wrote it, but we couldn't find anything. It took him a while to research it, and I figured you were too busy. I already missed the last full moon because we were so busy getting everything ready."

She felt guilty admitting it out loud. Despite her talk with Tanya, she hadn't felt bold enough to meet Anais on the full moon in November, instead throwing her energy into the Yule preparations and spending time with Jack and Nicolas. Not for the first time, she wondered if Anais had taken that as a sign that she wasn't coming. What if the mysterious woman was already gone, never to return? But she also would have seen that the letter was gone, and known someone had been there to take it.

"This could be my last chance to find out who I am. What do you think?"

Nicolas thrust the letter back at her as if it had scorched his hands through his gloves. Didn't she already have the love of a family? Wasn't that what she had wanted? Meanwhile he was left behind, still alone and unable to understand this, now suddenly unable to understand her. The pieces of the puzzle that he had

He hated the letter. It was the height of everything wrong with the current situation: the deceit, the loss of understanding, the danger, Ann being a world away from him.

"It is obvious what this is," Nicolas snapped. It all made perfect sense to him. The letter was bad, the letter was somehow the root of the pain he was feeling, and if he could get Ann to ignore it then their lives could return to normal. It was for her own good, too. Whoever had written that letter posed a threat to her well-being. "An evil witch wrote this letter to trick you into doing something foolish. It happens frequently in these

234

woods, magical beings luring unsuspecting humans to their doom."

Ann fumbled to get a hold of the letter in her shock. *A witch?*

She doubted he knew about the town legend. He didn't know much about humans in general, and she couldn't imagine him going into town for any reason. As far as she knew, he rarely left the castle at all. He couldn't know about Anais and the legacy she had left in the nameless town.

"You must be more careful," Nicolas said flatly. "Put it out of your mind. Nothing good can come of this letter. Besides, you have a new family now."

The last words came out as a whisper. He turned away from her, but Ann could see the unhidden misery in his frown.

Ann clutched the letter close, her hands shaking. Did he hate her now, the same way he'd hated Julius a century ago? Would this become a falling out? Would they be able to reconcile within her lifetime?

"I didn't know who Tanya was, or about being a princess, before tonight. I thought she was just a woman I met in the woods who was nice to me, and I liked her." She reached out a hand to him. "I didn't mean to embarrass you."

"I am..." Nicolas started, and seemed to choke on the words. "It does not matter if you embarrass me." He twined his fingers together in frantic motions. "There are rules for this. There are specific ways a faerie is supposed to treat members of the royal family, adopted or not. Your smallest whims are greater than my feelings. I am beneath you."

"You are not! You never will be!" Ann cried out and grabbed his hand, wincing at the chill that lanced through her ungloved hand.

Nicolas pulled away. On this, Bethilde had always been explicitly clear with him. The rules for talking to a peer or an underling were not the same as the rules for talking to a superior, and breaking those rules could cause a faerie to be disgraced and lose their rank. Nicolas already struggled so much with socializing in any way, he *had* to observe these rules to keep himself safe, to make sense of the world.

That did not make it any less painful to give up the connection he'd shared with Ann, for either of them. Shards of ice gathered at the corners of his eyes. He blinked them away, knowing he would summon a hailstorm to take their place later.

"I suppose there is no point in trying to explain. You are free from these worries. You do not have to care what anyone thinks of you."

"That isn't true," Ann said. She couldn't stop herself from reaching for him again, even though he stayed just beyond her grasp. "I care what my friends think of me. What *you* think of me."

"This *is* what I think."

Nicolas's voice was so weak. Ann couldn't stand to see him like this, miserable and suffering because of her, even if she'd never meant for it to happen. Was this why she'd been abandoned? Maybe she wasn't a bad person, but even good people could hurt their loved ones. She had broken something in Nicolas that she couldn't fix.

She started for the door.

Rarely had Nicolas thought of Ann as small since the

day they had met. She was physically small, of course, tiny enough for Jack to scoop her up and walk with her under one arm, or balance her on his shoulders without a care so she could reach a hook for a streamer. But she exuded a quality of largeness when she was happy and smiling. Her laughter could fill a room to the brim.

Now, wearing nothing but her nightgown and a pair of bunny fur slippers, the letter clutched tightly in one fist, she had never looked smaller or more fragile.

"Where are you going?" he asked, his throat so unexpectedly dry that he choked on the words. They died before they could reach Ann's ears.

Her fingers touched the doors, and she pushed them open. One of her slippers was caught on the edge of the ice slab and slipped off as she passed through.

"I—" The words stuck in his throat. He wanted to say, "Wait, it's night now and you could be attacked," or, "You're in your nightgown and you'll freeze." He wanted to seal the doors, do something, *anything* to keep her from going out into danger.

Yet no words would come. He tried to take a step toward her, but the same invisible chains that constricted his neck to prevent him from speaking also weighed down his arms and legs so he couldn't move.

Nicolas was stuck, unable to move or speak, until he could no longer see her shape amidst the shadows of the trees. It took him seconds to remember why—his oath. He had sworn that should Ann ever want to leave, he would not stop her, not with words or actions. Now he was being held to his promise.

"Stay, Ann!" he wanted to shout to her, "The rules can change, I can change! We can talk about this. We can talk about anything. Please, stay with me!"

But he knew it was too late. His paralysis was proof that she wanted to leave.

When the oath spell finally freed him, he was left holding an abandoned slipper in an empty castle.

Never had he felt so alone and so scared.

12

THE MANOR IN THE WOODS

ANN IGNORED THE TREE BRANCHES that whipped past her face and the stones that jabbed her bare foot as she ran. She ignored the sharp sting of winter air in her lungs as the frost fae set to work chilling the forest. The frigidness made her numb, so her small scratches and heaving breaths were nowhere near as painful as the tight squeezing around her heart.

She was all she had worried she was. She had hurt her best friend, brought him to tears on what should have been a triumphant and joyful night, and worse — she hadn't even *meant* to do it. That it was pure accident, pure coincidence, made it worse. She could do it again without even realizing what was happening until it was too late.

Nicolas would be happier without her. He hadn't even tried to convince her to stay.

She was doing the right thing for both of them by leaving.

Lost in thought, Ann smacked into a tree, its bark so dark that she could not distinguish it from the shadows. Pain burst across her nose and she rubbed it with a whine. She couldn't feel any open scratches, but it still

stung. It hurt enough to break through the numbness. Finally, the tears she'd been fighting back all the way from the castle arrived.

"How could this happen?" she whimpered, rubbing her eyes and nose until they were dry.

The jolt interrupted her single-minded determination to get away from the castle. She paused to feel each bruise and cut and scrape she had acquired on the way. She tried to hug herself for warmth, but even her thick nightgown was of little use against the winter chill overtaking the forest.

She would have to reach town before she got hypothermia. Cecil would always welcome her in with open arms and a cup of warm tea or hot chocolate. She was pretty sure she could climb over the town gate without much difficulty.

Ann looked around for a familiar landmark to point her in the right direction, only to realize she didn't recognize this part of the woods. It could just be because it was night, or because the last of the leaves had fallen, but she had no idea where she was.

Hurt, cold, sad, *and* lost.

"Some night this turned out to be," Ann said, biting back another sob. She began to sink to her knees, but when she detected the faintest sound of howling in the distance, she froze. She searched through the dark underbrush, but could see nothing other than branches reaching for her.

She had been warned of the dangerous creatures that prowled the forest at night. She remembered reading about them in Nicolas's library—imps, goblins, bogeys, banshees, vampires, and ghouls came out after the sun went down, and all of them would gladly snack on a human. They didn't care about the faerie royal family, or if Ann was a part of it now. Even without magical creatures skulking around in the dark, there were always wolves and other nocturnal predators that could make quick work of her. She didn't have an ax with which to defend herself, either.

Though thinking back on it now, Tanya probably didn't need the ax. She probably had powerful magic that could do all kinds of things, including defend herself from a few hungry wolves. Only Ann's boots and satchel were magical, and those were back at the castle with the rest of her few worldly possessions.

Ann forced herself to stay on her feet, keep quiet, and figure out where she was. By her reckoning, it would be dawn soon. If she could keep moving and at least make it close to town, she would be safe until the sun rose to banish the forest's more vile inhabitants.

The trickling sound of water moving over stones reached her ears. She'd ended up near the stream that cut through the forest from east to west. It opened a gap in the treetops, letting moonlight filter down to the forest floor. It would be easier to spot approaching enemies if she walked along the bank, and she could follow the flow of the water west toward the town.

Ann stepped into the soggy, sandy ground beside the creek and started walking across the soothingly soft earth.

If only she knew which way was east and which way was west.

Every rustle in the looming tree branches or snap of a twig made her jump. She knew she was small, but she hadn't ever *felt* small, except for maybe the first time she had met Tanya. Had she been planning on Nicolas and Ann becoming friends from those first few seconds? Had something in those brief moments assured her that her plan would work?

Ann wondered what would happen to Nicolas if Tanya's plan hadn't worked. Would he spend the rest of his life locked up in his castle, never to make another friend?

Jack and Julius and the other faeries would keep an eye on him and prevent him from doing anything he couldn't undo. She could at least be sure of that. He would move on and be just fine without her in his life.

She gazed at the moon. It would be full tomorrow night, and then she would find all the answers to her questions.

The stream swerved sharply and flowed into a short waterfall. Ann was certain there were no waterfalls near the town.

She groaned. She had gone the wrong way.

Ann was ready to sit down and wait out the night near the waterfall when lights caught her eye. Not the flashy flickering of faeries in flight or the mischievous blinking of wisps, but the structured, golden glow of light shining through windows.

She started toward the light. She hadn't been this far east in the forest before, since her wandering typically took her to the westernmost stretch between the palace and the town. It was possible someone *did* live here, after all. Maybe Anais!

The ground became painful to walk on as Ann abandoned the sandy bank, though occasionally she strayed across a smooth, long-forgotten cobblestone that offered her aching feet some comfort.

As she drew near, an imposing mansion formed around the squares of light from the windows. She wondered who would be up at this hour, but perhaps they were hosting a holiday party. With luck, it might have something to do with the plans Cecil said he and Graham had for the evening, and she would find them inside.

The cobblestones grew closer together and became less worn the closer she got to the porch, and she gladly hopped from one to the next until they were evenly spread across the ground. Once she reached the door, she dusted herself off as best she could and knocked firmly.

It didn't take long for someone to answer.

"Who's there?" the man asked. Ann couldn't get a clear look at him due to the glare of the light behind him, but his tone was more concerned than annoyed, which she took as a good sign. "Oh, goodness, you're filthy! Are you alright? Come inside, we'll get you cleaned up right away."

"Thank you," Ann said, allowing him to lead her into the house. From outside, he had appeared to be a dark, man-shaped blob, but once her eyes adjusted she saw a charming smile and the spark of good humor in his dark brown eyes. Black hair framed his face, curling slightly at the ends, and his thinly trimmed beard made him look a few years older than he probably was.

A thought lurched in the back of Ann's mind. She knew this face.

Someone I knew, she thought. *One of the faces in the*

crowd of my nightmares.

Ann wasn't sure what that meant. She had seen Nicolas in her nightmares, too. There was no telling if this man had caused her harm, or if they had been friends.

Or both.

The man's mouth dropped open once she stepped into the light. "Anais?" He broke into a beaming smile, scooped her up, and kissed her cheek. "Darling, you have no idea how much I've missed you! What on earth were you doing out here so late at night? You know how dangerous the local wildlife can be. What if a wolf had gotten you?"

Ann was surprised at the mention of the name, and she gently pushed back against his chest. "Excuse me, sir, but…I'm not Anais."

Am I? No, I can't be. I didn't write a letter to myself and leave it in the woods! Ann thought.

"Oh?" he set her down, leaning closer for a better look. He tried, but he couldn't mask his disappointment. "I suppose not. My apologies, Miss. You look *just* like my fiancé. Ah!" he snapped his fingers, "You must be a relative of hers, in town for the wedding, yes?"

A relative.

In town for the wedding.

That would explain it all. Ann lived somewhere else, maybe somewhere far away, and she'd come to the small town for her relative's wedding — which was happening out here at this woodland mansion, not the town, which explained why the townsfolk didn't know about it, and why Cecil hadn't seen Anais or her before — and she'd gotten lost in the woods, maybe hit her head, and forgotten where she was going and why she was there.

"Would she have told you who she was expecting?" Ann asked.

"Your name would be on the guest list," the man said. "Where are my manners? Allow me to introduce myself. My name is Earl Grey."

"Like the—"

"Yes, like the tea, so I would appreciate you calling me 'Grey.' Just 'Grey.' I am the owner of this manor, which has been in my family for some time. My fiancé isn't here right now, but her name is Anais Gagne, traveling doctor extraordinaire, though hopefully Anais *Grey* won't travel quite as much. I miss her terribly when she's away."

He extended his hand, and Ann took it. Instead of kissing the back of her hand like she expected, he gave it a firm shake. No stuffiness, no airs, just two people having as normal a conversation as one could have in the middle of the night.

Ann smiled. He was such a friendly man, and his easygoing demeanor reminded her of Jack. She introduced herself, no longer feeling the need to conceal anything. "My name is Ann, and I'm afraid I don't know much more than that. I woke up in the woods a few months ago with amnesia. I found a letter from Anais that I believe was addressed to me, and I've been looking forward to meeting her and finding out what she knows about me. I hope we were on good terms. I assume we must be, if I was invited to the wedding."

Or maybe I was coming to sabotage it, Ann thought. She brushed it aside. She couldn't imagine scheming or plotting anything. People didn't go around wringing their hands and smiling sinisterly at the idea of ruining someone else's life; they did it by accident.

"Perfect!" Grey clapped his hands in satisfaction. "She'll be back tomorrow for the wedding. You can catch up with her then, and find out everything you need to know."

Ann nodded, though she thought it strange that Anais wasn't there right now. Why wouldn't she be spending the eve of her wedding with her groom? Perhaps it was against custom for the bride and groom to spend time together on the eve of their wedding. Maybe Anais was traditional that way.

It would be nice if Ann knew anything about her.

"Let's not stand in the parlor all night," Grey said, ushering her farther inside with an arm wrapped around her shoulders.

The interior of the manor was, in a phrase, old-fashioned. Everything from the furniture to the wallpaper looked like an antique, though meticulously well-maintained. Ann supposed that was what people called 'vintage.' Even Grey's clothing looked like it wouldn't have been out of place at the turn of the century.

She caught Grey staring at her and gave him a confused look.

"Excuse me for being rude." He winced. "You really *do* look just like her, except maybe a little shorter, and your hair curls more than hers does. Aside from that, it's an uncanny resemblance. Here, let me show you." He went to one of the bookshelves and removed a charcoal drawing from a stack of papers, then showed Ann to a mirror and held up the sketch beside her. "You could be sisters."

It took Ann a moment to examine her reflection and the picture, but he was right. They had the same facial structure, the same nose, the same eyes. When Ann smiled, even that matched the woman's expression, right down to the creases under her eyes. "We could be twins," she gasped.

"I wonder why Anais never mentioned you," Grey said, frowning. "Most of our guests are from the community, or my relatives. My darling did not invite many members of her family, so one would think that those few she selected would be of particular note."

"Community?" Ann said. Then the townspeople, and Cecil, *would* know about the wedding. Why wouldn't he have brought that up, especially when Ann handed him a letter with Anais's name on it?

"Oh yes, Anais is ever so popular in the town," Grey went on. "Like I said, she's a wonderful doctor. Everyone adores her, though none more than I!"

'Popular' wasn't how Cecil had described *anyone* with the name 'Anais' in that town. Maybe Grey was talking about a different town?

"I thought that the people in the town west of here were all superstitious about people with that name because of the local legend," Ann said. If he would specify where this supposed loving community *was*, Ann would be a few steps closer to finding where she'd come from.

"Local legend?" Grey asked.

"About the witch named Anais."

Something dark flickered across Grey's expression, and he didn't answer. Ann decided she should change the subject, and fast. Maybe learning more about Grey himself would help her learn more about the kind of person Anais was. The kind of person she herself was. "Are you an artist? I have—I mean, had, maybe—a friend who paints."

Grey lightened up again. "Not a professional one. The opulence you see before you is the result of some smart business investments. Art is only my hobby, and Anais is my muse."

Ann looked around the living room again. There *were* a lot of pictures of Anais, some in charcoal, some in regular pencil. In fact, she didn't see any pictures that *weren't* Anais.

No paintings, though, she thought. She recalled all the artwork she had seen in Nicolas's study, and how much neater his room was. Here, papers and things were strewn everywhere. While she didn't personally mind the mess, she couldn't help but think of what Nicolas's reaction would be. *Probably disdain over using charcoal, since it smudges so easily…*

Ann froze and brought herself back to the present moment. She shouldn't be concerning herself with what Nicolas would think. She'd made up her mind that she would never see him again, and the less she thought of him, the less that decision hurt. But something about the charcoal itself upset her. Something deep inside her didn't want to connect Grey with fire, however remote the connection was.

Grey hadn't noticed Ann's flurry of emotions. "Before her, I did mostly landscapes. The sea, the beach, docks and harbors, that sort of thing. I'm a little surprised I can sketch a human being so well. I'll have to do a few of you, while you're here. I think having a sketch of you and Anais together would be prudent, don't you?" He looked down at her and chuckled. "After you're bathed and properly dressed. How did you manage to get so dirty? And what are you doing running around the forest in a nightgown?"

"I, um…" Ann faltered for an explanation that wouldn't make her sound crazy. "I got into an argument with a friend and had to leave immediately."

"That's not good," Grey said, giving her a sympathetic frown. "I'll show you to the guest bathroom. You can clean up, and I'll find a new nightgown for you. I'm sure Anais has some lying around that she wouldn't mind you using."

"Tell me more about Anais," Ann said, figuring that would be an easy topic of conversation on their walk to the bathroom.

Grey seemed like he could go on forever when it came to singing Anais's praises. He drew Ann's bath, helped her into the tub, and even washed her back and hair, never once closing his mouth for more than a few seconds. He didn't even seem to think it strange that he was still in the room while Ann washed, or perhaps he was simply so lost in thought that he didn't notice. She couldn't interrupt him long enough to remind him that she could wash up on her own.

The way he spoke about Anais made Ann believe she was perhaps the most wonderful person on the planet.

"Anais is brilliant. Just brilliant," he repeated for the twentieth time. "She saved the whole town from a horrible fever, working day and night to nurse her patients back to health. There were a few deaths, of course.

Regrettable, but not nearly as bad as if she hadn't been here. Half the town might have succumbed to the sickness if she hadn't helped them. So diligent!"

The talk of the fever piqued Ann's interest. That was the only part of Grey's chatter that aligned with Cecil's story. But the sickness in the legend had happened a hundred years ago, and this Anais was a doctor, alive and young.

Ann couldn't quite chalk it up to coincidence, though. She'd never known Cecil to be dishonest or tell her half-truths for the sake of a story.

Grey didn't pause long enough for her to ask him about it.

"I didn't meet her until after that nasty business was done. I had not gotten sick, thanks to my distance from town, but she had saved the lives of a number of my friends and their children. I wanted to do something to show everyone's appreciation. I had heard she was shy and humble, so I thought a masquerade ball would be perfect. That way she could come in costume, and not have to stand out while we all praised her work."

Ann stared down into the bubbly water. A masquerade ball? Maybe it was because she had just come from Yule, but that sounded familiar, too.

Grey sighed dreamily. "She was so adorable. So out of place at an extravagant party like that. I do tend to have luxurious tastes, and she was wearing the plainest dress you could imagine, but there was still *something* about her. Honest, but not quite…*earnest*, that's more like it. She was very *earnest*. I fell in love the moment I first spoke to her, and I begged her to stay just a little longer."

Grey was drying Ann's hair by the time he finally stopped talking about Anais. "Goodness, it's late! The sun will be up in a few hours. I'll go and get you that nightgown now. The wedding is in the evening, so I'm sure you'll be awake in plenty of time to talk to Anais before it starts. Of course she didn't choose a gown that requires too much handling before the ceremony, always so humble!"

Ann nodded, shivering. Grey's hands were even icier than Nicolas's, and the water had gotten cold while he talked, but it would have been rude to complain when he was going out of his way for her, and so late at night.

The nightgown Grey brought her was, unsurprisingly, vintage. The lace on the hems of the sleeve and skirt scratched her skin a little, and she was pretty sure there were some moth-eaten holes in places, but she thanked him all the same before climbing into the guest bed. The sheets smelled faintly musty, and everything looked a little dustier up close, but she was grateful to have a place to sleep, and the assurance that tomorrow she'd know who she was.

She curled up on the mattress and tried to get comfortable, but found it nearly impossible. With Grey gone, something about the house put her on edge, and she could have sworn she heard whispers of a magnificent masquerade ball through the walls, murmuring her name.

She dreamed of the two Nicolases again that night.

This time, the Nicolas on the throne was joined by Oberon. The two had their heads turned to face each other and were discussing something. Tanya stood by the Nicolas on the floor, trying to direct him on how to solve the puzzle, but whenever she pointed to a piece he lost the ability to pick it up.

Tanya looked at Ann. "Can you solve the puzzle?"

"I can't," Ann said.

"Why not?"

Ann shook her head. "It isn't my puzzle. My puzzle is—"

Coarse ropes around her torso and arms. Wood digging into her back as the heat of the flames made it crack and snap. Ann ignored the fire, along with the fear rising in her chest and throat, and looked through the crowd. Beyond, she saw her new adopted parents and the two Nicolases, still struggling with the puzzle. In the crowd, she saw her friends.

Not looking for them, she thought. Where was Grey? She knew she'd seen him here before, but so much of the crowd was now taken up by faces that had become important to Ann over the past few months. Another Tanya, another Nicolas, Cecil, Jack, and Julius, faeries she had met at the party, even the kittens were there.

"He betrayed you," she heard in what she knew to be Anais's voice. "He betrayed you."

Her eyes landed on Grey, who was standing closest to the pyre. She looked hard at his face.

His horrified, crying, guilty face.

He betrayed you.

By the time Ann woke, the sun was already starting to set. She'd slept all day.

Ann bolted up from the bed and searched the wardrobe for something appropriate to wear to a wedding. There were a few dresses within, sharing the same dusty smell as the sheets and everything else. She pulled on the layers of ill-fitting lace and fabric as best as she could, then found her way to the parlor downstairs.

She expected to see guests milling about, but the house was empty. Perhaps it wasn't as late as she thought. The sun *did* set fairly early in the day since it was close to the solstice.

Still, for none of the guests or wedding assistants to have arrived yet…

She looked around, searching for Grey, or Anais, or anyone else. The mansion was even bigger than she had thought, and she walked through hall after hall of offices, parlors, and spare bedrooms. She would have checked outside, but she couldn't find the way out, and she couldn't see from any of the windows whether the wedding had been set up outside.

I finally found my family, and now I'm going to miss the wedding, Ann thought.

She was beginning to wonder if she would ever find her way out of the maze-like house when she stepped into the entrance hall from the opposite side. She had wound her way through the entire manor and come back to where she'd begun.

She tried the center hallway, but that just took her

to an empty kitchen. A draft blew in through an open window and Ann clutched her arms, wishing she had her pink coat.

"There you are!"

Ann jumped. Grey was so close, yet she hadn't heard him approach.

"I'm sorry I startled you. I've been looking for you, actually. I wanted to let you know that the wedding is *tomorrow*, not today," Grey said with a self-conscious chuckle. "I must have gotten so excited that I mixed up the dates."

"I understand," Ann said, but that still didn't explain the complete lack of guests. The manor wasn't exactly in a convenient location, and she couldn't imagine people would stay in town and hike all the way through the woods when they could sleep in any of the numerous guest rooms that she had passed. And wedding guests aside, where were the maids and cooks?

Nicolas didn't have many servants, but his castle was also made of ice and glass, and he was able to keep it clean with little effort. This mansion, though nicely decorated, was covered in a layer of dust that Grey barely noticed. And while Nicolas loathed company, Grey seemed like he couldn't go more than a few hours without it.

So where were all the people that Ann felt should be there?

"Do you live alone?" Ann asked finally.

"Yes, and no. There are so many maids and guests around that even if they don't live here, I never feel lonely for long," Grey answered. "It's been unusually quiet as of late since the staff have taken a short holiday, but everyone will be here for the wedding. Then it will be impossible to find a peaceful moment."

"If the staff aren't here, then I guess we should clean up. I'd be happy to help," Ann offered. Having something to do might keep her mind off of how odd all of this was.

Grey blinked. "The maids left only yesterday. Everything should still be clean. You didn't track *that* much dirt in with you, my dear!"

Ann looked around. Maybe her senses were fooling her and the dusty look and smell were the result of so many antiques. She ran a finger over a nearby table to make sure. A thick layer of dust covered it, but Grey didn't notice. He was instead examining her dress.

"It doesn't fit very well, does it?" Grey commented. "I don't know if I have time to contact a tailor. We might have to settle for a few temporary fixes." He chuckled. "You honestly are Anais's double in face, but I suppose the fact that her dresses don't fit proves your difference. Fraternal twins, or just plain sisters, maybe." He looked at one of the nearby portraits of Anais. "But I still don't understand. Why wouldn't she tell me about you? We have no secrets."

"You can ask her today," Ann pointed out. "She'll be back today. Right?"

"Yes! Most likely. Maybe."

That wasn't the answer Ann wanted. Not in its entirety, anyway.

"I'm sorry. I know you must be eager to find out about your life before you lost your memory. My Anais is always busy with her work, but I'm sure she'll be home soon."

255

Ann tried not to let it show, but she wasn't so sure. According to the letter, Anais didn't like the town, and where else would she practice medicine? Ann would have spotted her by now if she were out in the forest regularly. Then again, she'd left the letter without Ann noticing her presence.

"She'll be back today," Grey insisted, though his tone was about as hopeful as Ann felt.

With nothing left to do, Grey took Ann on a tour of the manor, telling her about all the important people who had stayed there over the years. Despite how large the place was, it felt stifling to Ann, much like Nicolas's palace had at first. The way Grey spoke also set her on edge; his descriptions reminded her more of Cecil reading a story than a person talking about their real life.

Grey ended the tour by showing her outside, to the overgrown yard and dilapidated gazebo where he and Anais would exchange vows. Ann was relieved to be outside again; it was a welcome breath of fresh air after being cooped up inside the manor all day.

However, Grey also didn't seem to see the yard's state of disrepair. Ann was willing to write that off as embarrassment, or maybe a general lack of care in appearances — which did not fit the impression she had gotten of him so far — when he gestured to a rose bush and said, "Aren't the blooms lovely?"

Ann didn't know how to respond, firstly because it was far too late in the year for new blossoms, and secondly because the bush was dead. It had so thoroughly wilted that it barely rose from the ground. Grey's hand, which she assumed was holding a rose in his mind, was cupping empty air.

Thankfully, he didn't wait for her response before going back inside. Ann thought about bolting across the yard, finding the stream, and going to the town, but she wanted to see Anais. She would put up with Grey's eccentricities for another day if it meant getting answers.

Inside the mansion, Ann walked the halls again, and Grey stopped to tell stories and introduce her to his family members' portraits, even though he had just done so not an hour past.

Grey skipped over a locked door that Ann hadn't noticed the first time, probably because she was far less interested in the tour the second time around, and was more prone to let her gaze wander.

"What's in there?" she asked.

"Anais's room," Grey answered. "She's a private person and doesn't like the maids disturbing her things."

Ann stared hard at the door. Beyond it might be the key to her identity.

Grey caught her look, one of the only times he had really paid attention to her the entire evening. "She'll let you in if she wants to when she arrives. You are free to peruse any of the other rooms, but please stay out of this one. She'll be here tomorrow, for sure."

He walked away, leaving Ann alone with the door.

Ann went to bed early, but couldn't sleep. Maybe it was the fact that she had not eaten since the Yule celebration, and hunger was clawing at her stomach. Maybe it was the light of the nearly-full moon streaming through her window, and she itched with the desire to be outside. She'd been sure that that night should be the full moon, but perhaps the party had disoriented her sense of time; the moon outside her window definitely had a sliver missing.

Ann stood. She couldn't wait any longer. She had to go into Anais's room.

She opened her guest bedroom door and carefully looked down the hall, checking to see if Grey was keeping an eye on her. She didn't see him anywhere, and from the tour she knew that his room was quite a distance from Anais's room. Ordinarily she would have worried that he might notice a disturbance in the dust, but since he apparently couldn't see it, she abandoned that fear and set off down the hall.

She found her way without any trouble, grabbed a nearby chair, and stood on it to feel along the top of Anais's door frame. After a few moments of searching, her fingers connected with the cool metal that she knew would be there, and she pulled a brass key down.

Ann took note of where the key had been on the frame so she could put it back exactly where she had found it. Grey would never know she had been there.

With a deep breath, she slid the key into the lock. The door creaked, but the handle turned easily. She waited a moment to see if the squeak had woken Grey, but she heard no other doors opening, no footsteps coming her way.

Ann swallowed hard. The truth about Anais's identity and their relationship could be behind this door. Everything she'd spent the past few months wondering about and dreading might be revealed that night.

She stepped inside and regretted it immediately.

An old wedding dress lay across the bed, arms folded over the bodice and wrapped around a bouquet of long-dead roses. The walls, floor, and furniture were covered in overlapping sketches of Anais doing various things: picking flowers, reading a book, reclining on a sofa, asleep in bed. There were so many that they completely blanketed the room.

All of it struck Ann as deeply, terribly *wrong*, but what struck her most was the body.

Hanging from a thick rope in the center of the room was a decayed corpse. Clutched tightly in its hand was one final picture of Anais burning at the stake.

The body wore the same suit as Grey.

Ann took a shaky step back and closed the door.

The air behind her was cold.

"You went into her room."

Ann kept her eyes on the door and nodded. Her whole body shook, which was the only movement it could muster. If her hand hadn't been clinging to the handle of the door, she was fairly certain that she would have collapsed.

"I asked you not to do that," Grey said. His voice was barely a whisper, more like a breath than anything truly audible. Rather than shouting in anger, his tone was sorrowful.

"What are you?" Ann asked, turning to face him. The beam of moonlight that shone from the window at the end of the hall illuminated him in silver, and revealed that he was semi-translucent.

"A memory, perhaps, that refuses to move on." Grey frowned deeply. He reached for her, resting an icy hand against her cheek, and she realized that if not for the chill she would not be able to tell his hand was there at all. "You are so much like her…"

Ann trembled and moved away from his touch. "Where is Anais, really?"

"Gone," Grey answered simply.

Still shaking, Ann took a step away from him, down the hall. "Then I need to go, too."

"Wait!" Grey appeared in front of her in an instant. Of course he didn't need to move to catch up; he could simply materialize where he wanted. "*Please*. Please don't leave. It's been so long since I've had any company." He offered a strained smile. "If you stay, we can pretend this didn't happen. We can keep each other company, and neither of us will be alone again. You can forget all about your fight with your friend, and I can forget about…what I did. Wouldn't that be nicer?"

Ann stared at him, trying to ignore the fact that she could see the wallpaper behind him, *through* him. Perhaps, if he had been honest about being a ghost right away, she would not mind. But lying about what he was, about Anais? Suggesting they forget all their troubles and pretend everything was fine?

She shook her head. "No. That would just be running away." She put a hand on his arm, as well as she could. "I need to know more about Anais, the *real* Anais. I need to know who I really am."

Grey's form flickered. "Then, I wish you luck, Ann."

She blinked, and he was gone. The manor, too, disappeared. Only the few broken marble tiles embedded deep in the ground revealed that it had ever existed at all. When Ann looked up, she realized the forest was familiar, not far from the hill where she'd awoken months ago. The moon was indeed full above her.

She would have her answers tonight, after all.

13

THE WANDERER GOES HOME

THE MOON BATHED THE FOREST in silver light and seemed to guide Ann toward the underground room where she had discovered the letter. She followed the glow from one patch to the next as it glistened on the fresh snow. She passed a few frost faeries, no larger than butterflies, who bowed to her as she walked by.

The forest became more and more familiar with every step. She recognized her favorite climbing trees, a hole into which she had once chased a squirrel, and a now-bare patch of grass that had previously sported a cluster of blooming daisies. It was amazing how these little details were so clearly defined in her memory, yet all the important things about her identity were still lost to her.

A thin wisp of smoke rose from the hole, swirling and circling into the air.

They would not be lost for much longer.

She thought of Tanya and the other faeries who were now her siblings and in-laws; of Jack's smiling face; of how serious Nicolas looked when he was in his study, and of the beautiful things he made there. She thought of the reverence that she now held within the

faerie world as a princess, and wondered what it meant for her.

Did she want to be part of the Court? Did she have a choice?

Tanya had told her that no matter what, she would always see Ann as her daughter, and so would all the fair folk. Even so, Ann had a hard time believing she could be both a princess *and* whatever she was to Anais.

Ann wasn't sure how she was supposed to enter the subterranean room now that there was smoke coming out of the hole, which indicated a fire beneath, but she took a deep breath and stuck her head into the opening. Her eyes watered instantly, and she called, "Anais?"

She heard a startled cry, followed by a strict, "Get your face out of there!"

Ann was all too happy to pull back. She rubbed the ash from her face and heard a door open somewhere below. A woman appeared from under the hill, though Ann could only tell that based on her voice. Her whole body was cloaked in a dark gray shroud. The only part of her that was visible was a wrinkled hand, which gripped a wooden staff for support.

"What are you doing?" she demanded. "Sticking your face into chimneys! Have you no sense at all?"

"I'm looking for someone," Ann said, lowering her head. "Are you Anais?"

The figure took a step back. From the movement of the hood, Ann guessed the woman was looking her over. There was no rush to embrace, no outpouring of emotion or concern or relief. Another gnarled hand extended from beneath the cloak and motioned for Ann to follow. "Come inside, then."

"So, you are Anais?" Ann asked again.

The old woman led her into the room through a door in the side of the hill that Ann had never noticed before. Inside, a bubbling cauldron produced the smoke that rose through the hole. The cut-out shelves in the earth were lined with jars and plants, and the whole place smelled even more pleasant than before.

But it all pointed to one conclusion.

"You really are a witch!" Ann gasped.

"*Quiet!*" the woman hissed, a finger to her lips. Or at least, what Ann thought were her lips; she couldn't see through the shadow of her hooded cloak. The old woman glanced around, as if worried someone had heard them, before settling again. "I see you found your way back."

"I've been searching," Ann said. She had so many questions, and now she wasn't sure which to ask. So she asked the same one. "Are you Anais?"

"Yes, that is my name."

The floodgates opened. "You're a lot older than I thought you'd be," Ann blurted. "Why did you leave me in the woods? Why did you wait so long to come for me? Why didn't you look for me in town? And who am I, anyway? Am I your granddaughter? Grand-niece?"

Anais waved her bony hand and Ann closed her mouth, not entirely of her own accord.

"I see you have a lot of questions. Perhaps I can answer them all at once, if you are patient and listen well. But first—" She muttered an incantation over the cauldron and pulled Ann's bag out of it. She tossed it into Ann's arms with surprising force. "Get changed. That nightgown doesn't suit you."

Ann nodded her thanks and opened the satchel. Words couldn't tell how happy she was to see her pink coat inside. Donning it made her feel more at ease than she would have thought possible.

Anais gestured to a chair in the corner of the room. Ann sat and placed her hands in her lap, leaning forward intently. Anais waved a hand again, and the smoke moved. Through the haze, images appeared of a man, a woman, and a young girl who looked a lot like Ann.

"I was born over a century ago. My mother was gifted with green magic, and I inherited her powers, just as she had from her mother. We used our gifts to help heal the sick and wounded in our village by growing medicinal plants and putting them to good use in potions."

Flowers sprang up around the family, and Ann smiled. Everything was bright and happy, and the young Anais was learning how to make medicine augmented with magic to be even more effective. But soon the flowers wilted, and the man and woman vanished.

"Unfortunately, not even magic can change fate's design. I lost my parents to fever, and had to go my own way. I became a traveling doctor then. Thankfully, my mother had taught me that our kind were not accepted everywhere, so I moved from place to place and kept my magic a secret. I went wherever I was needed, collected what little payment my patients could offer. I mostly lived off the land, learned what plants I could eat, enchanted animals to stay still so I could hunt them. It was a good, quiet life.

"Near the end of the century, I came to a town in the woods that was suffering a deadly fever. Most of the victims were children, and some of their parents. I battled the fever for weeks as new patients came down with symptoms. I made sure they recovered. I stayed there longer than I did anywhere else. I should have left sooner."

Ann watched as the smoke formed into the familiar shapes of the library and its surrounding buildings, though the town back then had been much bigger than it was now. One by one the sick townspeople got better, rising from their beds and going outside as flowers sprouted in the square.

"On the eve of my scheduled departure, my patients informed me that one of the more affluent people in town was throwing a surprise masquerade ball in my honor."

Her voice softened the tiniest bit. The smoke formed an image of Grey's face, with a twinkle in his eye, just as Ann had seen him the night before.

"I didn't know what to do, but for the sake of being polite, I went. Me, with my plain clothes and plain face, out in that fancy mansion with all those fashionable people! I had never seen such abundance and wealth in my life. I was enchanted. And then *he* appeared and whisked me away to the dressing room to find me a suitable dress and mask and makeup, and he told me I was beautiful, and he danced with me. I was a young woman then, easily swept off my feet. I fell for his charms, and within a few months we were engaged."

The smoke showed the silhouettes of two embracing figures. Anais sighed. "We were happy. I truly believe that. But I couldn't marry Grey without him knowing the truth. On the eve of our wedding, I told him I was a witch."

The smoke picture shifted. Ann wasn't sure she wanted to see what it would become, but she kept her eyes on it nonetheless. Grey's expression changed from a handsome smile to a wounded frown, then to a vengeful scowl. Anais, as the young woman Ann had seen in the sketches, pleaded with him, but he stormed out of the mansion.

"He didn't take it well. As a man of good standing, Grey could not bear the thought of marrying a witch — or perhaps he believed I had put a spell on him, and that his feelings for me weren't true. Regardless, I was tied to a stake in the town square to be spat on and burned by the people I had saved, only a few hours after revealing to him my most closely guarded secret. They believed I perished in the flames, but I escaped, and cursed the town and Grey.

"It was a mistake. As you may well guess, I should have died many years ago, but the curse backfired, as curses always do. Until Grey's soul is at rest, I will continue to live and suffer."

"That's horrible!" Ann gasped. "How could they do that to you?"

"People do horrible things when they are afraid or angry," Anais answered. "But, as you can also guess, I did not want to spend the rest of my unnatural life suffering from my burns. I searched for more powerful spells that could reverse the effects of my curse. It took decades to find the spells and reagents I needed."

The smoke version of Anais transformed from a beautiful young woman into a burn-scarred hag, traveling the world in a cloak that hid her face and body.

A calico cat traveled at her side, bringing her plants for her spells and small animals to eat. Though the smoke made it appear instant, it must have been years, perhaps decades before she finally came upon an old book of spells, her red-welted fingers flipping through the yellowed pages.

"The spells were difficult. First, I had to make a vessel. I used the earth from Grey's grave and the heart of a cat, my familiar. Things that held significance to me. Then, I had to transfer my soul into the vessel. That was the most difficult spell of all, and everything had to be perfect—but the ritual was interrupted when clouds covered the moon. I left immediately to find more ingredients so I could repeat the spell once the clouds passed, but when I returned, I found that my vessel was gone."

The smoke reflected Ann's wide-eyed face back at her before dissipating. Anais tilted her head. "You can guess what happened to the vessel. From here, it is you who must explain to me where you've been."

Ann felt cold, despite the heat from the bubbling cauldron. "You mean I'm not human?"

"Physically, no. You are what is called a homunculus, a creation of alchemy and magic in human shape."

It took a moment for it all to sink in, but it made perfect sense. Ann wasn't an amnesiac; she didn't remember anything before waking up in the woods because there was nothing to remember. That had been her first conscious moment.

Her nightmares of burning at the stake must have been caused by the part of Anais's soul that had transferred to her. Their resemblance was due to the fact that Anais had created Ann as a vessel to be her new body.

The cat, Anais's familiar—Cecil's cat had left her kittens and disappeared right around the time Ann first came to town. She had been killed, not by a fox or a wolf, but by Anais for her spell.

It all added up.

Not human. No memories.

"Physically no, but what about *not* physically? What about on the inside?" Ann asked.

Anais looked her over again. "That remains to be seen. I can't tell you what you are."

Ann curled her fingers. None of this was what she had expected.

"I know it must be hard," Anais said, her harsh, scratchy voice gaining a note of sympathy. Maybe she had meant to be sympathetic all along, but her damaged voice didn't allow for it. "What matters is you're here now. I'll be leaving this area again soon. I don't like staying here, but it was necessary to gather the right ingredients and to reclaim you. I will try to make another vessel to transfer my soul into, without interruption this time, and we can travel Europe as a pair of doctors. We'll say we're sisters."

Say yes, Ann thought. *This is what you wanted. To know who you are and where your family is and be with them.*

But she also couldn't ignore Anais's story. She could travel and see the world, but she would be living in fear and suspicion wherever she went. She could never form attachments in the places they visited before they had to move on, perhaps never to return. She would be close to Anais—she didn't doubt that she could become close to Anais, if she spent enough time with her—but what about everyone else she'd be leaving behind? She

269

doubted Anais would ever want to visit the nameless town or surrounding forest again. She would have to live her life fleeing from everyone other than Anais.

"I don't know," Ann replied.

"Think on it," Anais said. "I'll be leaving in the morning. You can stay here until then if you like, or go on your way. I won't keep you."

Ann frowned. One night? Was that all she had to make the most important decision of her life?

Ann thought about the things she already had, the things she would lose if she left.

Cecil and the library and the kittens.

Jack, who had a smile for everyone. Nicolas, who smiled rarely and tried to hide behind his teacup when he did, usually because she'd said something clever or silly.

The Court, Titania, and her regality and gentleness.

All the faeries she had met at Yule—now her adopted siblings and friends. All the other faeries and friends she *would* meet.

As she thought, she stared into the smoke, and everything started to look a little clearer. She had never stopped thinking about any of those things, and though they remained a bit daunting, she didn't feel like running away anymore. She knew where she belonged.

"I can't go with you. I'm sorry," she answered at last.

Anais nodded, and said again, "I'll be gone in the morning, regardless. You can rest here for the night if you wish."

Ann looked around for a bed, but of course there was none. Still, sleeping on the dirt in a room heated by a bubbling cauldron was better than sleeping out in the open cold. In a way, it felt natural, probably due to some lingering bit of Cookie's memories. Anais hummed to her as she settled down, old songs, songs of love and loss…

When Ann woke the next morning, the room was chilly. Weak sunlight filtered in through the hole. The door had vanished and all of Anais's belongings were gone.

With a shake and a stretch, Ann got up, dusted herself off, and clambered out of the hole. She wasn't sure where to go next. She was tired and hungry and feeling a dozen conflicting emotions. She had made up her mind, but that hadn't brought her as much peace as she had hoped. There were still so many questions buzzing around her head, so many things she didn't know. How much of her was Cookie, or Anais, or herself? What exactly was a homunculus, and what did that mean for her?

No more running, she reminded herself. She would have to figure it all out, one way or another.

Ann looked at the trees, admiring the small piles of snow around their trunks and the powder dusting their branches. She crouched, felt the tension build in her thighs, and jumped into one of the snowbanks. She kept jumping from one snowbank to the next until she was well away from the conjuring room, and she no longer smelled like the aromatic smoke that had spun the pictures for Anais's tale.

She sat down next to a partially frozen pond and stared into it, studying her reflection. She tilted her head and scrunched up her nose, then growled, smiled, and frowned. No matter what face she made, she still looked just like the woman in the Grey's sketches.

Ann rubbed her face with her sleeves and a frustrated hiss escaped her clenched teeth. Even that sound was not entirely her own.

She curled her knees to her chest and rested her forehead on them.

How ironic, she thought. She'd finally found out who she was, but instead of the love and belonging she'd hoped would come with that discovery, she felt more like a misfit than ever before. Maybe that feeling would fade with time, with the help of those she loved.

Ann looked at her reflection again, just in time to see something strike the surface of the pond and break the thin sheets of ice floating on its surface. The ripples were small, but they distorted her image. As more of the things fell out of the sky, her reflection dissipated completely. Ann winced when one of them hit her head and bounced off—a tiny piece of ice.

Whoever she would be, wherever she was going, she knew where she needed to be at that moment. Everything else could come later, one step at a time.

Right then, her best friend needed her, and she needed him.

She almost started laughing and said, "I'm coming!"

Ann stood and started walking, hail hopping at her feet. The path was so familiar that she hardly needed to think about where she was going.

North until you see the mountains, then look for the castle towers.

The way home, she thought.

She didn't stop or slow down until the courtyard gates came into view. Only there did she pause, gazing at hills of fresh snow that had half-buried the statues, which still bore decorations for the Yule celebration. She remembered the awe she had felt when she had seen the palace for the first time, and how Nicolas had reacted back then.

It was a little scary how easily she could imagine Nicolas, sitting tall and regal on the ice throne, staring down at her with eyes colder than the whole palace. It almost felt like the person in that memory was someone else entirely.

He wasn't that person anymore. She knew he'd changed, whether she meant to nudge him toward that or not, just as he had changed her.

Ann pushed the gates open and stepped lightly across the snowbanks. Perfect consistency for packing into snowballs or building snowmen, she noticed. Winter was off to a joyous beginning for what she imagined must be the first time in decades. A good omen, maybe.

When she reached the imposing doors, she knocked once. The ice chilled her knuckles and hurt. She waited, but there was no answer.

A second knock, this time with her fist tucked inside her sleeve. It barely made a sound, and if the first knock hadn't alerted Nicolas to her presence, the second one definitely wouldn't.

Ann slammed her fist as hard as she dared into the ice, and she could faintly hear the echo it created inside the room beyond.

Still no answer.

She must have misunderstood the meaning of the hail, or maybe it had no meaning at all. Why should she expect that Nicolas would try to call her back to him? For all she knew, it was just part of his grand winter plan. It might not have come from him at all, but some other frost faerie doing their job.

Ann hung her head and turned away from the castle, taking slower steps down from the entryway and across the snow. It was tea time, and what she wanted more than anything was to sit in the parlor sharing a pastry and a pot of rose tea with Nicolas over a light conversation about the party, or how to form the perfect snowflake, or anything.

She had options. She could find Tanya and go away with her to wherever the Queen of the Faeries lived, but that could take a while. There was always the town, she supposed. Cecil might find a house for her there.

But those places weren't home. Not like the palace was.

It was strange how the castle, once intimidating and lonely, had become so full of happy memories over the past few months. She had come to the palace not knowing anything about herself, and yet almost everything she did know, she had learned here.

The wind kicked up and tugged at the edges of her coat, making her shiver. She hunched over and drew her arms in tight to combat the chill. The arctic wind grew stronger and stronger until it lifted her off her feet, pushing her back to the castle doors and into a pair of waiting arms.

For a moment, the only sound was that of the hail falling. Ann nuzzled her way into the surprising warmth of Nicolas's shoulder. When she lifted her head she saw that his wings were sparkling in a way she had never seen before, illuminating the dozens of curls and stars at their edges that had been invisible before.

He's so happy, she thought, and a laugh of pure joy escaped her.

He set her down as the hail stopped. Ann studied his face. She could now easily pick out the telltale signs of curiosity, concern, relief, joy, and for the first time, he let her see the warmth of a smile that refused to be hidden.

"Welcome home."

"Then Kay burst into tears, and he wept so that the splinter of glass swam out of his eye. Then he recognized Gerda, and said, joyfully, 'Gerda, dear little Gerda, where have you been all this time, and where have I been?' And he looked around him, and said, 'How cold it is, and how large and empty it all looks,' and he clung to Gerda, and she laughed and wept for joy... Then they took each other by the hand, and went forth from the great palace of ice."

- The Snow Queen, Hans Christian Andersen

ABOUT THE AUTHOR

Avalon Roselin (they/she) is an educator, writer, and independent author. Their favorite genres are Fantasy and Horror, especially when blended with other genres. Avalon is passionate about scary movies, the wonder of nature, and cats. She can most often be found writing from her lap desk in the company of her cat, Winnie, and her husband and illustrator, R. Hamlin. If Avalon were a faerie, they would be an autumnal floral faerie due to their love of the fall season and all things pumpkin spice.

To keep up with all that Avalon does, you can sign up for the official Roselin Books newsletter and find all her social media accounts by visiting www.roselinbooks.com.

OTHER BOOKS BY
AVALON ROSELIN

ALiCE

Stellar Eclipse #1: Cloudless Rain

Stellar Eclipse #2: Dark Lightning

Learn more at www.roselinbooks.com

9 798986 928401